ROTHERHAM LIBRARY & INFORMATION SERVICES

This book must be returned by the date specified at the time of issue
as the DATE DUE FOR RETURN.
The loan may be extended (personally, by post or telephone) for a
further period if the book is not required by another reader, by quoting
the above number / author / title.

LIS7a

The Everyman Wodehouse

P. G. WODEHOUSE

Plum Pie

EVERYMAN

Published by Everyman's Library
Northburgh House
10 Northburgh Street
London EC1V 0AT

First published in the UK by Herbert Jenkins Ltd, 1966
Published by Everyman's Library, 2007

Typography by Peter B. Willberg

ISBN 1-84159-153-X & 978-1-84159-153-7

A CIP catalogue record for this book is available from the British Library

Distributed by Random House (UK) Ltd.,
20 Vauxhall Bridge Road, London SW1V 2SA

Typeset by AccComputing, North Barrow, Somerset

Printed and bound in Germany
by GGP Media GmbH, Pössneck

Plum Pie

CONTENTS

The shades of night were falling fairly fast as I latchkeyed self and suitcase into the Wooster G.H.Q. Jeeves was in the sitting-room messing about with holly, for we would soon be having Christmas at our throats and he is always a stickler for doing the right thing. I gave him a cheery greeting.

'Well, Jeeves, here I am, back again.'

'Good evening, sir. Did you have a pleasant visit?'

'Not too bad. But I'm glad to be home. What was it the fellow said about home?'

'If your allusion is to the American poet John Howard Payne, sir, he compared it to its advantage with pleasures and palaces. He called it sweet and said there was no place like it.'

'And he wasn't so far out. Shrewd chap, John Howard Payne.'

'I believe he gave uniform satisfaction, sir.'

I had just returned from a week-end at the Chuffnell Regis clinic of Sir Roderick Glossop, the eminent loony doctor or nerve specialist as he prefers to call himself – not, I may add, as a patient but as a guest. My Aunt Dahlia's cousin Percy had recently put in there for repairs, and she had asked me to pop down and see how he was making out. He had got the idea, I don't know why, that he was being followed about by little men with black beards, a state of affairs which he naturally wished to have adjusted with all possible speed.

'You know, Jeeves,' I said some moments later, as I sat quaffing the whisky-and-s with which he had supplied me, 'life's odd, you can't say it isn't. You never know where you are with it.'

'There was some particular aspect of it that you had in mind, sir?'

'I was thinking of me and Sir R. Glossop. Who would ever have thought the day would come when he and I would be hobnobbing like a couple of sailors on shore leave? There was a time, you probably remember, when he filled me with a nameless fear and I leaped like a startled grasshopper at the sound of his name. You have not forgotten?'

'No, sir, I recall that you viewed Sir Roderick with concern.'

'And he me with ditto.'

'Yes, sir, a stiffness certainly existed. There was no fusion between your souls.'

'Yet now our relations are as cordial as they can stick. The barriers that separated us have come down with a bump. I beam at him. He beams at me. He calls me Bertie. I call him Roddy. To put the thing in a nutshell, the dove of peace is in a rising market and may quite possibly go to par. Of course, like Shadrach, Meshach and Abednego, if I've got the names right, we passed through the furnace together, and that always forms a bond.'

I was alluding to the time when – from motives I need not go into beyond saying that they were fundamentally sound – we had both blacked our faces, he with burned cork, I with boot polish, and had spent a night of terror wandering through Chuffnell Regis with no place to lay our heads, as the expression is. You don't remain on distant terms with somebody you've shared an experience like that with.

'But I'll tell you something about Roddy Glossop, Jeeves,' I said, having swallowed a rather grave swallow of the strengthening fluid. 'He has something on his mind. Physically I found him in excellent shape – few fiddles could have been fitter – but he was gloomy ... distrait ... brooding. Conversing with him, one felt that his thoughts were far away and that those thoughts were stinkers. I could hardly get a word out of him. It made me feel like that fellow in the Bible who tried to charm the deaf adder and didn't get to first base. There was a blighter named Blair Eggleston there, and it may have been this that depressed him, for this Eggleston ... Ever hear of him? He writes books.'

'Yes, sir. Mr Eggleston is one of our angry young novelists. The critics describe his work as frank, forthright and fearless.'

'Oh, do they? Well, whatever his literary merits he struck me as a fairly noxious specimen. What's he angry about?'

'Life, sir.'

'He disapproves of it?'

'So one would gather from his output, sir.'

'Well, I disapproved of him, which makes us all square. But I don't think it was having him around that caused the Glossop gloom. I am convinced that the thing goes deeper than that. I believe it's something to do with his love life.'

I must mention that while at Chuffnell Regis Pop Glossop, who was a widower with one daughter, had become betrothed to Myrtle, Lady Chuffnell, the aunt of my old crony Marmaduke ('Chuffy') Chuffnell, and that I should have found him still single more than a year later seemed strange to me. One would certainly have expected him by this time to have raised the price of a marriage licence and had the Bishop and assistant clergy getting their noses down to it. A red-blooded loony doctor under the influence of the divine passion ought surely to have put the thing through months ago.

'Do you think they've had a row, Jeeves?'

'Sir?'

'Sir Roderick and Lady Chuffnell.'

'Oh no, sir. I am sure there is no diminution of affection on either side.'

'Then why the snag?'

'Her ladyship refuses to take part in the wedding ceremony while Sir Roderick's daughter remains unmarried, sir. She has stated in set terms that nothing will induce her to share a home with Miss Glossop. This would naturally render Sir Roderick moody and despondent.'

A bright light flashed upon me. I saw all. As usual, Jeeves had got to the very heart of the matter.

A thing that always bothers me when compiling these memoirs of mine is the problem of what steps to take when I bring on the stage a dramatis persona, as I believe the expression is, who has already appeared in some earlier instalment. Will the customers, I ask myself, remember him or her, or will they have completely forgotten her or him, in which case they will naturally want a few footnotes to put them abreast. This difficulty arises in regard to Honoria Glossop, who got into the act in what I suppose would be about Chapter Two of the Wooster Story. Some will recall her, but there may be those who will protest that they have never heard of the beazel in their lives, so perhaps better be on the safe side and risk the displeasure of the blokes with good memories.

Here, then, is what I recorded with ref to this H. Glossop at the time when owing to circumstances over which I had no control we had become engaged.

'Honoria Glossop,' I wrote, 'was one of those large, strenuous, dynamic girls with the physique of a middleweight catch-as-catch-can wrestler and a laugh resembling the sound made by the Scotch Express going under a bridge. The effect she had on me was to make me slide into a cellar and lie low there till they blew the All Clear.'

One could readily, therefore, understand the reluctance of Myrtle, Lady Chuffnell to team up with Sir Roderick while the above was still a member of the home circle. The stand she had taken reflected great credit on her sturdy commonsense, I considered.

A thought struck me, the thought I so often have when Jeeves starts dishing the dirt.

'How do you know all this, Jeeves? Did he confer with you?' I said, for I knew how wide his consulting practice was. 'Put it up to Jeeves' is so much the slogan in my circle of acquaintance that it might be that even Sir Roderick Glossop, finding himself on a sticky wicket, had decided to place his affairs in his hands. Jeeves is like Sherlock Holmes. The highest in the land come to him with their problems. For all I know, they may give him jewelled snuff boxes.

It appeared that I had guessed wrong.

'No, sir, I have not been honoured with Sir Roderick's confidence.'

'Then how did you find out about his spot of trouble? By extra-whatever-it's-called?'

'Extra-sensory perception? No, sir. I happened to be glancing yesterday at the G section of the club book.'

I got the gist. Jeeves belongs to a butlers and valets club in Curzon Street called the Junior Ganymede, and they have a book there in which members are required to enter information about their employers. I remember how stunned I was when he told me one day that there are eleven pages about me in it.

'The data concerning Sir Roderick and the unfortunate situation in which he finds himself were supplied by Mr Dobson.'

'Who?'

'Sir Roderick's butler, sir.'

'Of course, yes,' I said, recalling the dignified figure into whose palm I had pressed a couple of quid on leaving that morning. 'But surely Sir Roderick didn't confide in him?'

'No, sir, but Dobson's hearing is very acute and it enabled him to learn the substance of conversations between Sir Roderick and her ladyship.'

'He listened at the keyhole?'

'So one would be disposed to imagine, sir.'

I mused awhile. So that was how the cookie crumbled. A pang of p for the toad beneath the harrow whose affairs we were discussing passed through me. It would have been plain to a far duller auditor than Bertram Wooster that poor old Roddy was in a spot. I knew how deep was his affection and esteem for Chuffy's Aunt Myrtle. Even when he was liberally coated with burned cork that night at Chuffnell Regis I had been able to detect the lovelight in his eyes as he spoke of her. And when I reflected how improbable it was that anyone would ever be ass enough to marry his daughter Honoria, thus making his path straight and ironing out the bugs in the scenario, my heart bled for him.

I mentioned this to Jeeves.

'Jeeves,' I said, 'my heart bleeds for Sir R. Glossop.'

'Yes, sir.'

'Does your heart bleed for him?'

'Profusely, sir.'

'And nothing to be done about it. We are helpless to assist.'

'One fears so, sir.'

'Life can be very sad, Jeeves.'

'Extremely, sir.'

'I'm not surprised that Blair Eggleston has taken a dislike to it.'

'No, sir.'

'Perhaps you had better bring me another whisky-and-s, to cheer me up. And after that I'll pop off to the Drones for a bite to eat.'

He gave me an apologetic look. He does this by allowing one eyebrow to flicker for a moment.

'I am sorry to say I have been remiss, sir. I inadvertently forgot to mention that Mrs Travers is expecting you to entertain her to dinner here tonight.'

'But isn't she at Brinkley?'

'No, sir, she has temporarily left Brinkley Court and taken up residence at her town house in order to complete her Christmas shopping.'

'And she wants me to give her dinner?'

'That was the substance of her words to me on the telephone this morning, sir.'

My gloom lightened perceptibly. This Mrs Travers is my good and deserving Aunt Dahlia, with whom it is always a privilege and pleasure to chew the fat. I would be seeing her, of course, when I went to Brinkley for Christmas, but getting this preview was an added attraction. If anyone could take my mind off the sad case of Roddy Glossop, it was she. I looked forward to the reunion with bright anticipation. I little knew that she had a bombshell up her sleeve and would be touching it off under my trouser seat while the night was yet young.

*   *   *

On these occasions when she comes to town and I give her dinner at the flat there is always a good deal of gossip from Brinkley Court and neighbourhood to be got through before other subjects are broached, and she tends not to allow a nephew to get a word in edgeways. It wasn't till Jeeves had brought the coffee that any mention of Sir Roderick Glossop was made. Having lit a cigarette and sipped her first sip, she asked me how he was, and I gave her the same reply I had given Jeeves.

'In robust health,' I said, 'but gloomy. Sombre. Moody. Despondent.'

'Just because you were there, or was there some other reason?'

'He didn't tell me,' I said guardedly. I always have to be very careful not to reveal my sources when Jeeves gives me information he has gleaned from the club book. The rules about preserving secrecy concerning its contents are frightfully strict at the Junior Ganymede. I don't know what happens to you if you're caught giving away inside stuff, but I should imagine that you get hauled up in a hollow square of valets and butlers and have your buttons snipped off before being formally bunged out of the institution. And it's a very comforting thought that such precautions are taken, for I should hate to think that there was any chance of those eleven pages about me receiving wide publicity. It's bad enough to know that a book like that – pure dynamite, as you might say – is in existence. 'He didn't let me in on what was eating him. He just sat there being gloomy and despondent.'

The old relative laughed one of those booming laughs of hers which in the days when she hunted with the Quorn and Pytchley probably lifted many a sportsman from the saddle. Her vocal delivery when amused always resembles one of those explosions in London street you read about in the papers.

'Well, Percy had been with him for several weeks. And then you on top of Percy. Enough to blot the sunshine from any man's life. How is Percy, by the way?'

'Quite himself again. A thing I wouldn't care to be, but no doubt it pleases him.'

'Little men no longer following him around?'

'If they are, they've shaved. He hasn't seen a black beard for quite a while, he tells me.'

'That's good. Percy'll be all right if he rids himself of the idea that alcohol is a food. Well, we'll soon buck Glossop up when he comes to Brinkley for Christmas.'

'Will he be there?'

'He certainly will, and joy will be unconfined. We're going to have a real old-fashioned Christmas with all the trimmings.'

'Holly? Mistletoe?'

'Yards of both. And a children's party complete with Santa Claus.'

'With the vicar in the stellar role?'

'No, he's down with flu.'

'The curate?'

'Sprained his ankle.'

'Then who are you going to get?'

'Oh, I'll find someone. Was anyone else at Glossop's?'

'Only a fellow of the name of Eggleston.'

'Blair Eggleston, the writer?'

'Yes, Jeeves tells me he writes books.'

'And articles. He's doing a series for me on the Modern Girl.'

For some years, helped out by doles from old Tom Travers, her husband, Aunt Dahlia had been running a weekly paper for women called *Milady's Boudoir*, to which I once contributed a 'piece', as we journalists call it, on What The Well-Dressed Man Is Wearing. The little sheet has since been sold, but at that time it was still limping along and losing its bit of money each week, a source of considerable spiritual agony to Uncle Tom, who had to foot the bills. He has the stuff in sackfuls, but he hates to part.

'I'm sorry for that boy,' said Aunt Dahlia.

'For Blair Eggleston? Why?'

'He's in love with Honoria Glossop.'

'What!' I cried. She amazed me. I wouldn't have thought it could be done.

'And is too timid to tell her so. It's often that way with these frank, fearless young novelists. They're devils on paper, but put them up against a girl who doesn't come out of their fountain pen and their feet get as cold as a dachshund's nose. You'd think, when you read his novels, that Blair Eggleston was a menace to the sex and ought to be kept on a chain in the interests of pure womanhood, but is he? No, sir. He's just a rabbit. I don't know if he has ever actually found himself in an incense-scented boudoir alone with a girl with sensual lips and dark smouldering eyes, but if he did, I'll bet he would take a chair as far away from her as possible and ask her if she had read any good books lately. Why are you looking like a half-witted fish?'

'I was thinking of something.'

'What?'

'Oh, just something,' I said warily. Her character sketch of Blair Eggleston had given me one of those ideas I do so often get quick as a flash, but I didn't want to spill it till I'd had time to think it over and ponder on it. It never does to expose these brain waves to the public eye before you've examined them from every angle. 'How do you know all this?' I said.

'He told me in a burst of confidence the other day when we were discussing his Modern Girl Series. I suppose I must have one of those sympathetic personalities which invite confidences. You will recall that you have always told me about your various love affairs.'

'That's different.'

'In what way?'

'Use the loaf, old flesh and blood. You're my aunt. A nephew naturally bares his soul to a loved aunt.'

'I see what you mean. Yes, that makes sense. You do love me dearly, don't you?'

'Like billy-o. Always have.'

'Well, I'm certainly glad to hear you say that—'

'Well deserved tribute.'

'– because there's something I want you to do for me.'

'Consider it done.'

'I want you to play Santa Claus at my children's Christmas party.'

Should I have seen it coming? Possibly. But I hadn't, and I tottered where I sat. I was trembling like an aspen. I don't know if you've ever seen an aspen – I haven't myself as far as I can remember – but I knew they were noted for trembling like the dickens. I uttered a sharp cry, and she said if I was going to sing, would I kindly do it elsewhere, as her ear drum was sensitive.

'Don't say such things even in fun,' I begged her.

'I'm not joking.'

I gazed at her incredulously.

'You seriously expect me to put on white whiskers and a padded stomach and go about saying "Ho, ho, ho" to a bunch of kids as tough as those residing near your rural seat?'

'They aren't tough.'

'Pardon me. I've seen them in action. You will recollect that I was present at the recent school treat.'

'You can't go by that. Naturally they wouldn't have the Christmas spirit at a school treat in the middle of summer. You'll find them as mild as newborn lambs on Christmas Eve.'

I laughed a sharp, barking laugh.

'*I* shan't.'

'Are you trying to tell me you won't do it?'

'I am.'

She snorted emotionally and expressed the opinion that I was a worm.

'But a prudent, level-headed worm,' I assured her. 'A worm who knows enough not to stick its neck out.'

'You really won't do it?'

'Not for all the rice in China.'

'Not to oblige a loved aunt?'

'Not to oblige a posse of loved aunts.'

'Now listen, young Bertie, you abysmal young blot...'

As I closed the front door behind her some twenty minutes later, I had rather the feeling you get when parting company with a tigress of the jungle or one of those fiends with hatchet who are always going about slaying six. Normally the old relative is as genial a soul as ever downed a veal cutlet, but she's apt to get hot under the collar when thwarted, and in the course of the recent meal, as we have seen, I had been compelled to thwart her like a ton of bricks. It was with quite a few beads of persp bedewing the brow that I went back to the dining-room, where Jeeves was cleaning up the debris.

'Jeeves,' I said, brushing away the b of p with my cambric handkerchief, 'you were off stage towards the end of dinner, but did you happen to drink in any of the conversation that was taking place?'

'Oh yes, sir.'

'Your hearing, like Dobson's, is acute?'

'Extremely, sir. And Mrs Travers has a robust voice. I received the impression that she was incensed.'

'She was as sore as a gumboil. And why? Because I stoutly refused to portray Santa Claus at the Christmas orgy she is giving down at Brinkley for the children of the local yokels.'

'So I gathered from her obiter dicta, sir.'

'I suppose most of the things she called me were picked up on the hunting field in her hunting days.'

'No doubt, sir.'

'Members of the Quorn and Pytchley are not guarded in their speech.'

'Very seldom, sir, I understand.'

'Well, her efforts were . . . what's that word I've heard you use?'

'Bootless, sir?'

'Or fruitless?'

'Whichever you prefer, sir.'

'I was not to be moved. I remained firm. I am not a disobliging man, Jeeves. If somebody wanted me to play Hamlet, I would do my best to give satisfaction. But at dressing up in white whiskers and a synthetic stomach I draw the line and draw it sharply. She huffed and puffed, as you heard, but she might have known that argument would be bootless. As the wise old saying has it, you can take a horse to the water, but you can't make it play Santa Claus.'

'Very true, sir.'

'You think I was justified in being adamant?'

'Fully justified, sir.'

'Thank you, Jeeves.'

I must say I thought it pretty decent of him to give the young master the weight of his support like this, for though I haven't mentioned it before it was only a day or two since I had been compelled to thwart him as inflexibly as I had thwarted the recent aunt. He had been trying to get me to go to Florida after Christmas, handing out a lot of talk about how pleasant it would be for my many American friends, most of whom make a bee line for Hobe Sound in the winter months, to have me with them again, but I recognized this, though specious, as merely the old oil. I knew what was the thought behind his words. He likes the fishing in Florida and yearns some day to catch a tarpon.

Well, I sympathized with his sporting aspirations and would have pushed them along if I could have managed it, but I particularly wanted to be in London for the Drones Club Darts Tournament, which takes place in February and which I confidently expected to win this year, so I said Florida was out and he said 'Very good, sir', and that was that. The point I'm making is that there was no dudgeon or umbrage or anything of that sort on his part, as there would have been if he had been a lesser man, which of course he isn't.

'And yet, Jeeves,' I said, continuing to touch on the affair of the stricken aunt, 'though my firmness and resolution enabled me to emerge victorious from the battle of wills, I can't help feeling a pang.'

'Sir?'

'Of remorse. It's always apt to gnaw you when you've crushed someone beneath the iron heel. You can't help thinking that you ought to do something to bind up the wounds and bring the sunshine back into the poor slob's life. I don't like the thought of Aunt Dahlia biting her pillow tonight and trying to choke back the rising sobs because I couldn't see my way to fulfilling her hopes and dreams. I think I should extend something in the way of an olive branch or *amende honorable*.'

'It would be a graceful act, sir.'

'So I'll blow a few bob on flowers for her. Would you mind nipping out tomorrow morning and purchasing say two dozen long-stemmed roses?'

'Certainly, sir.'

'I think they'll make her face light up, don't you?'

'Unquestionably, sir. I will attend to the matter immediately after breakfast.'

'Thank you, Jeeves.'

I was smiling one of my subtle smiles as he left the room, for in the recent exchanges I had not been altogether frank, and it tickled me to think that he thought that I was merely trying to apply a soothing poultice to my conscience.

Mark you, what I had said about wanting to do the square thing by the aged relative and heal the breach and all that sort of thing was perfectly true, but there was a lot more than that behind the gesture. It was imperative that I get her off the boil, because her co-operation was essential to the success of a scheme or plan or plot which had been fizzing in the Wooster brain ever since the moment after dinner when she had asked me why I was looking like a half-witted fish. It was a plan designed to bring about the happy ending for Sir R. Glossop, and now that I had had time to give it the once over it seemed to me that it couldn't miss.

Jeeves brought the blooms while I was in my bath, and having dried the frame and donned the upholstery and breakfasted and smoked a cigarette to put heart into me I started out with them.

I wasn't expecting a warm welcome from the old flesh and blood, which was lucky, because I didn't get one. She was at her haughtiest, and the look she gave me was the sort of look which in her Quorn and Pytchley days she would have given some fellow-sportsman whom she had observed riding over hounds.

'Oh, it's you?' she said.

Well, it was, of course, no argument about that, so I endorsed her view with a civil good morning and a smile – rather a weak smile, probably, for her aspect was formidable. She was plainly sizzling.

'I hope you thoroughly understand,' she said, 'that after your craven exhibition last night I'm not speaking to you.'

'Oh, aren't you?'

'Certainly not. I'm treating you with silent contempt. What's that you've got there?'

'Some long-stemmed roses. For you.'

She sneered visibly.

'You and your long-stemmed roses! It would take more than long-stemmed roses to change my view that you're a despicable cowardy custard and a disgrace to a proud family. Your ancestors fought in the Crusades and were often mentioned in despatches, and you cringe like a salted snail at the thought of appearing as Santa Claus before an audience of charming children who wouldn't hurt a fly. It's enough to make an aunt turn her face to the wall and give up the struggle. But perhaps,' she said, her manner softening for a moment, 'you've come to tell me you've changed your mind?'

'I fear not, aged relative.'

'Then buzz off, and on your way home try if possible to get run over by a motor bus. And may I be there to hear you go pop.'

I saw that I had better come to the *res* without delay.

'Aunt Dahlia,' I said, 'it is within your power to bring happiness and joy into a human life.'

'If it's yours, I don't want to.'

'Not mine. Roddy Glossop's. Sit in with me in a plan or scheme which I have in mind, and he'll go pirouetting about his clinic like a lamb in Springtime.'

She drew a sharp breath and eyed me keenly.

'What's the time?' she asked.

I consulted the wrist-w.

'A quarter to eleven. Why?'

'I was only thinking that it's very early for anyone, even you, to get pie-eyed.'

'I'm not pie-eyed.'

'Well, you're talking as if you were. Have you got a piece of chalk?'

I tut-tutted impatiently.

'Of course I haven't. Do you think I go about with pieces of chalk on my person? What do you want it for?'

'I would like to draw a line on the carpet and see if you can walk along it, because it's being borne in upon me more emphatically every moment that you're stewed to the gills. Say "Truly rural".'

I did so.

'And "She stood at the door of Burgess's fish sauce shop, welcoming him in".'

Again I passed the test.

'Well,' she said grudgingly, 'you seem as sober as you ever are. What do you mean about bringing happiness and joy into old Glossop's life?'

'The matter is susceptible of a ready explanation. I must begin by saying that Jeeves told me a story yesterday that shocked me to the core. No,' I said in answer to her query, 'it was not the one about the young man of Calcutta. It had to do with Roddy's love life. It's a long story, but I'll condense it into a short-story, and I would like to stress before embarking on my narrative that you can rely on it being accurate, for when Jeeves tells you anything, it's like getting it straight from the mouth of the stable cat. Furthermore, it's substantiated by Mr Dobson, Roddy's butler. You know Myrtle, Lady Chuffnell?'

'I've met her.'

'She and Roddy are betrothed.'

'So I've heard.'

'They love each other fondly.'

'So what's wrong with that?'

'I'll tell you what's wrong. She stoutly declines to go centre-aisleing with him until his daughter Honoria gets married.'

I had expected this to make her sit up, and it did. For the first time her demeanour conveyed the impression that she wasn't labelling my utterances as just delirious babble from the sick bed. She has always been fond of R. Glossop and it came as a shock to her to learn that he was so firmly established in the soup. I wouldn't say she turned pale, for after years of following the hounds in all weathers she can't, but she snorted and I could see that she was deeply moved.

'For heaven's sake! Is this true?'

'Jeeves has all the facts.'

'Does Jeeves know everything?'

'I believe so. Well, you can understand Ma Chuffnell's attitude. If you were a bride, would you want to have Honoria a permanent resident of your little nest?'

'I wouldn't.'

'Exactly. So obviously steps must be taken by Roddy's friends and well-wishers to get her married. And that brings me to the nub. I have a scheme.'

'I'll bet it's rotten.'

'On the contrary, it's a ball of fire. It flashed on me last night, when you were telling me that Blair Eggleston loves Honoria. That is where hope lies.'

'You mean you're thinking that he will marry her and take her off the strength?'

'Precisely.'

'Not a chance. I told you he was too much of a rabbit to suggest a merger. He'll never have the nerve to propose.'

'Unless helped by a push from behind.'

'And who's going to give him that?'

'I am. With your co-operation.'

She gave me another of those long keen looks, and I could see that she was again asking herself if her favourite nephew wasn't steeped to the tonsils in the juice of the grape. Fearing more tests and further references to pieces of chalk, I hastened to explain.

'Here's the idea. I start giving Honoria the rush of a lifetime. I lush her up at lunch and dinner. I take her to theatres and night clubs. I haunt her like a family spectre and cling to her closer than a porous plaster.'

I thought I heard her mutter 'Poor girl', but I ignored the slur and continued.

'You meanwhile . . . Will you be seeing something of Eggleston?'

'I see him daily. He brings me his latest views on the Modern Girl.'

'Then the thing's in the bag. You say he has already confided in you about his warmer-and-deeper-than-ordinary-friendship feelings concerning Honoria, so it won't be difficult for you to bring the subject up in the course of conversation. You warn him in a motherly way that he's a sap if he goes on not telling his love and letting concealment like a worm in the bud feed on his damask cheek – one of Jeeves's gags. I thought he put it rather well – and stress the fact that he had better heat up his feet and grab the girl while the grabbing's good, because you happen to know that your nephew Bertram is making a heavy play in her direction and may sew up the deal at any moment. Use sufficient eloquence, and I can't see how he can fail to respond. He'll be pouring out his love before you know where you are.'

'And suppose she doesn't feel like getting engaged to him?'

'Absurd. Why, she was once engaged to *me*.'

She was silent for a space, plunged in thought, as the expression is.

'I'm not sure,' she said at length, 'that you haven't got something.'

'It's a snip.'

'Yes, I think you're right. Jeeves has a great brain.'

'What's Jeeves got to do with it?'

'Wasn't it his idea?'

I drew myself up rather haughtily – not an easy thing to do when you're sitting in an arm chair. I resent this universal tendency to take it for granted that whenever I suggest some particularly ripe scheme, it must be Jeeves's.

'The sequence was entirely mine.'

'Well, it's not at all a bad one. I've often said that you some-times have lucid intervals.'

'And you'll sit in and do your bit?'

'It will be a pleasure.'

'Fine. Can I use your phone? I want to ask Honoria Glossop to lunch.'

I should imagine that it has often been said of Bertram Wooster that when he sets his hand to the plough he does not readily sheathe the sword. I had told Aunt Dahlia that I was going to give Honoria the rush of a lifetime, and the rush of a lifetime was precisely what I gave her. I lunched, dined and on two occasions nightclubbed her. It ran into money, but you can put up with a few punches in the pocketbook when you're working in a good cause. Even when wincing at the figures at the foot of the bill I was able to console myself with the thought of what all this was in aid of. Nor did I grudge the hours spent in the society of a girl whom in normal circs I would willingly have run a mile in tight shoes to avoid. Pop Glossop's happiness was at stake, and when a pal's happiness is at stake, the undersigned does not count the cost.

Nor were my efforts bootless. Aunt Dahlia was always ringing me up to tell me that Blair Egglestone's temperature was rising steadily day by day and it seemed to her only a question of time before the desired object would be achieved. And came a day when I was able to go to her with the gratifying news that the d.o. had indeed been a.

I found her engrossed in an Erle Stanley Gardner, but she lowered the volume courteously as I entered.

'Well, ugly,' she said, 'what brings you here? Why aren't you off somewhere with Honoria Glossop, doing your South American Joe act? What's the idea of playing hooky like this?'

I smiled one of my quiet smiles.

'Aged relative,' I said, 'I have come to inform you that I think we have reached the end of the long long trail,' and without further preamble I gave her the low-down. 'Have you been out today?'

'I went for a stroll, yes.'

'The weather probably struck you as extraordinarily mild for the latter part of December. More like spring than winter.'

'You haven't come here to talk about the weather?'

'You will find it is germane to the issue. Because the afternoon was so balmy—'

'Like others I could name.'

'I beg your pardon?'

'I didn't speak. Go on.'

'Well, as it was such a nice day I thought I would take a walk in the Park. I did so, and blowed if the first thing I saw wasn't Honoria. She was sitting on a chair by the Serpentine. I was about to duck, but it was too late. She had seen me, so I had to heave alongside and chat. And suddenly who should come along but Blair Eggleston.'

I had enchained her interest. She uttered a yip.

'He saw you?'

'With the naked eye.'

'Then that was your moment. If you'd had an ounce of sense, you'd have kissed her.'

I smiled another of my quiet ones.

'I did.'

'You *did*?'

'Yes, sir, I folded her in a close embrace and let her have it.'

'And what did Eggleston say?'

'I didn't wait to hear. I pushed off.'

'But you're sure he saw you?'

'He couldn't have missed. He was only a yard or two away, and the visibility was good.'

It isn't often that I get unstinted praise from my late father's sister, she as a rule being my best friend and severest critic, but on this occasion she gave me a rave notice. It was a pleasure to listen to her.

'That should have done it,' she said after handing me some stately compliments on my ingenuity and resource. 'I saw Eggleston yesterday, and when I mentioned what fun you and Honoria were having going about together, he looked like a blond Othello. His hands were clenched, his eyes burning, and if he wasn't grinding his teeth, I don't know a ground tooth when I hear one. That kiss was just what he needed to push him over the edge. He probably proposed to her the moment you were out of the way.'

'That's how I had it figured out.'

'Oh, hell,' said the old ancestor, for at this moment the telephone rang, interrupting us just when we wanted to go on discussing the thing undisturbed. She reached for it, and a long one-sided conversation ensued. I say one-sided because her contribution to it consisted merely of Ohs and Whats. Eventually whoever was at the other end appeared to have said his or her say, for she replaced the receiver and turned a grave face in my direction.

'That was Honoria,' she said.

'Oh, really?'

'And what she had to tell me was fraught with interest.'

'Did matters work out according to plan?'

'Not altogether.'

'How do you mean, not altogether?'

'Well, to begin with, it seems that Blair Eggleston, no doubt inflamed by what I told you I had said to him yesterday, proposed to her last night.'

'He did?'

'And was accepted.'

'That's good.'

'Not so good.'

'Why not?'

'Because when he saw you kiss her, he blew his top and broke the engagement.'

'Oh, my God!'

'Nor is that all. The worst is yet to come. She now says she's going to marry you. She said she quite realized your many defects but is sure she can correct them and mould you, and even though you aren't the mate of her dreams, she feels that your patient love should be rewarded. Obviously what happened was that you made yourself too fascinating. There was always that risk, I suppose.'

Long before she had concluded these remarks I had gone into my aspen act again. I goggled at her, stunned.

'But this is frightful!'

'I told you it wasn't so good.'

'You aren't pulling my leg?'

'No, it's official.'

'Then what shall I do for the best?'

She shrugged a moody shoulder.

'Don't ask me,' she said. 'Consult Jeeves. He may be able to suggest something.'

Well, it was all very well to say consult Jeeves, but it wasn't as simple as she seemed to think. The way I looked at it was that to place him in possession of the facts in what you might call pitiless detail would come under the head of bandying a woman's name, which, as everybody knows, is the sort of thing that gets you kicked out of clubs and cut by the County. On the other hand, to be in a jam like this and not seek his counsel would be a loony proceeding. It was only after profound thought that I saw how the thing could be worked. I gave him a hail, and he presented himself with a courteous 'Sir?'.

'Oh, Jeeves,' I said, 'I hope I'm not interrupting you when you were curled up with your Spinoza's Ethics or whatever it is but I wonder if you could spare me a moment of your valuable time?'

'Certainly, sir.'

'A problem has arisen in the life of a friend of mine who shall be nameless, and I want your advice. I must begin by saying that it's one of those delicate problems where not only my friend must be nameless but all the other members of the personnel. In other words, I can't mention names. You see what I mean?'

'I understand you perfectly, sir. You would prefer to term the protagonists A and B.'

'Or North and South?'

'A and B is more customary, sir.'

'Just as you say. Well, A is male, B female. You follow me so far?'

'You have been lucidity itself, sir.'

'And owing to . . . what's that something of circumstances you hear people talking about? Cats enter into it, if I remember rightly.'

'Would concatenation be the word for which you are groping?'

'That's it. Owing to a concatenation of circumstances B has got it into her nut that A's in love with her. But he isn't. Still following?'

'Yes, sir.'

I had to pause here for a moment to marshal my thoughts. Having done so, I proceeded.

'Now until quite recently B was engaged to—'

'Shall we call him C, sir?'

'Caesar's as good a name as any, I suppose. Well, as I was saying, until quite recently B was engaged to Caesar and A hadn't a worry in the world. But now there has been a rift within the lute, the fixture has been scratched, and B is talking freely of teaming up with A, and what I want you to bend your brain to is the problem of how A can oil out of it. Don't get the idea that it's simple, because A is what is known as a preux chevalier, and this hampers him. I mean when B comes to him and says "A, I will be yours", he can't just reply "You will, will you? That's what *you* think". He has his code, and the code rules that he must kid her along and accept the situation. And frankly, Jeeves, he would rather be dead in a ditch. So there you are. The facts are before you. Anything stirring?'

'Yes, sir.'

I was astounded. Experience has taught me that he generally knows all the answers, but this was certainly quick service.

'Say on, Jeeves. I'm all agog.'

'Obviously, sir, B's matrimonial plans would be rendered null and void if A were to inform her that his affections were engaged elsewhere.'

'But they aren't.'

'It would be necessary merely to convey the impression that such was the case.'

I began to see what he was driving at.

'You mean if I – or, rather, A – were to produce some female and have her assert that she was betrothed to me – or I should say him – the peril would be averted?'

'Precisely, sir.'

I mused.

'It's a thought,' I agreed, 'but there's the dickens of a snag – viz, how to get hold of the party of the second part. You can't rush about London asking girls to pretend they're engaged to you. At least, I suppose you can, but it would be quite a nervous strain.'

'That, sir, *is* the difficulty.'

'You haven't an alternative plan to suggest?'

'I fear not, sir.'

I confess I was baffled, but it's pretty generally recognized at the Drones and elsewhere that while you can sometimes baffle Bertram Wooster for the nonce, he rarely stays baffled long. I happened to run into Catsmeat Potter-Pirbright at the Drones that night, and I suddenly saw how the snag to which I had alluded could be got around.

Catsmeat is on the stage and now in considerable demand for what are called juvenile roles, but in his early days he had been obliged, like all young hams, to go from agent to agent seeking employment – or trying to get a shop, as I believe the technical term is, and he was telling me anecdotes about them after dinner. And it struck me like a blow in the midriff that if you wanted a girl to exhibit as your fiancée, a theatrical agent was the very man to help you out. Such a bloke would be in an admirable position to supply some resting artiste who would be glad to sit in on an innocent deception in return for a moderate fee.

Catsmeat had told me where these fauna were to be found. The Charing Cross Road is apparently where most of them hang out, and on the following morning I might have been observed entering the premises of Jas Waterbury on the top floor of a building about half-way up that thoroughfare.

The reason my choice had fallen on Jas was not that I had

heard glowing reports of him from every side, it was simply because all the other places I had tried had been full of guys and dolls standing bumper to bumper and it hadn't seemed worth while waiting. Entering *chez* Waterbury I found his outer office completely empty. It was as if he had parted company with the human herd.

It was possible, of course, that he had stepped across the road for a quick one, but it was also possible that he was lurking behind the door labelled Private, so I rapped on it. I hadn't expected anything to start into life, but I was wrong. A head popped out.

I've seen heads that were more of a feast for the eye. It was what I would describe as a greasy head. Its summit was moist with hair oil and the face, too, suggested that its proprietor after the morning shave had thought fit to rub his cheeks with butter. But I'm a broad-minded man and I had no objection to him being greasy, if he liked being greasy. Possibly, I felt, if I had had the privilege of meeting Kenneth Molyneux, Malcolm McCullen, Edmund Ogilvy and Horace Furnival, the other theatrical agents I had visited, I would have found them greasy, too. It may be that all theatrical agents are. I made a mental note to ask Catsmeat Potter-Pirbright about this.

'Oh, hullo, cocky,' said this oleaginous character, speaking thickly, for he was making an early lunch on what looked like a ham sandwich. 'Something I can do for you?'

'Jas Waterbury?'

'That's me. You want a shop?'

'I want a girl.'

'Don't we all? What's your line? Are you running a touring company?'

'No, it's more like amateur theatricals.'

'Oh, those? Well, let's have the inside story.'

I had told myself that it would be embarrassing confiding one's intimate private affairs to a theatrical agent, and it was embarrassing, but I stiffened the upper lip and had at it, and as my narrative proceeded it was borne in upon me that I had sized up Jas Waterbury all wrong. Misled by his appearance, I had assumed him to be one of those greasy birds who would be slow on the uptake and unable to get hep to the finer points. He proved to be both quick and intelligent. He punctuated my remarks with understanding nods, and when I had finished said I had come to the right man, for he had a niece called Trixie who would fill the bill to my complete satisfaction. The whole project, he said, was right up Trixie's street. If I placed myself in her hands, he added, the act must infallibly be a smash hit.

It sounded good, but I pursed my lips a bit dubiously. I was asking myself if an uncle's love might not have made him give the above Trixie too enthusiastic a build-up.

'You're sure,' I said, 'that this niece of yours would be equal to this rather testing job? It calls for considerable histrionic skill. Can she make her role convincing?'

'She'll smother you with burning kisses, if that's what you're worrying about.'

'What I had in mind was more the dialogue. We don't want her blowing up in her lines. Don't you think we ought to get a seasoned professional?'

'That's just what Trixie is. Been playing Fairy Queens in panto for years. Never got a shop in London owing to jealousy in high places, but ask them in Leeds and Wigan what they think of her. Ask them in Hull. Ask them in Huddersfield.'

I said I would, always provided I happened to come across them, and he carried on in a sort of ecstasy.

' "This buxom belle" – *Leeds Evening Chronicle*. "A talented bit of all right" – *Hull Daily News*. "Beauty and dignity combined" – *Wigan Intelligencer*. Don't you fret yourself, cocky, Trix'll give you your money's worth. And talking of that, how much does the part pay?'

'I was thinking of a fiver.'

'Make it ten.'

'Right ho.'

'Or, rather, fifteen. That way you'll get every ounce of zest and co-operation.'

I was in no mood to haggle. Aunt Dahlia had rung up while I was breakfasting to tell me that Honoria Glossop had told her that she would be looking in on me at four o'clock, and it was imperative that the reception committee be on hand to greet her. I dished out the fifteen quid and asked how soon he could get hold of his niece, as time was of the essence. He said her services would be at my disposal well ahead of zero hour, and I said Fine.

'Give me a ring when it's all set,' I said. 'I'll be lunching at the Drones Club.'

This seemed to interest him quite a bit.

'Drones Club, eh? You a member there? I've got some good friends at the Drones Club. You know a Mr Widgeon?'

'Freddie Widgeon? Yes, very well.'

'And Mr Prosser?'

'Yes, I know Oofy Prosser.'

'Give them my best, if you see them. Nice lads, both. And now you can trot along and feed your face without a care in the world. I'll have contacted Trixie before you're half-way through your fish and chips.'

And I was called to the phone while having the after-luncheon coffee in the smoking-room. It was, as I had anticipated, Jas Waterbury.

'That you, cocky?'

I said it was, and he said everything was under control. Trixie had been contacted and would be up and doing with a heart for any fate in good time for the rise of the curtain. What, he asked, was the address they were to come to, and I told him and he said they would be there at a quarter to four without fail. So that was all fixed, and I was full of kindly feelings towards Jas Waterbury as I made my way back to the smoking-room. He was a man whom I would have hesitated to invite to come with me on a long walking tour and I still felt that he would have been well advised to go easier on the grease as regarded both his hair and his person, but there was no getting away from it that if circumstances rendered it necessary for you to plot plots, he was the ideal fellow to plot them with.

During my absence from the smoking-room Catsmeat Potter-Pirbright had taken the chair next to mine, and I lost no time in sounding him out on the subject of Jas Waterbury.

'You remember you were telling me about theatrical agents, Catsmeat. Did you ever happen to come across one called Waterbury?'

He pondered awhile.

'The name seems vaguely familiar. What does he look like?'

'Nothing on earth.'

'That doesn't place him. All theatrical agents look like nothing on earth. But it's odd that I seem to know the name. "Waterbury? Waterbury?" Ha! Is he a greasy bird?'

'Very greasy.'

'And is his first name Jas?'

'That's right.'

'Then I know the chap you mean. I never met him myself –
I doubt if he was going at the time when I was hoofing it from
agent to agent – but I've heard of him from Freddie Widgeon
and Oofy Prosser.'

'Yes, he said they were friends of his.'

'He'd revise that view if he could listen to them talking about
him. Oofy in particular. Jas Waterbury once chiselled him out
of two thousand pounds.'

I was amazed.

'He chiselled *Oofy* out of two thousand pounds?' I gasped,
wondering if I could believe my e. Oofy is the Drones Club
millionaire, but it is well known that it's practically impossible
to extract as much as five bob from him without using chloro-
form and a forceps. Dozens have tried it and failed.

'That's what Freddie Widgeon told me. Freddie says that once
Jas Waterbury enters your life, you can kiss at least a portion of
your holdings goodbye. Has he taken anything off you?'

'Fifteen quid.'

'You're lucky it wasn't fifteen hundred.'

If you're saying to yourself that these words of Catsmeat's must
have left me uneasy and apprehensive, you are correct to the last
drop. A quarter to four found me pacing the Wooster carpet
with furrowed brow. If it had been merely a matter of this grease-
coated theatrical agent tapping Freddie Widgeon for a couple
of bob, it would have been different. A child can tap Freddie.
But when it came to him parting Oofy Prosser, a man in whose
wallet moths nest and raise large families, from a colossal sum
like two thousand pounds, the brain reeled and one sought in
vain for an explanation. Yet so it was. Catsmeat said it was
impossible to get the full story, because every time Jas's name

was mentioned Oofy just turned purple and spluttered, but the stark fact remained that Jas's bank balance was that amount up and Oofy's that amount down, and it made me feel like a fellow in a novel of suspense who suddenly realizes that he's up against an Octopus of Crime and hasn't the foggiest how he's going to avoid the menacing tentacles.

But it wasn't long before Reason returned to its throne and I saw that I'd been alarming myself unnecessarily. Nothing like that was going to happen to me. It might be that Jas Waterbury would have a shot at luring me into some business venture with the ultimate aim of leaving me holding the baby, but if he did he would find himself stymied by a firm nolle prosequi, so, to cut a long story s, by the time the front door bell rang Bertram was himself again.

I answered the bell, for it was Jeeves's afternoon off. Once a week he downs tools and goes off to play Bridge at the Junior Ganymede. I opened the door and Jas and his niece came in, and I stood gaping dumbly. For an instant, you might say I was spellbound.

Not having attended the performance of a pantomime since fairly early childhood, I had forgotten how substantial Fairy Queens were, and the sight of Trixie Waterbury was like a blow from a blunt instrument. A glance was enough to tell me why the dramatic critic of the *Leeds Evening Chronicle* had called her buxom. She stood about five feet nine in her short French vamps and bulged in every direction. Also the flashing eyes and the gleaming teeth. It was some moments before I was able to say Good Afternoon.

'Afternoon,' said Jas Waterbury. He looked about him approvingly. 'Nice little place you've got here. Costs a packet to keep up, I'll bet. This is Mr Wooster, Trixie. You call him Bertie.'

The Fairy Queen said wouldn't 'sweetie-pie' be better, and Jas Waterbury told her with a good deal of enthusiasm that she was quite right.

'Much more box office,' he agreed. 'Didn't I say she would be right for the part, cocky? You can rely on her to give a smooth West End performance. When do you expect your lady friend?'

'Any moment now.'

'Then we'd better be dressing the stage. Discovered, you sitting in that chair there with Trixie on your lap.'

'What!'

He seemed to sense the consternation in my voice, for he frowned a little under the grease.

'We're all working for the good of the show,' he reminded me austerely. 'You want the scene to carry conviction, and there's nothing like a sight gag.'

I could see there was much in what he said. This was not a time for half measures. I sat down. I don't say I sat blithely, but I sat, and Wigan's favourite Fairy Queen descended on my lap with a bump that made the stout chair tremble like an aspen. And scarcely had she started to nestle when the door bell rang.

'Curtain going up,' said Jas Waterbury. 'Let's have that passionate embrace, Trixie, and make it good.'

She made it good, and I felt like a Swiss mountaineer engulfed by an avalanche smelling of patchouli. Jas Waterbury flung wide the gates, and who should come in but Blair Eggleston, the last caller I was expecting.

He stood goggling. I sat goggling. Jas Waterbury goggled, too. One could understand how he was feeling. Anticipating the entrance of the female star and observing coming on left centre a character who wasn't a member of the cast at all, he was pardonably disconcerted. No impresario likes that sort of thing.

I was the first to speak. After all, I was the host and it was for me to get the conversation going.

'Oh, hullo, Eggleston,' I said. 'Come along in. I don't think you've met Mr Waterbury, have you. Mr Eggleston, Mr Jas Waterbury. And his niece Miss Trixie Waterbury, my fiancée.'

'Your *what*?'

'Fiancée. Betrothed. Affianced.'

'Good Lord!'

Jas Waterbury appeared to be feeling that as the act had been shot to pieces like this, there was no sense in hanging around.

'Well, Trix,' he said, 'your Bertie'll be wanting to talk to his gentleman friend, so give him a kiss and we'll be getting along. Pleased to have met you, Mr What-is-it,' and with a greasy smile he led the Fairy Queen from the room.

Blair Eggleston seemed still at a loss. He looked at the door through which they had passed as if asking himself if he had really seen what he thought he had seen, then turned to me with the air of one who intends to demand an explanation.

'What's all this, Wooster?'

'What's all what, Eggleston? Be more explicit.'

'Who on earth is that female?'

'Weren't you listening? My fiancée.'

'You're really engaged to her?'

'That's right.'

'Who is she?'

'She plays Fairy Queens in pantomime. Not in London owing to jealousy in high places, but they think a lot of her in Leeds, Wigan, Hull and Huddersfield. The critic of the *Hull Daily News* describes her as a talented bit of all right.'

He was silent for a space, appearing to be turning this over in his mind. Then he spoke in the frank, forthright and fearless way these modern novelists have.

'She looks like a hippopotamus.'

I conceded this.

'There is a resemblance, perhaps. I suppose Fairy Queens have to be stoutish if they are to keep faith with their public in towns like Leeds and Huddersfield. Those audiences up North want lots for their money.'

'And she exudes a horrible scent which I am unable at the moment to identify.'

'Patchouli. Yes, I noticed that.'

He mused again.

'I can't get over you being engaged to her.'

'Well, I am.'

'It's official?'

'Absolutely.'

'Well, this will be great news for Honoria.'

I didn't get his drift.

'For Honoria?'

'Yes. It will relieve her mind. She was very worried about you, poor child. That's why I'm here. I came to break it to you that she can never be yours. She's going to marry me.'

I stared at him. My first impression was that even though the hour was only about four-thirty he was under the influence of alcoholic stimulants.

'But I learned from a usually reliable source that that was all off.'

'It was, but now it's on again. We have had a complete reconciliation.'

'Well, fancy that!'

'And she shrank from coming and telling you herself. She

said she couldn't bear to see the awful dumb agony in your eyes. When I tell her you're engaged, she'll go singing about the West End of London, not only because of the relief of knowing that she hasn't wrecked your life but because she'll be feeling what a merciful escape she's had. Just imagine being married to you! It doesn't bear thinking of. Well, I'll be going along and telling her the good news,' he said, and took his departure.

A moment later the bell rang. I opened the door and found him on the mat.

'What,' he asked, 'was that name again?'

'Name?'

'Your fiancée's.'

'Trixie Waterbury.'

'Good God!' he said, and pushed off. And I returned to the reverie he had interrupted.

There was a time when if somebody had come to me and said 'Mr Wooster, I have been commissioned by a prominent firm of publishers to write your biography and I need some intimate stuff which only you can supply. Looking back, what would you consider the high spot in your career?', I would have had no difficulty in slipping him the info. It occurred, I would have replied, in my fourteenth year when I was a resident pupil at Malvern House, Bramley-on-Sea, the private school conducted by that prince of stinkers, Aubrey Upjohn, M.A. He had told me to present myself in his study on the following morning, which always meant six of the juiciest with a cane that bit like a serpent and stung like an adder, and blowed if when morning came I wasn't all over pink spots. I had contracted measles and the painful interview was of course postponed *sine die*, as the expression is.

That had always been my supreme moment. Only now was I experiencing to an even greater extent the feeling of quiet happiness which comes to you when you've outsmarted the powers of darkness. I felt as if a great weight had been lifted off me. Well, it had of course in one sense, for the Fairy Queen must have clocked in at fully a hundred and sixty pounds ringside, but what I mean is that a colossal burden had been removed from the Wooster soul. It was as though the storm clouds had called it a day and the sun come smiling through.

The only thing that kept the moment from being absolutely perfect was that Jeeves was not there to share my hour of triumph. I toyed with the idea of ringing him up at the Junior Ganymede, but I didn't want to interrupt him when he was probably in the act of doubling six no trumps.

The thought of Aunt Dahlia presented itself. She of all people should be the one to hear the good news, for she was very fond of Roddy Glossop and had shown herself deeply concerned when informed of his in-the-soup-ness. Furthermore, she could scarcely not be relieved to learn that a loved nephew had escaped the fate that is worse than death – viz. marrying Honoria. It was true that my firm refusal to play Santa Claus at her children's party must still be rankling, if that's the word, but at our last meeting I had found her far less incandescent than she had been, so there was reason to suppose that if I looked in on her now I should get a cordial reception. Well, not absolutely cordial, perhaps, but something near enough to it. So I left a note for Jeeves saying where I'd gone and hared off to her address in a swift taxi.

It was as I had anticipated. I don't say her face lit up when she saw me, but she didn't throw her Perry Mason at me and she called me no new names, and after I had told my story she was all joviality and enthusiasm. We were saying what a wonderful

Christmas present the latest development would be for Pop Glossop and speculating as to what it would feel like being married to his daughter Honoria and, for the matter of that, being married to Blair Eggleston, and we had just agreed that both Honoria and Blair had it coming to them, when the telephone rang. The instrument was on a table near her chair, and she reached for it.

'Hullo?' she boomed. 'Who?' Or, rather, WHO, for when at the telephone her vocal delivery is always of much the same calibre as it used to be on the hunting field. She handed me the receiver. 'One of your foul friends wants you. Says his name's Waterbury.'

Jas Waterbury, placed in communication with self, seemed perplexed. In rather an awed voice he asked:

'Where are you, cocky? At the Zoo?'

'I don't follow you, Jas Waterbury.'

'A lion just roared at me.'

'Oh, that was my aunt.'

'Sooner yours than mine. I thought the top of my head had come off.'

'She has a robust voice.'

'I'll say she has. Well, cully, I'm sorry I had to disturb her at feeding time, but I thought you'd like to know that Trix and I have been talking it over and we both think a simple wedding at the registrar's would be best. No need for a lot of fuss and expense. And she says she'd like Brighton for the honeymoon. She's always been fond of Brighton.'

I was at something of a loss to know what on earth he was talking about, but reading between the lines I gathered that the Fairy Queen was thinking of getting married. I asked if this was so, and he chuckled greasily.

'Always kidding, Bertie. You will have your joke. If you don't know she's going to get married, who does?'

'I haven't a notion. Who to?'

'Why, you, of course. Didn't you introduce her to your gentleman friend as your fiancée?'

I lost no time in putting him straight.

'But that was just a ruse. Surely you explained it to her?'

'Explained what?'

'That I just wanted her to pretend that we were engaged.'

'What an extraordinary idea. What would I have done that for?'

'Fifteen quid.'

'I don't remember any fifteen quid. As I recall it, you came to me and told me you'd seen Trixie as the Fairy Queen in Cinderella at the Wigan Hippodrome and fallen in love with her at first sight, as so many young fellows have done. You had found out somehow that she was my niece and you asked me to bring her to your address. And the moment we came in I could see the love light in your eyes, and the love light was in her eyes, too, and it wasn't five minutes after that that you'd got her on your lap and there you were, as snug as two bugs in a rug. Just a case of love at first sight, and I don't mind telling you it touched me. I like to see the young folks getting together in Springtime. Not that it's Springtime now, but the principle's the same.'

At this point Aunt Dahlia, who had been simmering gently, intervened to call me a derogatory name and ask what the hell was going on. I waved her down with an imperious hand. I needed every ounce of concentration to cope with this misunderstanding which seemed to have arisen.

'You're talking through your hat, Jas Waterbury.'

'Who, me?'

'Yes, you. You've got your facts all wrong.'

'You think so, do you?'

'I do, and I will trouble you to break it to Miss Waterbury that those wedding bells will not ring out.'

'That's what I was telling you. Trixie wants it to be at the registrar's.'

'Well, that registrar won't ring out, either.'

He said I amazed him.

'You don't want to marry Trixie?'

'I wouldn't marry her with a ten-foot pole.'

An astonished 'Lord love a duck' came over the wire.

'If that isn't the most remarkable coincidence,' he said. 'Those were the very words Mr Prosser used when refusing to marry another niece of mine after announcing his betrothal before witnesses, same as you did. Shows what a small world it is. I asked him if he hadn't ever heard of breach of promise cases, and he shook visibly and swallowed once or twice. Then he looked me in the eye and said "How much?" I didn't get his meaning at first, and then it suddenly flashed on me. "Oh, you mean you want to break the engagement," I said, "and feel it's your duty as a gentleman to see that the poor girl gets her bit of heart balm," I said. "Well, it'll have to be something substantial," I said, "because there's her despair and desolation to be taken into account." So we talked it over and eventually settled on two thousand quid, and that's what I'd advise in your case. I think I can talk Trixie into accepting that. Nothing, mind you, can ever make life anything but a dreary desert for her after losing you, but two thousand quid would help.'

'BERTIE!' said Aunt Dahlia.

'Ah,' said Jas Waterbury, 'there's that lion again. Well, I'll leave you to think it over. I'll come and see you tomorrow and get your decision, and if you feel that you don't like writing that cheque, I'll ask a friend of mine to try what he can do to persuade you. He's an all-in wrestler of the name of Porky Jupp. I used to manage him at one time. He's retired now because he broke a fellow's spine and for some reason that gave him a distaste for the game. But he's still in wonderful condition. You ought to see him crack Brazil nuts with his fingers. He thinks the world of me and there's nothing he wouldn't do for me. Suppose, for instance, somebody had done me down in a business transaction, Porky would spring to the task of plucking him limb from limb like some innocent little child doing She-loves-me she-loves-me-not with a daisy. Good night, good night,' said Jas Waterbury, and rang off.

I would have preferred, of course, after this exceedingly unpleasant conversation to have gone off into a quiet corner somewhere and sat there with my head between my hands, reviewing the situation from every angle, but Aunt Dahlia was now making her desire for explanatory notes so manifest that I had to give her my attention. In a broken voice I supplied her with the facts and was surprised and touched to find her sympathetic and understanding. It's often this way with the female sex. They put you through it in no uncertain manner if you won't see eye to eye with them in the matter – to take an instance at random – of disguising yourself in white whiskers and stomach padding, but if they see you are really up against it, their hearts melt, rancour is forgotten and they do all they can to give you a shot in the arm. It was so with the aged relative. Having expressed the opinion that I was the king of the fatheads and ought never to be allowed out without a nurse, she continued in gentler strain.

'But after all you are my brother's son whom I frequently

dandled on my knee as a baby, and a subhuman baby you were if ever I saw one, though I suppose you were to be pitied rather than censured if you looked like a cross between a poached egg and a ventriloquist's dummy, so I can't let you sink in the soup without a trace. I must rally round and lend a hand.'

'Well, thanks, old flesh and blood. Awfully decent of you to want to assist. But what can you do?'

'Nothing by myself, perhaps, but I can confer with Jeeves and between us we ought to think of something. Ring him up and tell him to come here at once.'

'He won't be home yet. He's playing Bridge at his club.'

'Give him a buzz, anyway.'

I did so, and was surprised when I heard a measured voice say, 'Mr Wooster's residence.'

'Why, hullo, Jeeves,' I said. 'I didn't expect you to be home so early.'

'I left in advance of my usual hour, sir. I did not find my Bridge game enjoyable.'

'Bad cards?'

'No, sir, the hands dealt to me were uniformly satisfactory, but I was twice taken out of business doubles, and I had not the heart to continue.'

'Too bad. So you're at a loose end at the moment?'

'Yes, sir.'

'Then will you hasten to Aunt Dahlia's place? You are sorely needed.'

'Very good, sir.'

'Is he coming?' said Aunt Dahlia.

'Like the wind. Just looking for his bowler hat.'

'Then you pop off.'

'You don't want me for the conference?'

'No.'

'Three heads are better than two,' I argued.

'Not if one of them is solid ivory from the neck up,' said the aged relative, reverting to something more like her customary form.

I slept fitfully that night, my slumbers much disturbed by dreams of being chased across country by a pack of Fairy Queens with Jas Waterbury galloping after them shouting Yoicks and Tally ho. It was past eleven when I presented myself at the breakfast table.

'I take it, Jeeves,' I said as I started to pick at a moody fried egg, 'that Aunt Dahlia has told you all?'

'Yes, sir, Mrs Travers was most informative.'

Well, that was a relief in a way, because all that secrecy and A-and-B stuff is always a strain.

'Disaster looms, wouldn't you say?'

'Certainly your predicament is one of some gravity, sir.'

'I can't face a breach of promise action with a crowded court giving me the horse's laugh and the jury mulcting.... Is it mulcting?'

'Yes, sir, you are quite correct.'

'And the jury mulcting me in heavy damages. I wouldn't be able to show my face in the Drones again.'

'The publicity would certainly not be agreeable, sir.'

'On the other hand, I thoroughly dislike the idea of paying Jas Waterbury two thousand pounds.'

'I can appreciate your dilemma, sir.'

'But perhaps you have already thought of some terrific scheme for foiling Jas and bringing his greasy hairs in sorrow to the grave. What do you plan to do when he calls?'

'I shall attempt to reason with him, sir.'

The heart turned to lead in the bosom. I suppose I've become so used to having Jeeves wave his magic wand and knock the stuffing out of the stickiest crises that I expect him to produce something brilliant from the hat every time, and though never at my brightest at breakfast I could see that what he was proposing to do was far from being what Jas Waterbury would have called box office. Reason with him, forsooth! To reason successfully with that king of the twisters one would need brass knuckles and a stocking full of sand. There was reproach in my voice as I asked him if that was the best he could do.

'You do not think highly of the idea, sir?'

'Well, I don't want to hurt your feelings—'

'Not at all, sir.'

'– but I wouldn't call it one of your top thoughts.'

'I am sorry, sir. Nevertheless—'

I leaped from the table, the fried egg frozen on my lips. The front door bell had given tongue. I don't know if my eyes actually rolled as I gazed at Jeeves, but I should think it extremely likely, for the sound had got in amongst me like the touching off of an ounce or so of trinitrotoluol.

'There he is!'

'Presumably, sir.'

'I can't face him as early in the morning as this.'

'One appreciates your emotion, sir. It might be advisable if you were to conceal yourself while I conduct the negotiations. Behind the piano suggests itself as a suitable locale.'

'How right you are, Jeeves!'

To say that I found it comfortable behind the piano would be to give my public a totally erroneous impression, but I secured privacy, and privacy was just what I was after. The facilities, too, for keeping in touch with what was going on in the great world outside were excellent. I heard the door opening and then Jas Waterbury's voice.

'Morning, cocky.'

'Good morning, sir.'

'Wooster in?'

'No, sir, he has just stepped out.'

'That's odd. He was expecting me.'

'You are Mr Waterbury?'

'That's me. Where's he gone?'

'I think it was Mr Wooster's intention to visit his pawn-broker, sir.'

'What!'

'He mentioned something to me about doing so. He said he hoped to raise, as he expressed it, a few pounds on his watch.'

'You're kidding! What's he want to pop his watch for?'

'His means are extremely straitened.'

There was what I've heard called a pregnant silence. I took it that Jas Waterbury was taking time off to allow this to sink in. I wished I could have joined in the conversation, for I would have liked to say 'Jeeves, you are on the right lines' and offer him an apology for ever having doubted him. I might have known that when he said he was going to reason with Jas he had the ace up his sleeve which makes all the difference.

It was some little time before Jas Waterbury spoke, and when he did his voice had a sort of tremolo in it, as if he'd begun to realize that life wasn't the thing of roses and sunshine he'd been thinking it. I knew how he must be feeling. There is no anguish like that of the man who, supposing that he has found the pot of gold behind the rainbow, suddenly learns from an authoritative source that he hasn't, if you know what I mean. To him until now Bertram Wooster had been a careless scatterer of fifteen quids, a thing you can't do if you haven't a solid bank balance behind you, and to have him presented to him as a popper of watches must have made the iron enter into his soul, if he had one. He spoke as if stunned.

'But what about this place of his?'

'Sir?'

'You don't get a Park Lane flat for nothing.'

'No, indeed, sir.'

'Let alone a vally.'

'Sir?'

'You're a vally, aren't you?'

'No, sir. I was at one time a gentleman's personal gentleman, but at the moment I am not employed in that capacity. I represent Messrs Alsopp and Wilson, wine merchants, goods supplied to the value of three hundred and four pounds, fifteen shillings and eightpence, a bill which Mr Wooster finds it far beyond his fiscal means to settle. I am what is technically known as the man in possession.'

A hoarse 'Gorblimey' burst from Jas's lips. I thought it rather creditable of him that he did not say anything stronger.

'You mean you're a broker's man?'

'Precisely, sir. I am sorry to say I have come down in the world and my present situation was the only one I could secure. But while not what I have been accustomed to, it has its compensations. Mr Wooster is a very agreeable young gentleman and takes my intrusion in an amiable spirit. We have long and interesting conversations, and in the course of these he has confided his financial position to me. It appears that he is entirely dependent on the bounty of his aunt, a Mrs Travers, a lady of uncertain temper who has several times threatened unless he curbs his extravagance to cancel his allowance and send him to Canada to subsist on a small monthly remittance. She is of course under the impression that I am Mr Wooster's personal attendant. Should she learn of my official status, I do not like to envisage the outcome, though if I may venture on a pleasantry, it would be a case of outgo rather than outcome for Mr Wooster.'

There was another pregnant s, occupied, I should imagine, by Jas Waterbury in wiping his brow, which one presumes had by this time become wet with honest sweat.

Finally he once more said 'Gorblimey'.

Whether or not he would have amplified the remark I cannot say, for his words, if he had intended uttering any, were dashed from his lips. There was a sound like a mighty rushing wind and a loud snort informed me that Aunt Dahlia was with us. In letting Jas Waterbury in, Jeeves must have omitted to close the front door.

'Jeeves,' she boomed, 'can you look me in the face?'

'Certainly, madam, if you wish.'

'Well, I'm surprised you can. You must have the gall of an Army mule. I've just found out that you're a broker's man in valet's clothing. Can you deny it?'

'No, madam. I represent Messrs Alsopp and Wilson, wines, spirits and liqueurs supplied to the value of three hundred and four pounds fifteen shillings and eightpence.'

The piano behind which I cowered hummed like a dynamo as the aged relative unshipped a second snort.

'Good God! What does young Bertie do – bathe in the stuff? Three hundred and four pounds fifteen shillings and eightpence! Probably owes as much, too, in a dozen other places. And in the red to that extent he's planning, I hear, to marry the fat woman in a circus.'

'A portrayer of Fairy Queens in pantomime, madam.'

'Just as bad. Blair Eggleston says she looks like a hippopotamus.'

I couldn't see him, of course, but I imagine Jas Waterbury drew himself to his full height at this description of a loved niece, for his voice when he spoke was stiff and offended.

'That's my Trixie you're talking about, and he's going to marry her or else get sued for breach of promise.'

It's just a guess, but I think Aunt Dahlia must have drawn herself to her full height, too.

'Well, she'll have to go to Canada to bring her action,' she thundered, 'because that's where Bertie Wooster'll be off to on the next boat, and when he's there he won't have money to fritter away on breach of promise cases. It'll be as much as he can manage to keep body and soul together on what I'm going to allow him. If he gets a meat meal every third day, he'll be lucky. You tell that Trixie of yours to forget Bertie and go and marry the Demon King.'

Experience has taught me that except in vital matters like playing Santa Claus at children's parties it's impossible to defy Aunt Dahlia, and apparently Jas Waterbury realized this, for a moment later I heard the front door slam. He had gone without a cry.

'So that's that,' said Aunt Dahlia. 'These emotional scenes take it out of one, Jeeves. Can you get me a drop of something sustaining?'

'Certainly, madam.'

'How was I? All right?'

'Superb, madam.'

'I think I was in good voice.'

'Very sonorous, madam.'

'Well, it's nice to think our efforts were crowned with success. This will relieve young Bertie's mind. I use the word mind loosely. When do you expect him back?'

'Mr Wooster is in residence, madam. Shrinking from confronting Mr Waterbury, he prudently concealed himself. You will find him behind the piano.'

I was already emerging, and my first act was to pay them both a marked tribute. Jeeves accepted it gracefully, Aunt Dahlia with another of those snorts. Having snorted, she spoke as follows.

'Easy enough for you to hand out the soft soap, but what I'd like to see is less guff and more action. If you were really grateful, you would play Santa Claus at my Christmas party.'

I could see her point. It was well taken. I clenched the hands. I set the jaw. I made the great decision.

'Very well, aged relative.'

'You will?'

'I will.'

'That's my boy. What's there to be afraid of? The worst those kids will do is rub chocolate eclairs on your whiskers.'

'Chocolate eclairs?' I said in a low voice.

'Or strawberry jam. It's a tribal custom. Pay no attention, by the way, to stories you may have heard of them setting fire to the curate's beard last year. It was purely accidental.'

I had begun to go into my aspen act, when Jeeves spoke.

'Pardon me, madam.'

'Yes, Jeeves?'

'If I might offer the suggestion, I think that perhaps a maturer artist than Mr Wooster would give a more convincing performance.'

'Don't tell me you're thinking of volunteering?'

'No, madam. The artist I had in mind was Sir Roderick Glossop. Sir Roderick has a fine presence and a somewhat deeper voice than Mr Wooster. His Ho-ho-ho would be more dramatically effective, and I am sure that if you approached him, you could persuade him to undertake the role.'

'Considering,' I said, putting in my oar, 'that he is always blacking up his face with burned cork.'

'Precisely, sir. This will make a nice change.'

Aunt Dahlia pondered.

'I believe you're right, Jeeves,' she said at length. 'It's tough on those children, for it means robbing them of the biggest laugh they've ever had, but they can't expect life to be one round of pleasure. Well, I don't think I'll have that drink after all. It's a bit early.'

She buzzed off, and I turned to Jeeves, deeply moved. He had saved me from an ordeal at the thought of which the flesh crept, for I hadn't believed for a moment the aged r's story of the blaze in the curate's beard having been an accident. The younger element had probably sat up nights planning it out.

'Jeeves,' I said, 'you were saying something not long ago about going to Florida after Christmas.'

'It was merely a suggestion, sir.'

'You want to catch a tarpon, do you not?'

'I confess that it is my ambition, sir.'

I sighed. It wasn't so much that it pained me to think of some tarpon, perhaps a wife and mother, being jerked from the society of its loved ones on the end of a hook. What gashed me like a knife was the thought of missing the Drones Club Darts Tournament, for which I would have been a snip this year. But what would you? I fought down my regret.

'Then will you be booking the tickets?'

'Very good, sir.'

I struck a graver note.

'Heaven help the tarpon that tries to pit its feeble cunning against you, Jeeves,' I said. 'Its efforts will be bootless.'

Our Man in America

'Not guilty!' spectators pouring out of a Denver, Colorado, court-room shouted to the waiting crowds in the street, and a great cheer went up, for public sympathy during the trial had been solidly with the prisoner in the dock, a parrot charged with using obscene language in a public spot.

The bird, it seems, had been accustomed to sit outside its owner's house watching the passers-by, and one of these, a woman of strict views, had it arrested, claiming that every time she passed by it used what she delicately described as 'Waterfront language'.

The jury would have liked to hear a few samples, but the parrot was too smart for that. Throughout the proceedings, no doubt on advice of counsel, it maintained a dignified silence, with the result that the rap could not be pinned on it. Later, when talking to reporters, it is said to have expressed itself with a good deal of frankness, being particularly candid about the ancestry of the deputy district attorney, who had conducted the prosecution.

*

Talking of reporters, considerable anxiety is being caused just now by the new trend which is creeping into the Presidential

Press conferences, if creeping is what trends do. Until recently the gentlemen of the Press just sat around and asked questions, and everything was fine, but now that these conferences are televised it has become the practice to switch the camera off the President and turn it on to the reporter as he speaks, and this has brought out all the ham in the young fellows. As nice a bunch of modest, unassuming chaps as you could wish to meet they used to be, but today you find them out in the corridors peering into pocket mirrors and practising the quick, keen glance with which they hope to slay their public. They call each other 'Laddie' and ask friends if they caught them on the screen last Friday when they jumped in and saved the show.

*

A rather interesting story comes from Toledo, Ohio, where Cyril Murphy (aged eight) was up before the Juvenile Court, accused of having tried to purloin a tin of fruit juice from a parked delivery truck.

He admitted the charge, but pleaded in extenuation that he had been egged on to the crime by the Devil. The Devil, he said, got into conversation with him and hearing that he was thirsty, for the day was warm, suggested that what he needed to correct this thirst was a good swig of fruit juice, which, he went on to point out, could be obtained from that delivery truck over there. Juvenile Court Referee Wade McBride advised him next time to make contact with an angel.

Cyril described the Devil as covered with hair, big balls of fire in his eyes, three horns, a long tail and four hooved feet, and the theory in New York theatrical circles is that what he met must have been a dramatic critic.

*

The news that Wayburn Mace, aged six, has been given a flash-light will probably have escaped the notice of the general public, but it is going to mean a lot to Mr Mace senior and the residents of Long Beach, California, for life for them should from now on become much more tranquil. It seems that Junior, suspecting the presence under his bed of Red Indians, went after them with a lighted candle, and the subsequent activities of the local fire brigade blocked traffic on all roads leading to the Mace home for several hours.

It is generally felt that no blame attaches to the little fellow. Nothing is more annoying than to have Red Indians under your bed, and the verdict is that he did the right and spirited thing in taking a firm line with them.

*

It is not lightly that one describes anyone as belonging to the old bulldog breed but surely George Clemens of Riverhead N.Y. is entitled to the accolade. He is fond of motoring and the other day this led to him appearing in the Riverside court before Justice of the Peace Otis J. Pike.

'H'm,' said Mr Pike. 'Driving without a licence, eh? Anything to say?'

George had. He explained that every time he takes a driving test he gets so nervous that everything goes black and they turn him down, leaving him no option but to cut the red tape and carry on without the papers which mean so much to the rest of us. He had been driving without a licence for twenty years, he said.

Mr Pike consulted the charge sheet.

'Reckless driving? Speeding? Improper turns? Going through seven red lights and refusing to stop when ordered to by a police-man? Looks bad, George.'

Mr Clemens admitted that superficially his actions might seem to call for comment, but not if you got the full story.

'It wasn't really my fault, your honour,' he said. 'I was drunk at the time.'

In his office on the premises of Popgood and Grooly, publishers of the Book Beautiful, Madison Avenue, New York, Cyril Grooly, the firm's junior partner, was practising putts into a tooth glass and doing rather badly even for one with a twenty-four handicap, when Patricia Binstead, Mr Popgood's secretary, entered, and dropping his putter he folded her in a close embrace. This was not because all American publishers are warm-hearted impulsive men and she a very attractive girl, but because they had recently become betrothed. On his return from his summer vacation at Paradise Valley, due to begin this afternoon, they would step along to some convenient church and become man, if you can call someone with a twenty-four handicap a man, and wife.

'A social visit?' he asked, the embrace concluded. 'Or business?'

'Business. Popgood had to go out to see a man about subsidiary rights, and Count Dracula has blown in. Well, when I say Count Dracula, I speak loosely. He just looks like him. His name is Professor Pepperidge Farmer, and he's come to sign his contract.'

'He writes books?'

'He's written one. He calls it *Hypnotism As A Device To Uncover The Unconscious Drives and Mechanism In An Effort*

To Analyse The Functions Involved Which Give Rise To Emotional Conflicts In The Waking State, but the title's going to be changed to *Sleepy Time*. Popgood thinks it's snappier.'

'Much snappier.'

'Shall I send him in?'

'Do so, queen of my soul.'

'And Popgood says be sure not to go above two hundred dollars for the advance,' said Patricia, and a few moments later the visitor made his appearance.

It was an appearance, as Patricia had hinted, of a nature to chill the spine. Sinister was the adjective that automatically sprang to the lips of those who met Professor Pepperidge Farmer for the first time. His face was gaunt and lined and grim, and as his burning eyes bored into Cyril's the young publisher was conscious of a feeling of relief that this encounter was not taking place down a dark alley or in some lonely spot in the country. But a man used to mingling with American authors, few of whom look like anything on earth, is not readily intimidated and he greeted him with his customary easy courtesy.

'Come right in,' he said. 'You've caught me just in time. I'm off to Paradise Valley this afternoon.'

'A golfing holiday?' said the Professor, eyeing the putter.

'Yes, I'm looking forward to getting some golf.'

'How is your game?'

'Horrible,' Cyril was obliged to confess. 'Mine is a sad and peculiar case. I have the theory of golf at my fingertips, but once out in the middle I do nothing but foozle.'

'You should keep your head down.'

'So Tommy Armour tells me, but up it comes.'

'That's Life.'

'Or shall we say hell?'

'If you prefer it.'

'It seems the *mot juste*. But now to business. Miss Binstead tells me you have come to sign your contract. I have it here. It all appears to be in order except that the amount of the advance has not been decided on.'

'And what are your views on that?'

'I was thinking of a hundred dollars. You see,' said Cyril, falling smoothly into his stride, 'a book like yours always involves a serious risk for the publisher owing to the absence of the Sex Motif, which renders it impossible for him to put a nude female of impressive vital statistics on the jacket and no hope of getting banned in Boston. Add the growing cost of paper and the ever-increasing demands of printers, compositors, binders and . . . why are you waving your hands like that?'

'I have French blood in me. On the mother's side.'

'Well, I wish you wouldn't. You're making me sleepy.'

'Oh, am I? How very interesting. Yes, I can see that your eyes are closing. You are becoming drowsy. You are falling asleep . . . you are falling asleep . . . asleep . . . asleep . . . asleep . . .'

It was getting on for lunch time when Cyril awoke. When he did so, he found that the recent gargoyle was no longer with him. Odd, he felt, that the fellow should have gone before they had settled the amount of his advance, but no doubt he had remembered some appointment elsewhere. Dismissing him from his mind, Cyril resumed his putting, and soon after lunch he left for Paradise Valley.

On the subject of Paradise Valley the public relations representative of the Paradise Hotel has expressed himself very frankly. It is, he says in his illustrated booklet, a dream world of breathtaking beauty, and its noble scenery, its wide open spaces, its soft mountain breezes and its sun-drenched pleasances impart to the jaded city worker a new vim and vigour and fill him so full of red corpuscles that before a day has elapsed in these delightful surroundings he is conscious of a *je ne sais quoi* and a *bien être* and goes about with his chin up and both feet on the ground, feeling as if he had just come back from the cleaner's. And, what is more, only a step from the hotel lies the Squashy Hollow golf course, of whose amenities residents can avail themselves on payment of a green fee.

What, however, the booklet omits to mention is that the Squashy Hollow course is one of the most difficult in the country. It was constructed by an exiled Scot who, probably from some deep-seated grudge against the human race, has modelled the eighteen holes on the nastiest and most repellent of his native land, so that after negotiating – say – the Alps at Prestwick, the pleasure-seeker finds himself confronted by the Stationmaster's Garden at St Andrews, with the Eden and the Redan just around the corner.

The type of golfer it attracts, therefore, is the one with high ideals and an implicit confidence in his ability to overcome the toughest obstacles; the sort who plays in amateur championships and mutters to himself 'Why this strange weakness?' if he shoots worse than a seventy-five, and one look at it gave Cyril that uncomfortable feeling known to scientists as the heeby-jeebies. He had entered for the medal contest which was to take place tomorrow, for he always entered for medal contests, never being able to forget that he had once shot a ninety-eight and that this, if repeated, would with his handicap give him a sporting chance of success. But the prospect of performing in front of all these hardened experts created in him the illusion that caterpillars to the number of about fifty-seven were parading up and down his spinal cord. He shrank from exposing himself to their bleak contemptuous stares. His emotions when he did would, he knew, be similar in almost every respect to those of a mongrel which has been rash enough to wander into some fashionable Kennel Show.

As, then, he sat on the porch of the Paradise Hotel on the morning before the contest, he was so far from being filled with *bien être* that he could not even achieve *je ne sais quoi*, and at this moment the seal was set on his despondency by the sight of Agnes Flack.

Agnes Flack was a large young woman who on the first day of his arrival had discovered that he was a partner in a publishing firm and had immediately begun to speak of a novel which she had written and would be glad to have his opinion of when he had a little time to spare. And experience had taught him that when large young women wrote novels they were either squashily sentimental or so Chatterleyesque that it would be necessary to print them on asbestos, and he had spent much of his leisure avoiding her. She seemed now to be coming in his direction, so rising hastily he made on winged feet for the bar. Entering it at a rapid gallop, he collided with a solid body, and this proved on inspection to be none other than Professor Pepperidge Farmer, looking more sinister than ever in Bermuda shorts, a shirt like a Turner sunset and a Panama hat with a pink ribbon round it.

He stood amazed. There was, of course, no reason why the other should not have been there, for the hotel was open to all whose purses were equal to the tariff, but somehow he seemed out of place, like a ghoul at a garden party or a vampire bat at a picnic.

'You!' he exclaimed. 'What ever became of you that morning?'

'You allude to our previous meeting?' said the Professor. 'I saw you had dozed off, so I tiptoed out without disturbing you. I thought it would be better to resume our acquaintance in these more agreeable surroundings. For if you are thinking that my presence here is due to one of those coincidences which are so strained and inartistic, you are wrong. I came in the hope that I might be able to do something to improve your golf game. I feel I owe you a great deal.'

'You do? Why?'

'We can go into that some other time. Tell me, how is the golf going? Any improvement?'

If he had hoped to receive confidences, he could not have put the question at a better moment. Cyril did not habitually bare his soul to comparative strangers, but now he found himself unable to resist the urge. It was as though the Professor's query had drawn a cork and brought all his doubts and fears and inhibitions foaming out like ginger pop from a ginger pop bottle. As far as reticence was concerned, he might have been on a psychoanalyst's couch at twenty-five dollars the half-hour. In burning words he spoke of the coming medal contest, stressing his qualms and the growing coldness of his feet, and the Professor listened attentively, clicking a sympathetic tongue from time to time. It was plain that though he looked like something Charles Addams might have thought up when in the throes of a hangover, if Mr Addams does ever have hangovers, he had a feeling heart.

'I'm paired with a fellow called Sidney McMurdo, who they tell me is the club champion, and I fear his scorn. It's going to take me at least a hundred and fifteen shots for the round, and on each of those hundred and fifteen shots Sidney McMurdo will look at me as if I were something slimy and obscene that had crawled out from under a flat stone. I shall feel like a crippled leper, and so,' said Cyril, concluding his remarks, 'I have decided to take my name off the list of entrants. Call me weak if you will, but I can't face it.'

The Professor patted him on the shoulder in a fatherly manner and was about to speak, but before he could do so Cyril heard his name paged and was told that he was wanted on the telephone. It was some little time before he returned, and when he did the dullest eye could see that something had occurred to ruffle him. He found Professor Farmer sipping a lemon squash, and when the Professor asked him if he would care for one of the same, he thundered out a violent No.

'Blast and damn all lemon squashes!' he cried vehemently. 'Do you know who that was on the phone? It was Popgood, my senior partner. And do you know what he said? He wanted to know what had got into me to make me sign a contract giving you five thousand dollars advance on that book of yours. He said you must have hypnotized me.'

A smile, probably intended to be gentle, but conveying the impression that he was suffering from some internal disorder, played over the Professor's face.

'Of course I did, my dear fellow. It was one of the ordinary business precautions an author has to take. The only way to get a decent advance from a publisher is to hypnotize him. That was what I was referring to when I said I owed you a great deal. But for you I should never have been able to afford a holiday at a place like Paradise Valley where even the simplest lemon squash sets you back a prince's ransom. Was Popgood annoyed?'

'He was.'

'Too bad. He should have been rejoicing to think that his money had been instrumental in bringing a little sunshine into a fellow creature's life. But let us forget him and return to this matter of your golfing problems.'

He had said the one thing capable of diverting Cyril's thoughts from his incandescent partner. No twenty-four handicap man is ever deaf to such an appeal.

'You told me you had all the theory of the game at your fingertips. Is that so? Your reading has been wide?'

'I've read every golf book that has been written.'

'You mentioned Tommy Armour. Have you studied his preachings?'

'I know them by heart.'

'But lack of confidence prevents you putting them into practice?'

'I suppose that's it.'

'Then the solution is simple. I must hypnotize you again. You should still be under the influence, but the effects may have worn off and it's best to be on the safe side. I will instil into you the conviction that you can knock spots off the proudest McMurdo. When you take club in hand, it will be with the certainty that your ball is going to travel from Point A to Point B by the shortest route and will meet with no misadventures on the way. Whose game would you prefer yours to resemble? Arnold Palmer's? Gary Player's? Jack Nicklaus's? Palmer's is the one I would recommend. Those spectacular finishes of his. You agree? Palmer it shall be, then. So away we go. Your eyes are closing. You are feeling drowsy. You are falling asleep . . . asleep . . . asleep . . .'

Paradise Valley was at its best next day, its scenery just as noble, its mountain breezes just as soft, its spaces fully as wide and open as the public relations man's booklet had claimed them to be, and Cyril, as he stood beside the first tee of the Squashy Hollow course awaiting Sidney McMurdo's arrival, was feeling, as he had confided to the caddy master when picking up his clubs, like a million dollars. He would indeed scarcely have been exaggerating if he had made it two million. His chin was up, both his feet were on the ground, and the red corpuscles of which the booklet had spoken coursed through his body like students rioting in Saigon, Moscow, Cairo, Panama and other centres. Professor Farmer, in assuring him that he would become as confident as Arnold Palmer, had understated it. He was as confident as Arnold Palmer, Gary Player, Ray Venturi, Jack Nicklaus and Tony Lema all rolled into one.

He had not been waiting long when he beheld a vast expanse of man approaching and presumed that this must be his partner for the round. He gave him a sunny smile.

'Mr McMurdo? How do you do? Nice day. Very pleasant, those soft mountain breezes.'

The newcomer's only response was a bronchial sound such as might have been produced by an elephant taking its foot out of a swamp in a teak forest. Sidney McMurdo was in dark and sullen mood. On the previous night Agnes Flack, his fiancée, had broken their engagement owing to a trifling disagreement they had had about the novel she had written. He had said it was a lot of prune juice and advised her to burn it without delay, and she had said it was not, too, a lot of prune juice, adding that she never wanted to see or speak to him again, and this had affected him adversely. It always annoyed him when Agnes Flack broke their engagement, because it made him overswing, particularly off the tee.

He did so now, having won the honour, and was pained to see that his ball, which he had intended to go due north, was travelling nor'-nor'-east. And as he stood scowling after it, Cyril spoke.

'I wonder if you noticed what you did wrong there, Mr McMurdo,' he said in the friendliest way. 'Your backswing was too long. Length of backswing does not have as much effect on distance as many believe. You should swing back only just as far as you can without losing control of the club. Control is all-important. I always take my driver to about the horizontal position on the backswing. Watch me now.'

And so saying Cyril with effortless grace drove two hundred and eighty yards straight down the fairway.

'See what I mean?' he said.

It was on the fourth green, after he had done an eagle, that he spoke again. Sidney McMurdo had had some difficulty in getting out of a sand trap and he hastened to give him the benefit of his advice. There was nothing in it for him except the glow that comes from doing an act of kindness, but it distressed him to see a quite promising player like McMurdo making mistakes of which a wiser head could so easily cure him.

'You did not allow for the texture of the sand,' he said. 'Your sand shot should differ with the texture of the sand. If it is wet, hard or shallow, your clubhead will not cut into it as deeply as it would into soft and shifting sand. If the sand is soft, try to dig into it about two inches behind the ball, but when it is hard penetrate it about one and a half inches behind the ball. And since firm sand will slow down your club considerably, be sure to give your swing a full follow-through.'

The game proceeded. On the twelfth Cyril warned his partner to be careful to remember to bend the knees slightly for greater flexibility throughout the swing, though – on the sixteenth – he warned against bending them too much, as this often led to topping. When both had holed out at the eighteenth, he had a word of counsel to give on the subject of putting.

'Successful putting, Sidney,' he said, for he felt that they might now consider themselves on first name terms, 'depends largely on the mental attitude. Confidence is everything. Never let anxiety make you tense. Never for an instant harbour the thought that your shot may miss. When I sank that last fifty-foot putt, I *knew* it was going in. My mind was filled with a picture of the ball following a proper line to the hole, and it is that sort of picture I should like to encourage in you. Well, it has been a most pleasant round. We must have another soon. I shot a sixty-two, did I not? I thought so. I was quite on my game today, quite on my game.'

Sidney McMurdo's eyebrows, always beetling, were beetling still more darkly as he watched Cyril walking away with elastic tread. He turned to a friend who had just come up.

'Who is that fellow?' he asked hoarsely.

'His name's Grooly,' said the friend. 'One of the summer visitors.'

'What's his handicap?'

'I can tell you that, for I was looking at the board this morning. It's twenty-four.'

'Air!' cried Sidney McMurdo, clutching his throat. 'Give me air!'

Cyril, meanwhile, had rounded the clubhouse and was approaching the practice green that lay behind it. Someone large and female was engaged there in polishing her chip shots, and as he paused to watch he stood astounded at her virtuosity. A chip shot, he was aware, having read his Johnny Farrell, is a crisp hit with the clubhead stopping at the ball and not following through. 'Open your stance,' says the venerable Farrell, 'place your weight on the left foot and hit down at the ball,' and this was precisely what this substantial female was doing. Each ball she struck dropped on the green like a poached egg, and as she advanced to pick them up he saw that she was Agnes Flack.

A loud gasp escaped Cyril. The dream world of breathtaking beauty pirouetted before his eyes as if Arthur Murray were teaching it dancing in a hurry. He was conscious of strange, tumultuous emotions stirring within him. Then the mists cleared, and gazing at Agnes Flack he knew that there before him stood his destined mate. A novelist she might be and no doubt as ghastly a novelist as ever set finger to typewriter key, but what of that? Quite possibly she would grow out of it in time, and in any case he felt that as a man who went about shooting sixty-twos in medal contests he owed it to himself to link his lot with a golfer of her calibre. Theirs would be the ideal union.

In a situation like this no publisher hesitates. A moment later, Cyril was on the green, his arms as far around Agnes Flack as they would go.

'Old girl,' he said. 'You're a grand bit of work!'

Two courses were open to Agnes Flack. She could draw herself to her full height, say 'Sir!' and strike this clinging vine with her number seven iron, or, remembering that Cyril was a publisher and that she had a top copy and two carbons of a novel in her suitcase, she could co-operate and accept his addresses. She chose the latter alternative, and when Cyril suggested that they should spend the honeymoon in Scotland, playing all the famous courses there, she said that that would suit her perfectly. If, as she plighted her troth, a thought of Sidney McMurdo came into her mind, it was merely the renewed conviction that he was an oaf and a fathead temperamentally incapable of recognizing good literature when it was handed to him on a skewer.

These passionate scenes take it out of a man, and it is not surprising that Cyril's first move on leaving Agnes Flack should have been in the direction of the bar. Arriving there, he found Professor Farmer steeping himself, as was his custom, in lemon squashes. The warm weather engendered thirst, and since he had come to the Paradise Hotel the straw had seldom left his lips.

'Ah, Cyril, if you don't mind me calling you Cyril, though you will be the first to admit that it's a hell of a name,' said the Professor. 'How did everything come out?'

'Quite satisfactorily, Pepperidge. The returns are not all in, but I think I must have won the medal. I shot a sixty-two, which, subtracting my handicap, gives me a thirty-eight. I doubt if anyone will do better than thirty-eight.'

'Most unlikely.'

'Thirty-four under par takes a lot of beating.'

'Quite a good deal. I congratulate you.'

'And that's not all. I'm engaged to the most wonderful girl.'

'Really? I congratulate you again. Who is she?'

'Her name is Agnes Flack.'

The Professor started, dislodging a drop of lemon squash from his lower lip.

'Agnes Flack?'

'Yes.'

'You couldn't be mistaken in the name?'

'No.'

'H'm!'

'Why do you say H'm?'

'I was thinking of Sidney McMurdo.'

'How does he get into the act?'

'He is – or was – betrothed to Agnes Flack, and I am told he has rather a short way with men who get engaged to his fiancée, even if technically ex. Do you know a publisher called Pickering?'

'Harold Pickering? I've met him.'

'He got engaged to Agnes Flack, and it was only by butting Sidney McMurdo in the stomach with his head and disappearing over the horizon that he was able to avoid being torn by the latter into little pieces. But for his ready resource he would have become converted into, as one might say, a sort of publishing hash, though, of course, McMurdo might simply have jumped on him with spiked shoes.'

It was Cyril's turn to say H'm, and he said it with a good deal of thoughtful fervour. He had parted so recently from Sidney McMurdo that he had not had time to erase from his mental retina what might be called the over-all picture of him. The massive bulk of Sidney McMurdo rose before his eyes, as did the other's rippling muscles. The discovery that in addition to possessing the physique of a gorilla he had also that animal's easily aroused temper was not one calculated to induce a restful peace of mind. Given the choice between annoying Sidney McMurdo and stirring up a nest of hornets with a fountain pen, he would unhesitatingly have cast his vote for the hornets.

And it was as he sat trying to think what was to be done for the best that the door flew open and the bar became full of McMurdo. He seemed to permeate its every nook and cranny. Nor had Professor Farmer erred in predicting that his mood would be edgy. His eyes blazed, his ears wiggled and a clicking sound like the manipulation of castanets by a Spanish dancer told that he was gnashing his teeth. Except that he was not beating his chest with both fists, he resembled in every respect the gorilla to which Cyril had mentally compared him.

'Ha!' he said, sighting Cyril.

'Oh, hullo, Sidney.'

'Less of the Sidney!' snarled McMurdo. 'I don't want a man of your kidney calling me Sidney,' he went on, rather surprisingly dropping into poetry. 'Agnes Flack tells me she is engaged to you.'

Cyril replied nervously that there had been some informal conversation along those lines.

'She says you hugged her.'

'Only a little.'

'And kissed her.'

'In the most respectful manner.'

'In other words, you have sneaked behind my back like a slithery serpent and stolen from me the woman I love. Perhaps, if you have a moment to spare, you will step outside.'

Cyril did not wish to step outside, but it seemed that there was no alternative. He preceded Sidney McMurdo through the door, and was surprised on reaching the wide open spaces to find that Professor Farmer had joined the party. The Professor was regarding Sidney with that penetrating gaze of his which made him look like Boris Karloff on one of his bad mornings.

'Might I ask you to look me in the eye for a moment, Mr McMurdo,' he said. 'Thank you. Yes, as I thought. You are drowsy. Your eyes are closing. You are falling asleep.'

'No, I'm not.'

'Yes, you are.'

'By Jove, I believe you're right,' said Sidney McMurdo, sinking slowly into a conveniently placed deck chair. 'Yes, I think I'll take a nap.'

The Professor continued to weave arabesques in the air with his hands, and suddenly Sidney McMurdo sat up. His eye rested on Cyril, but it was no longer the flaming eye it had been. Almost affectionate it seemed, and when he spoke his voice was mild.

'Mr Grooly.'

'On the spot.'

'I have been thinking it over, Mr Grooly, and I have reached a decision which, though painful, I am sure is right. It is wrong to think only of self. There are times when a man must make the great sacrifice no matter what distress it causes him. You love Agnes Flack, Agnes loves you, and I must not come between you. Take her, Mr Grooly. I yield her to you, yield her freely. It breaks my heart, but her happiness is all that matters. Take her, Grooly, and if a broken man's blessing is of any use to you, I give it without reserve. I think I'll go to the bar and have a gin and tonic,' said Sidney McMurdo, and proceeded to do so.

'A very happy conclusion to your afternoon's activities,' said Professor Farmer as the swing door closed behind him. 'I often say that there is nothing like hypnotism for straightening out these little difficulties. I thought McMurdo's speech of renunciation was very well phrased, didn't you? In perfect taste. Well, as you will now no longer have need of my services, I suppose I had better de-hypnotize you. It will not be painful, just a momentary twinge,' said the Professor, blowing a lemon-squash-charged breath in Cyril's face, and Cyril was aware of an odd feeling of having been hit by an atom bomb while making a descent in an express elevator. He found himself a little puzzled by his companion's choice of the expression 'momentary twinge', but he had not leisure to go into what was after all a side issue. With the removal of the hypnotic spell there had come to him the realization of the unfortunate position in which he had placed himself, and he uttered a sharp 'Oh, golly!'

'I beg your pardon?' said the Professor.

'Listen,' said Cyril, and his voice shook like a jelly in a high wind. 'Does it count if you ask a girl to marry you when you're hypnotized?'

'You are speaking of Miss Flack?'

'Yes, I proposed to her on the practice green, carried away by the super-excellence of her chip shots, and I can't stand the sight of her. And, what's more, in about three weeks I'm supposed to be marrying someone else. You remember Patricia Binstead, the girl who showed you into my office?'

'Very vividly.'

'She holds the copyright. What am I to do? You couldn't go and hypnotize Agnes Flack and instil her, as you call it, with the idea that I'm the world's leading louse, could you?'

'My dear fellow, nothing easier.'

'Then do it without an instant's delay,' said Cyril. 'Tell her I'm scratch and pretended to have a twenty-four handicap in order to win the medal. Tell her I'm sober only at the rarest intervals. Tell her I'm a Communist spy and my name's really Groolinsky. Tell her I've two wives already. But you'll know what to say.'

He waited breathlessly for the Professor's return.

'Well?' he cried.

'All washed up, my dear Cyril. I left her reunited to McMurdo. She says she wouldn't marry you if you were the last publisher on earth and wouldn't let you sponsor her novel if you begged her on bended knees. She says she is going to let Simon and Schuster have it, and she hopes that will be a lesson to you.'

Cyril drew a deep breath.

'Pepperidge, you're wonderful!'

'One does one's best,' said the Professor modestly. 'Well, now that the happy ending has been achieved, how about returning to the bar? I'll buy you a lemon squash.'

'Do you really like that stuff?'

'I love it.'

It was on the tip of Cyril's tongue to say that one would have thought he was a man who would be more likely to share Count Dracula's preference for human blood when thirsty, but he refrained from putting the thought into words. It might, he felt, be lacking in tact, and after all, why criticize a man for looking like something out of a horror film if his heart was so patently of the purest gold. It is the heart that matters, not the features, however unshuffled.

'I'm with you,' he said. 'A lemon squash would be most refreshing.'

'They serve a very good lemon squash here.'

'Probably made from contented lemons.'

'I shouldn't wonder,' said the Professor.

He smiled a hideous smile. It had just occurred to him that if he hypnotized the waiter, he would be spared the necessity of disbursing money, always a consideration to a man of slender means.

Our Man in America

The trend in Television Westerns is now towards sweetness and light. 'Adult Westerns' they call them, an adult Western broadly speaking, being one where gun play is kept down to a minimum and the good guy does not kill the bad guy but tries to understand him. The sheriff who used to start the conversational ball rolling with some such remark as 'Best say your prayers, Hank Spivis, 'cos Ah'm a-goin' to drill yer like a dawg' is out of vogue. Today he leads the man to the office couch and psychoanalyses him. It turns out in the end that the reason why Hank rustles cattle and shoots up the Malemute saloon on Saturday nights is that, when he was three, his mother took away his all-day sucker, and we fade out on a medium shot of him, a reformed character in a morning coat and top hat, selling his life story to a motion picture studio for a hundred thousand dollars.

Indians, too, rarely bite the dust nowadays on the Television screen. They have a quiet talk with the Commandant of the U.S. Cavalry at the fort ('Is your scalping really necessary?') as the result of which they toddle off and go into the hay, corn and feed business and do well.

*

The mystery, which has puzzled so many, of where all these darned American novels come from, is partially solved by an interview in one of the papers with a Mrs Handy, who runs the Handy Colony for Writers at Marshall, Illinois, and encourages young authors in their dark work, taking in twenty at a time.

'Everybody's up at five each morning,' says Mrs Handy, 'then a quick bite and right to work on their novels. I go over everything they write, keeping after them, making them rewrite. Everybody writes around the camp. My mother-in-law is ninety. She learned to type at eighty-five and has just finished her first novel. It's not right. She'll have to do it again.'

To me the interesting thing about this is that it makes it plain that American novels are produced deliberately. For years I had been looking on them as just Acts of God like those waterspouts, attacks by pirates and mutiny on the high seas which you are warned to look out for when you travel on the White-Star-Cunard line.

*

Dieting continues to be all the go on this side of the Atlantic, and the number of those who hope to become streamlined by pushing their plates away untasted increases daily. But there are still some sturdy souls who enjoy a square meal, notably in Detroit, Michigan. The health commissioner of that city has just published a list of the peculiar things eaten and drunk by the citizens during his three years of office. It includes insecticides, detergents, laundry bleaches, chalk and charcoal (washed down with ink) and lighter fluid. I have never actually attended any of these Detroit parties, but the picture I conjure up is of a sort of Dickens Christmas, the detergent bowl circulating freely and the air ringing with merry cries of 'Don't spare the shoe-polish,

Percy' and 'After you with the insecticide, George'. And the extraordinary thing is that the revellers seem to thrive on the stuff. The rosy cheeks and sparkling eyes to be seen in Detroit would reach, if placed end to end, for miles and miles and miles.

*

Good news for those who want rabbits' ears to droop limply instead of sticking up as they do at present comes from the New York Heart Association, whose Doctor Lewis Thomas has discovered that all you have to do is inject enzyme-papain into the rabbit. The Association chaps are pretty pleased about it, but in my opinion too easily pleased. It is all very well to go slapping Doctor Lewis Thomas on the back and standing him drinks, but when all the smoke has cleared away, what has he got? Merely a rabbit from whose ears the starch has been removed. If he likes that sort of rabbit, well and good, and I have nothing to say. But I think children and nervous people should be warned in case they meet one accidentally.

*

And now let us take a quick glance at the cat situation in Tennessee. We learn that Mrs Chester Missey of Knoxville in that state had put some towels in her automatic clothes dryer the other day when she was called to the telephone. She had not been talking long before a suspicion floated into her mind that something was amiss.

'I glanced at the dryer,' she told reporters, 'and saw this white thing going around inside. I knew I hadn't put anything white in there, just brown towels.'

So she opened the door, and there was her cat Murphy doing, like a South American republic, sixty revolutions to the minute.

It is pleasant to be able to record that after five minutes, during which he was getting back his breath, Murphy was 'just as alive as he can be' – which, if you know Tennessee cats, is saying a lot.

It was a beautiful afternoon. The sky was blue, the sun yellow, butterflies flitted, birds tooted, bees buzzed and, to cut a long story short, all Nature smiled. But on Lord Emsworth's younger son Freddie Threepwood, as he sat in his sports model car at the front door of Blandings Castle, a fine Alsatian dog at his side, these excellent weather conditions made little impression. He was thinking of dog biscuits.

Freddie was only an occasional visitor at the castle these days. Some years before, he had married the charming daughter of Mr Donaldson of Donaldson's Dog Joy, the organization whose aim it is to keep the American dog one hundred per cent red-blooded by supplying it with wholesome and nourishing biscuits, and had gone off to Long Island City, U.S.A., to work for the firm. He was in England now because his father-in-law, anxious to extend Dog Joy's sphere of influence, had sent him back there to see what he could do in the way of increasing sales in the island kingdom. Aggie, his wife, had accompanied him, but after a week or so had found life at Blandings too quiet for her and had left for the French Riviera. The arrangement was that at the conclusion of his English campaign Freddie should join her there.

He was drying his left ear, on which the Alsatian had just

bestowed a moist caress, when there came down the front steps a small, dapper elderly gentleman with a black-rimmed monocle in his eye. This was that notable figure of London's Bohemia, his Uncle Galahad, at whom the world of the theatre, the race-course and the livelier type of restaurant had been pointing with pride for years. He greeted him cordially. To his sisters Constance, Julia, Dora and Hermione Gally might be a blot on the escutcheon, but in Freddie he excited only admiration. He considered him a man of infinite resource and sagacity, as indeed he was.

'Well, young Freddie,' said Gally. 'Where are you off to with that dog?'

'I'm taking him to the Fanshawes.'

'At Marling Hall? That's where that pretty girl I met you with the other day lives, isn't it?'

'That's right. Valerie Fanshawe. Her father's the local Master of Hounds. And you know what that means.'

'What does it mean?'

'That he's the managing director of more dogs than you could shake a stick at, each dog requiring the daily biscuit. And what could be better for them than Donaldson's Dog Joy, containing as it does all the essential vitamins?'

'You're going to sell him dog biscuits?'

'I don't see how I can miss. Valerie is the apple of his eye, to whom he can deny nothing. She covets this Alsatian and says if I'll give it to her, she'll see that the old man comes through with a substantial order. I'm about to deliver it F.O.B.'

'But, my good Freddie, that dog is Aggie's dog. She'll go up in flames.'

'Oh, that's all right. I've budgeted for that. I have my story all set and ready. I shall tell her it died and I'll get her another just as good. That'll fix Aggie. But I mustn't sit here chewing the fat with you, I must be up and about and off and away. See you later,' said Freddie, and disappeared in a cloud of smoke.

He left Gally pursing his lips. A lifetime spent in the society of bookies, racecourse touts and skittle sharps had made him singularly broadminded, but he could not regard these tactics with approval. Shaking his head, he went back into the house and in the hall encountered Beach, the castle butler. Beach was wheezing a little, for he had been hurrying, and he was no longer the streamlined young butler he had been when he had first taken office.

'Have I missed Mr Frederick, sir?'

'By a hair's breadth. Why?'

'This telegram has arrived for him, Mr Galahad. I thought it might be important.'

'Most unlikely. Probably somebody just wiring him the result of the four o'clock race somewhere. Give it to me. I'll see that he gets it on his return.'

He continued on his way, feeling now rather at a loose end. A sociable man, he wanted someone to talk to. He could of course go and chat with his sister Lady Constance, who was reading a novel on the terrace, but something told him that there would be little profit and entertainment in this. Most of his conversation consisted of anecdotes of his murky past, and Connie was not a good audience for these. He decided on consideration to look up his brother Clarence, with whom it was always a pleasure to exchange ideas, and found that mild and dreamy peer in the library staring fixedly at nothing.

'Ah, there you are, Clarence,' he said, and Lord Emsworth sat up with a startled 'Eh, what?', his stringy body quivering.

'Oh, it's you, Galahad.'

PLUM PIE

'None other. What's the matter, Clarence?'

'Matter?'

'There's something on your mind. The symptoms are un-mistakable. A man whose soul is at rest does not leap like a nymph surprised while bathing when somebody tells him he's there. Confide in me.'

Lord Emsworth was only too glad to do so. A sympathetic listener was precisely what he wanted.

'It's Connie,' he said. 'Did you hear what she was saying at breakfast?'

'I didn't come down to breakfast.'

'Ah, then you probably missed it. Well, right in the middle of the meal – I was eating a kippered herring at the time – she told me she was going to get rid of Beach.'

'What! Get rid of *Beach*?'

'"He is so slow," she said. "He wheezes. We ought to have a younger, smarter butler." I was appalled. I choked on my kippered herring.'

'I don't blame you. Blandings without Beach is unthinkable. So is Blandings with what she calls a young, smart butler at the helm. Good God! I can picture the sort of fellow she would get, some acrobatic stripling who would turn somersaults and slide down the banisters. You must put your foot down, Clarence.'

'Who, me?' said Lord Emsworth.

The idea seemed to him too bizarre for consideration. He was, as has been said, a mild, dreamy man, his sister Constance a forceful and imperious woman modelled on the lines of the late Cleopatra. Nominally he was the master of the house and as such entitled to exercise the Presidential Veto, but in practice Connie's word was always law. Look at the way she made him wear a top hat at the annual village school treat. He had reasoned and pleaded, pointing out in the clearest possible way that for a purely rural festivity of that sort a simple fishing hat would be far more suitable, but every year when August came around there he was, balancing the beastly thing on his head again and just asking the children in the tea tent to throw rock cakes at it.

'I can't put my foot down with Connie.'

'Well, I can, and I'm going to. Fire Beach, indeed! After eighteen years' devoted service. The idea's monstrous.'

'He would of course receive a pension.'

'It's no good her thinking she can gloss it over with any talk about pensions. Wrap it up as she may, the stark fact remains that she's planning to fire him. She must not be allowed to do this frightful thing. Good heavens, you might just as well fire the Archbishop of Canterbury.'

He would have spoken further, but at this moment there came from the stairs outside the slumping of feet, announcing that Freddie was back from the Fanshawes and on his way to his room. Lord Emsworth winced. Like so many aristocratic fathers, he was allergic to younger sons, and since going to live in America Freddie had acquired a brisk, go-getter jumpiness which jarred upon him.

'Frederick,' he said with a shudder, and Gally started.

'I've got a telegram for Freddie,' he said. 'I'd better take it up to him.'

'Do,' said Lord Emsworth. 'And I think I will be going and having a look at my flowers.'

He left the room and making for the rose garden pottered slowly to and fro, sniffing at its contents. It was a procedure which as a rule gave him great pleasure, but today his heavy heart found no solace in the scent of roses. Listlessly he returned to the library and took a favourite pig book from its shelf. But even pig books were no palliative. The thought of Beach fading from the Blandings scene, if a man of his bulk could be said to fade, prohibited concentration.

He had sunk into a sombre reverie, when it was interrupted by the entrance of the subject of his gloomy meditations.

'Pardon me, m'lord,' said Beach. 'Mr Galahad desires me to ask if you would step down to the smoking-room and speak to him.'

'Why can't he come up here?'

'He has sprained his ankle, m'lord. He and Mr Frederick fell downstairs.'

'Oh?' said Lord Emsworth, not particularly interested. Freddie was always doing odd things. So was Galahad. 'How did that happen?'

'Mr Galahad informs me that he handed Mr Frederick a telegram. Mr Frederick, having opened and perused it, uttered a sharp exclamation, reeled, clutched at Mr Galahad, and they both fell downstairs. Mr Frederick, too, has sprained his ankle. He has retired to bed.'

'Bless my soul. Are they in pain?'

'I gather that the agony has to some extent abated. They have been receiving treatment from the kitchen maid. She is a Brownie.'

'She's a *what*?'

'A Brownie, m'lord. I understand it is a species of female Boy Scout. They are instructed in the fundamentals of first aid.'

'Eh? First aid? Oh, you mean first aid,' said Lord Emsworth, reading between the lines. 'Bandages and that sort of thing, what?'

'Precisely, m'lord.'

By the time Lord Emsworth reached the smoking-room the Brownie had completed her ministrations and gone back to her *Screen Gems*. Gally was lying on a sofa, looking not greatly disturbed by his accident. He was smoking a cigar.

'Beach tells me you had a fall,' said Lord Emsworth.

'A stinker,' Gally assented. 'As who wouldn't when an ass of a nephew grabs him at the top of two flights of stairs.'

'Beach seems to think Frederick's action was caused by some bad news in the telegram which you gave to him.'

'That's right. It was from Aggie.'

'Aggie?'

'His wife.'

'I thought her name was Frances.'

'No, Niagara.'

'What a peculiar name.'

'A gush of sentiment on the part of her parents. They spent the honeymoon at Niagara Falls.'

'Ah yes, I have heard of Niagara Falls. People go over them in barrels, do they not? Now there is a thing I would not care to do myself. Most uncomfortable, I should imagine, though no doubt one would get used to it in time. Why was her telegram so disturbing?'

'Because she says she's coming here and will be with us the day after tomorrow.'

'I see no objection to that.'

'Freddie does, and I'll tell you why. He's gone and given her dog to Valerie Fanshawe.'

'Who is Valerie Fanshawe?'

'The daughter of Colonel Fanshawe of Marling Hall, the tally-ho and view-halloo chap. Haven't you met him?'

'No,' said Lord Emsworth, who never met anyone, if he could

help it. 'But why should Frances object to Frederick giving this young woman a dog?'

'I didn't say *a* dog, I said *her* dog. Her personal Alsatian, whom she loves to distraction. However, that could be straightened out, I imagine, with a few kisses and a remorseful word or two if Valerie Fanshawe were a girl with a pasty face and spectacles, but unfortunately she isn't. Her hair is golden, her eyes blue, and years of huntin', shootin', and fishin', not to mention swimmin', tennis-playin' and golfin', have rendered her figure lissom and slender. She looks like something out of a beauty chorus, and as you are probably aware the little woman rarely approves of her mate being on chummy terms with someone of that description. Let Aggie get one glimpse of Valerie Fanshawe and learn that Freddie has been showering dogs on her, and she'll probably divorce him.'

'Surely not?'

'It's on the cards. American wives get divorces at the drop of a hat.'

'Bless my soul. What would Frederick do then?'

'Well, her father obviously wouldn't want him working at his dog biscuit emporium. I suppose he would come and live here.'

'What, at the castle?' cried Lord Emsworth, appalled. 'Good God!'

'So you see how serious the situation is. However, I've been giving it intense thought, turning here a stone, exploring there an avenue, and I am glad to say I have found the solution. We must get that dog back before Aggie arrives.'

'You will ask Rosalie Fanshawe to return it?'

'Not quite that. She would never let it go. It will have to be pinched, and that's where you come in.'

'I?'

'Who else is there? Freddie and I are both lying on beds of pain, unable to move, and we can hardly ask Connie to oblige. You are our only mobile force. Your quick intelligence has probably already told you what you have to do. What do people do when they've got a dog? They instruct the butler to let it out for a run last thing at night.'

'Do they?'

'Invariably. Or bang go their carpets. Every dog has its last-thing-at-night outing, and I think we can safely assume that it will be via the back door.'

'What the back door?'

'Via.'

'Oh, via? Yes, yes, quite.'

'So you must pop over to the Fanshawes – say around ten o'clock – and lurk outside their back door till the animal appears, and bring it back here.'

Lord Emsworth stared, aghast.

'But, Galahad!'

'It's no good saying "But, Galahad!". It's got to be done. You don't want Freddie's whole future to turn blue at the edges and go down the drain, do you? Let alone having him at the castle for the rest of his life. Ah, I see you shudder. I thought you would. And, dash it, it's not much I'm asking of you. Merely to go and stand in a back garden and scoop in a dog. A child could do it. If it wasn't that we want to keep the thing a secret just between ourselves, I'd hand the job over to the Brownie.'

'But what if the dog refuses to accompany me? After all, we've scarcely met.'

'I've thought of that. You must sprinkle your trouser legs with aniseed. Dogs follow aniseed to the ends of the earth.'

'But I have no aniseed.'

'Beach is bound to be able to lay his hands on some. And Beach never asks questions. Unlike Connie's young, smart butler, who would probably be full of them. Oh, Beach,' said Gally, who had pressed the bell. 'Have we aniseed in the house?'

'Yes, Mr Galahad.'

'Bring me a stoup of it, will you?'

'Very good, sir,' said Beach.

If the request surprised him, he did not show it. Your experienced butler never allows himself to look surprised at anything. He brought the aniseed. At the appointed hour Lord Emsworth drove off in Freddie's sports model car, smelling to heaven. And Gally, left alone, lit another cigar and turned his attention to the *Times* crossword puzzle.

He found it, however, difficult to concentrate on it. This was not merely because these crossword puzzles had become so abstruse nowadays and he was basically a Sun-god-Ra and Large-Australian-bird-emu man. Having seen Lord Emsworth off on his journey, doubts and fears were assailing him. He was wishing he could feel more confident of his brother's chances of success in the mission which had been entrusted to him. A lifetime association with him had left him feeling that the head of the family was a frail reed on which to lean in an emergency. His genius for doing the wrong thing was a byword in his circle of acquaintance.

Which, he was asking himself, of the many ways open to him for messing everything up would Lord Emsworth select? Drive the car into a ditch? Go to the wrong house? Or would he forget all about his assignment and sit by the roadside musing on pigs? It was impossible to say, and Gally's emotions were similar to those of a General who, having planned a brilliant piece of strategy, finds himself dubious as to the ability of his troops to carry it out. Generals in such circumstances chew their moustaches in an overwrought sort of way, and Gally would have chewed his, if he had had one.

Heavy breathing sounded outside the door. Beach entered.

'Miss Fanshawe, sir,' he announced.

Gally's acquaintance with Valerie Fanshawe was only a slight one and in the interval since they had last met he had forgotten some of her finer points. Seeing her now, he realized how accurate had been his description of her to Lord Emsworth. In the best and deepest sense of the words she was a dish and a pippin – in short, the very last type of girl to whom a young husband should have given his wife's Alsatian.

'Good evening,' he said. 'You must forgive me for not rising as directed in the books of etiquette. I've sprained my ankle.'

'Oh, I'm sorry,' said Valerie. 'I hope I'm not disturbing you.'

'Not at all.'

'I asked for Mr Threepwood, forgetting there were two of you. I came to see Freddie.'

'He's gone to bed. He has sprained his ankle.'

The girl seemed puzzled.

'Aren't you getting the cast of characters mixed up?' she said. 'It was you who sprained the ankle.'

'Freddie also.'

'What, both of you? What happened?'

'We fell downstairs together.'

'What made you do that?'

'Oh, we thought we would. Can I give Freddie a message?'

'If you wouldn't mind. Tell him that all is well. Did he mention to you that he was trying to sell Father those dog biscuits of his?'

'He did.'

'Well, I approached Father on the subject and he said Oh, all right, he would give them a try. He said he didn't suppose they would actually poison the dumb chums and as I was making such a point of it he'd take a chance.'

'Splendid.'

'And I've brought back the dog.'

It was only the most sensational piece of news that could make Gally's monocle drop from his eye. At these words it fell like a shooting star.

'You've done *what*?' he exclaimed, retrieving the monocle and replacing it in order the better to goggle at her.

'He gave me an Alsatian dog this afternoon, and I've brought it back.'

'You mean you don't want it?'

'I want it all right, but I can't have it. The fathead's first act on clocking in was to make a bee line for Father's spaniel and try to assassinate it, the one thing calculated to get himself socially ostracized. Father thinks the world of that spaniel. "Who let this canine paranoiac into the house?" he thundered, foaming at the mouth. I said I had. "Where did you get the foul creature?" he demanded. "Freddie gave him to me," I said. "Then you can damn well take him back to this Freddie, whoever he is" he—'

'Vociferated?'

'Yes, vociferated. "And let me add," he said, "that I am about to get my gun and count ten, and if the animal's still around when I reach that figure, I shall blow his head off at the roots and the Lord have mercy on his soul." Well, I'm pretty quick and I saw right away that what he was hinting at was that he preferred not to associate with the dog, so I've brought him back. I think he went off to the Servants' Hall to have a bite of supper. I shall miss him, of course. Still, easy come, easy go.'

And so saying Valerie Fanshawe, reverting to the subject of

Gally's ankle, expressed a hope that he would not have to have it amputated, and withdrew.

If at this moment somebody had started to amputate Gally's ankle, it is hardly probable that he would have noticed it, so centred were his thoughts on this astounding piece of good luck which had befallen a nephew of whom he had always been fond. If, as he supposed, it was the latter's guardian angel who had engineered the happy ending like a conjuror pulling a rabbit out of a hat, he would have liked to slap him on the back and tell him how greatly his efforts were appreciated. Joy cometh in the morning, he told himself, putting the clock forward a little, and by way of celebrating the occasion he rang for Beach and asked him to bring him a whisky and soda.

It was some considerable time before the order was filled, and Beach was full of apologies for his tardiness.

'I must express my regret for being so long, Mr Galahad. I was detained on the telephone by Colonel Fanshawe.'

'The Fanshawe family seem very much with us tonight. Is there a Mrs Fanshawe?'

'I understand so, Mr Galahad.'

'No doubt she will be dropping in shortly. What did the Colonel want?'

'He was asking for his lordship, but I have been unable to locate him.'

'He's gone for a stroll.'

'Indeed? I was not aware. Colonel Fanshawe wished him to come to Marling Hall tomorrow morning in his capacity of Justice of the Peace. It appears that the butler at Marling Hall apprehended a prowler who was lurking in the vicinity of the back door and has locked him in the cellar. Colonel Fanshawe is hoping that his lordship will give him a sharp sentence.'

For the second time that night Gally's monocle had fallen from the parent eye socket. He had not, as we have seen, been sanguine with regard to the possibility of his brother getting through the evening without mishap, but he had not foreseen anything like this. This was outstanding, even for Clarence.

'Beach,' he said, 'this opens up a new line of thought. You speak of a prowler.'

'Yes, sir.'

'Who was lurking at the Fanshawe back door and is now in the Fanshawe cellar.'

'Yes, sir.'

'Well, here's something for your files. The prowler you have in mind was none other than Clarence, ninth Earl of Emsworth.'

'Sir!'

'I assure you. I sent him to Marling Hall on a secret mission, the nature of which I am not empowered to disclose, and how he managed to get copped we shall never know. Suffice it that he did and is now in the cellar. Wine cellar or coal?'

'Coal, I was given to understand, sir.'

'Our task, then, is to get him out of it. Don't speak. I must think, I must think.'

When an ordinary man is trying to formulate a scheme for extricating his brother from a coal cellar, the procedure is apt to be a lengthy one involving the furrowed brow, the scratched head and the snapped finger, but in the case of a man like Gally this is not so. Only a minimum of time had elapsed before he was able to announce that he had got it.

'Beach!'

'Sir?'

'Go to my bedroom, look in the drawer where the

handkerchiefs are, and you will find a small bottle containing white tablets. Bring it to me.'

'Very good, sir. Would this be the bottle to which you refer, sir?' asked Beach, returning a few minutes later.

'That's the one. Now a few necessary facts. Is the butler at the Fanshawes a pal of yours?'

'We are acquainted, sir.'

'Then he won't be surprised if you suddenly pay him a call?'

'I imagine not, Mr Galahad. I sometimes do when I find myself in the neighbourhood of Marling Hall.'

'And on these occasions he sets them up?'

'Sir?'

'You drain a cup or two?'

'Oh yes, sir. I am always offered refreshment.'

'Then it's all over but the cheering. You see this bottle, Beach? It contains what are known as Mickey Finns. The name is familiar to you?'

'No, sir.'

'They are a recognized sedative in the United States. When I last went to New York, a great friend of mine, a bartender on Eighth Avenue, happened to speak of them and was shocked to learn that I had none in my possession. They were things, he said, which nobody should be without. He gave me a few, assuring me that sooner or later they were bound to come in useful. Hitherto I have had no occasion to make use of them, but I think you will agree that now is the time for them to come to the aid of the party. You follow me, Beach?'

'No, sir.'

'Come, come. You know my methods, apply them. Slip one of these into this butler's drink, and almost immediately you will see him fold up like a tired lily. Your path thus made straight, you proceed to the cellar, unleash his lordship and bring him home.'

'But, Mr Galahad!'

'Now what?'

'I hardly like—'

'Don't stand there making frivolous objections. If Clarence is not extracted from that cellar before tomorrow morning, his name will be mud. He will become a hissing and a byword.'

'Yes, sir, but—'

'And don't overlook another aspect of the matter. Perform this simple task, and there will be no limit to his gratitude. Purses of gold will change hands. Camels bearing apes, ivory and peacocks, all addressed to you, will shortly be calling at the back door of Blandings Castle. You will clean up to an unimaginable extent.'

It was a powerful plea. Beach's two chins, which had been waggling unhappily, ceased to waggle. A light of resolution came into his eyes. He looked like a butler who has stiffened the sinews and summoned up the blood, as recommended by Henry the Fifth.

'Very good, Mr Galahad,' he said.

Gally resumed his crossword puzzle, more than ever convinced that the compiler of the clues was suffering from softening of the brain, and in due course heavy breathing woke him from the light doze into which he had fallen while endeavouring to read sense into '7 across' and he found that Beach was back from the front. He had the air of one who has recently passed through some great spiritual experience.

'Well?' said Gally. 'All washed up? Everything nice and smooth?'

'Yes, Mr Galahad.'

'You administered the medium dose for an adult?'

'Yes, Mr Galahad.'

'And released his lordship?'

'Yes, Mr Galahad.'

'That's my boy. Where is he?'

'Taking a bath, Mr Galahad. He was somewhat begrimed. Would there be anything further, sir?'

'Not a thing. You can go to bed and sleep peacefully. Good night.'

'Good night, sir.'

It was some minutes later, while Gally was wrestling with '12 down', that he found his privacy invaded by a caller with whom he had not expected to hobnob. It was very seldom that his sister Constance sought his society. Except for shivering austerely whenever they met, she rarely had much to do with him.

'Oh, hullo, Connie,' he said. 'Are you any good at crossword puzzles?'

Lady Constance did not say 'To hell with crossword puzzles,' but it was plain that only her breeding restrained her from doing so. She was in one of those moods of imperious wrath which so often had reduced Lord Emsworth to an apologetic jelly.

'Galahad,' she said. 'Have you seen Beach?'

'Just been chatting with him. Why?'

'I have been ringing for him for half an hour. He really is quite past his duties.'

'Clarence was telling me that that was how you felt about him, He said you were thinking of firing him.'

'I am.'

'I shouldn't.'

'What do you mean?'

'You'll rue the day.'

'I don't understand you.'

'Then let me tell you a little bedtime story.'

'Please do not drivel, Galahad. Really I sometimes think that you have less sense than Clarence.'

'It is a story,' Gally proceeded, ignoring the slur, 'of a feudal devotion to the family interests which it would be hard to over-praise. It shows Beach in so favourable a light that I think you will agree that when you speak of giving him the heave-ho you are talking, if you will forgive me saying so, through the back of your neck.'

'Have you been drinking, Galahad?'

'Only a series of toasts to a butler who will go down in legend and song. Here comes the story.'

He told it well, omitting no detail however slight, and as his narrative unfolded an ashen pallor spread over Lady Constance's face and she began to gulp in a manner which would have interested any doctor specializing in ailments of the thoracic cavity.

'So there you are,' said Gally, concluding. 'Even if you are not touched by his selfless service and lost in admiration of his skill in slipping Mickey Finns into people's drinks, you must realize that it would be madness to hand him the pink slip. You can't afford to have him spreading the tale of Clarence's activities all over the county, and you know as well as I do that, if sacked, he will dine out on the thing for months. If I were you, Connie, I would reconsider.'

He eyed the wreck of what had once been a fine upstanding sister with satisfaction. He could read the message of those gulps, and could see that she was reconsidering.

Our Man in America

One of the disadvantages you fellows have who live in England and don't see the New York papers regularly is that you miss a lot of interesting stuff. I don't suppose, for instance, that any of you have been able to follow the Fooshe-Harris case, have you? It culminated in the headline in the press:

WOMAN WHO CAME TO DINNER DEPARTS AFTER 11-YEAR STAY

and the ensuing brief announcement:

> St Louis, April 30. Mrs Eleanor Elaine Lee Harris, who stretched a dinner invitation into an eleven-year stay at the home of Mr and Mrs Fuller Fooshe of this city, packed up and departed today on a judge's order. The Fooshes, who are now separated, joined in the eviction suit against her.

Now one can understand that correspondence which has been going on so long between Worried (St Louis) and Loretta Biggs Tuttle, the well-known adviser on social etiquette whose column is so widely syndicated.

October 10, 1947

DEAR LORETTA BIGGS TUTTLE, – I am hoping that you will be able to tell me what to do in a case like this, for I have no mother to advise me.

Here are the facts very briefly. On April 14, 1944, I was invited to dinner by some friends of mine ... well, I suppose they were more acquaintances at that time ... and it was all most enjoyable. My host and hostess could not have been more charming. But now that I have been with them three years and six months something seems to have happened. Their manner has changed. I do my best to be bright and entertaining, and have even gone to the trouble of learning a few simple card tricks, but they keep falling into long silences and Mr F., my host, groans a good deal. Do you think that without knowing it I can have done something to offend them?

(You must not be so sensitive, Worried. We are all a little inclined to be diffident and to think ourselves responsible when some trifling thing goes wrong. There are a hundred reasons why Mr F. should groan ... high taxation, increased cost of living, heavy day at the office and so on. As for the long silences, so many people go into long silences these days. All this Yogi meditation stuff, you know.)

August 3, 1952

Dear Loretta Biggs Tuttle, – I am *sure* there is something wrong. Mrs F. has not spoken to me since 1949, and Mr F. is still groaning. He seems to have aged a good deal, and I am afraid his memory is failing him. This afternoon a friend of his called, and when introducing me he said: 'Shake hands with Mrs Barnacle-Limpet.' I thought it so odd, because after more than eight years he *must* know what my name is.

(You must not let your imagination run away with you, Worried. Mr F.'s little slip is so easily explained. His mind was on his work and he was thinking of the representative of some English

firm with which he is doing business. Barnacle-Limpet is obviously an English name like Knatchbull-Hugessen or Binks-Binks-Binks. May I say in passing what a pleasure it is to me to learn that you are still visiting the F.'s. So difficult to find an apartment nowadays. If Mr F. seems to have aged, surely that is quite natural. We none of us get younger.)

April 15, 1954

So you have been with the F.'s ten years, Worried! How the time does fly, does it not? Yes, I suppose, as you say, it *has* been quite a long dinner party, but I am sure that the F.'s have enjoyed every minute of it. The bottle containing a sample of the arrow-root which Mr F. so kindly brought to your room to help you sleep, and which you thought tasted kind of funny, has not yet reached me, but I will, of course, send it to the analyst, as you ask, the moment it arrives.

April 10, 1955

No, Worried, I see no reason for your suspicions. The man who you say attacked you in the street with a bludgeon was probably just some casual passer-by filling in time before lunch. I cannot agree with you when you call it odd that you should have seen him on the previous day in conversation with Mr F., and that Mr F. was giving him money. No doubt some old acquaintance of his who had fallen on evil times. To the rattle-snake you say you found in your bed I attach little importance. Do what you will, it is almost impossible to keep rattlesnakes from coming into the house.

May 1, 1955

You could knock me down with a feather, Worried! 'Judge's order' indeed! Is this our boasted American hospitality! But cheer up, my poor Worried. I am sure you will soon find someone else to put you up for the next few years. No, I am sorry, I am afraid I cannot break my rule of never giving correspondents my private address.

4 UKRIDGE STARTS A BANK ACCOUNT

Except that he was quite well-dressed and plainly prosperous, the man a yard or two ahead of me as I walked along Piccadilly looked exactly like my old friend Stanley Featherstonehaugh Ukridge, and I was musing on these odd resemblances and speculating idly as to what my little world would be like if there were two of him in it, when he stopped to peer into a tobacconist's window and I saw that it was Ukridge. It was months since I had seen that battered man of wrath, and though my guardian angel whispered to me that it would mean parting with a loan of five or even ten shillings if I made my presence known, I tapped him on the shoulder.

Usually if you tap Ukridge on the shoulder, he leaps at least six inches into the air, a guilty conscience making him feel that the worst has happened and his sins have found him out, but now he merely beamed, as if being tapped by me had made his day.

'Corky, old horse!' he cried. 'The very man I wanted to see. Come in here while I buy one of those cigarette lighters, and then you must have a bite of lunch with me. And when I say lunch, I don't mean the cup of coffee and roll and butter to which you are accustomed, but something more on the lines of a Babylonian orgy.'

We went into the shop and he paid for the lighter from a wallet stuffed with currency.

'And now,' he said, 'that lunch of which I was speaking. The Ritz is handy.'

It was perhaps tactless of me, but when we had seated ourselves and he had ordered spaciously, I started to probe the mystery of this affluence of his. It occurred to me that he might have gone to live again with his aunt, the wealthy novelist Miss Julia Ukridge, and I asked him if this was so. He said it was not.

'Then where did you get all that money?'

'Honest work, laddie, or anyway I thought it was honest when I took it on. The pay was good. Ten pounds a week and no expenses, for of course Percy attended to the household bills. Everything I got was velvet.'

'Who was Percy?'

'My employer, and the job with which he entrusted me was selling antique furniture. It came about through my meeting Stout, my aunt's butler, in a pub, and the advice I would give to every young man starting life is Always go into pubs, for you never know whether there won't be someone there who can do you a bit of good. For some minutes after entering the place I had been using all my eloquence and persuasiveness to induce Flossie, the barmaid, to chalk my refreshment up on the slate, my finances at the time being at a rather low ebb. It wasn't easy. I had to extend all my powers. But I won through at last, and I was returning to my seat with a well-filled flagon, when a bloke accosted me and with some surprise I saw it was my Aunt Julia's major domo.

'Hullo,' I said. 'Why aren't you buttling?'

It appeared that he no longer held office. Aunt Julia had given him the sack. This occasioned me no astonishment, for she is a confirmed sacker. You will probably recall that she has bunged me out of the home not once but many times. So I just said

'Tough luck' or something to that effect, and we chatted of this and that. He asked me where I was living now, and I told him, and after a pleasant quarter of an hour we parted, he to go and see his brother, or that's where he said he was going, I to trickle round to the Foreign Office and try to touch George Tupper for a couple of quid, which I was fortunately able to do, he luckily happening to be in amiable mood. Sometimes when you approach Tuppy for a small loan you find him all agitated because mysterious veiled women have been pinching his secret treaties, and on such occasions it is difficult to bend him to your will.

With this addition to my resources I was in a position to pay my landlady the trifling sum I owed her, so when she looked in on me that night as I sat smoking my pipe and wishing I could somehow accumulate a bit of working capital I met her eye without a tremor.

But she had not come to talk finance. She said there was a gentleman downstairs who wanted to see me, and I confess this gave me pause. What with the present worldwide shortage of money – affecting us all these days – I had been compelled to let one or two bills run up, and this might well be some creditor whom it would have been embarrassing to meet.

'What sort of man is he?' I asked, and she said he was husky in the voice, which didn't get me much further, and when she added that she had told him I was in, I said she had better send him up, and a few moments later in came a bloke who might have been Stout's brother. Which was as it should have been, for that was what he turned out to be.

'Evening,' he said, and I could see why Mrs Whatever-her-name-was had described him as husky. His voice was hoarse and muffled. Laryngitis or something, I thought.

'Name of Stout,' he proceeded. 'I think you know my brother Horace.'

'Good Lord!' I said. 'Is his name Horace?'

'That's right. And mine's Percy.'

'Are you a butler, too?'

'Silver ring bookie. Or was.'

'You've retired?'

'For a while. Lost my voice calling the odds. And that brings me to what I've come about.'

It was a strange story he had to relate. It seemed that a client of his had let his obligations pile up – a thing I've often wished bookies would let me do – till he owed this Percy a pretty considerable sum, and finally he had settled by handing over a lot of antique furniture. The stuff being no good to Percy, he was anxious to dispose of it if the price was right, and the way to make the price right, he felt, was to enlist the services of someone of persuasive eloquence – someone with the gift of the gab was the way he put it – to sell it for him. Because of course he couldn't do it himself, his bronchial cords having turned blue on him. And his brother Horace, having heard me in action, was convinced that they need seek no further. Any man, Horace said, who could persuade Flossie to give credit for two pints of mild and bitter was the man for Percy. He knew Flossie to be a girl of steel and iron, adamant to the most impassioned pleas, and he said that if he hadn't heard it with his own ears, he wouldn't have believed it possible.

So how about it, Percy asked.

Well, you know me, Corky. First and foremost the level-headed man of business. What, I enquired, was there in it for me, and he said he would give me a commission. I said that I would prefer a salary, and when he suggested five pounds a week with board and lodging thrown in, it was all I could do to keep from jumping at it, for, as I told you, my financial position was not good. But I managed to sneer loftily, and in the end I got him up to ten.

'You say board and lodging,' I said. 'Where do I board and lodge?'

That, he said, was the most attractive part of the assignment. He wasn't going to take a shop in the metropolis but planned to exhibit his wares in a cottage equipped with honeysuckle, roses and all the fittings down in Kent. One followed his train of thought. Motorists would be passing to and fro in droves and the betting was that at least some of them, seeing the notice on the front gate 'Antique furniture for sale. Genuine period. Guaranteed', would stop off and buy. My Aunt Julia is an aficionada of old furniture and I knew that she had often picked up some good stuff at these wayside emporia. The thing looked to me like a snip, and he said he thought so, too. For mark you, Corky, though you and I wouldn't be seen dead in a ditch with the average antique, there are squads of half-wits who value them highly – showing, I often say, that it takes all sorts to make a world. I told myself that this was going to be good. I slapped him on the back. He slapped me on the back. I shook his hand. He shook my hand. And – what made the whole thing a real love feast – he slipped me an advance of five quid. And the following afternoon found me at Rosemary Cottage in the neighbourhood of Tunbridge Wells, all eagerness to get my nose down to it.

My rosy expectations were fulfilled. For solid comfort there is nothing to beat a jolly bachelor establishment. Women have their merits, of course, but if you are to live the good life, you don't want them around the home. They are always telling you to wipe your boots and they don't like you dining in your shirt sleeves. At Rosemary Cottage we were hampered by none of these restrictions. Liberty Hall about sums it up.

We were a happy little community. Percy had a fund of good stories garnered from his years on the turf, while Horace, though less effervescent as a conversationalist, played the harmonica with considerable skill, a thing I didn't know butlers ever did. The other member of our group was a substantial character named Erb, who was attached to Percy in the capacity of what is called a minder. In case the term is new to you, it meant that if you owed Percy a fiver on the two o'clock at Plumpton and didn't brass up pretty quick, you got Erb on the back of your neck. He was one of those strong silent men who don't speak till they're spoken to, and not often then, but he was fortunately able to play a fair game of Bridge, so we had a four for after supper. Erb was vice-president in charge of the cooking, and I never wish to bite better pork chops than the ones he used to serve up. They melted in the mouth.

Yes, it was an idyllic life, and we lived it to the full. The only thing that cast a shadow was the fact that business might have been brisker. I sold a few of the ghastly objects, but twice I let promising prospects get away from me, and this made me uneasy. I didn't want to get Percy thinking that in entrusting the selling end of the business to me he might have picked the wrong man. With a colossal sum like ten quid a week at stake it behoved me to do some quick thinking, and it wasn't long before I spotted where the trouble lay. My patter lacked the professional note.

You know how it is when you're buying old furniture. You expect the fellow who's selling it to weigh in with a lot of abstruse stuff which doesn't mean a damn thing to you but which you know ought to be there. It's much the same as when you're buying a car. If you aren't handed plenty of applesauce about springs and cam shafts and differential gears and sprockets, you suspect a trap and tell the chap you'll think it over and let him know.

And fortunately I was in a position to correct this flaw in my technique without difficulty. Aunt Julia had shelves of books about old furniture which I could borrow and bone up on, thus acquiring the necessary double-talk, so next morning I set out for The Cedars, Wimbledon Common, full of zeal and the will to win.

I was sorry to be informed by Horace's successor on my arrival that she was in bed with a nasty cold, but he took my name up and came back to say that she could give me five minutes – not longer, because she was expecting the doctor. So I went up and found her sniffing eucalyptus and sneezing a good deal, plainly in rather poor shape. But her sufferings had not impaired her spirit, for the first thing she said to me was that she wouldn't give me a penny, and I was pained to see that that matter of the ormulu clock still rankled. What ormulu clock? Oh, just one which, needing a bit of capital at the time, I pinched from one of the spare rooms, little thinking that its absence would ever be noticed. I hastened to disabuse her of the idea that I had come in the hope of making a touch, and the strain that had threatened to mar the conversation became eased.

'Though I did come to borrow something, Aunt Julia,' I said. 'Do you mind if I take two or three books of yours about antique furniture? I'll return them shortly.'

She sneezed sceptically.

'Or pawn them,' she said. 'Since when have you been interested in antique furniture?'

'I'm selling it.'

'You're *selling* it?' she exclaimed like an echo in the Swiss mountains. 'Do you mean you are working in a shop?'

'Well, not exactly a shop. We conduct our business at a cottage – Rosemary Cottage, to be exact – on the roadside not far from Tunbridge Wells. In this way we catch the motoring trade. The actual selling is in my hands and so far I've done pretty well, but I have not been altogether satisfied with my work. I feel I need more technical stuff, and last night it occurred to me that if I read a few of your books I'd be able to make my sales talk more convincing. So if you will allow me to take a selection from your library—'

She sneezed again, but this time more amiably. She said that if I was really doing some genuine work, she would certainly be delighted to help me, adding in rather poor taste, I thought, that it was about time I stopped messing about and wasting my life as I had been doing. I could have told her, of course, that there is not a moment of the day, except possibly when relaxing over a mild and bitter at the pub, when I am not pondering some vast scheme which will bring me wealth and power, but it didn't seem humane to argue with a woman suffering from a nasty cold.

'Tomorrow, if I am well enough,' she said, 'I will come and see your stock myself.'

'Will you really? That'll be fine.'

'Or perhaps the day after tomorrow. But it's an extraordinary coincidence that you should be selling antique furniture, because—'

'Yes, it was odd that I should have happened to run into Stout.'

'Stout? You mean my butler?'

'Your late butler. He gave me to understand that you had sacked him.'

She sneezed grimly.

'I certainly did. Let me tell you what happened.'

'No, let me tell *you* what happened,' I said, and I related the circumstances of my meeting with Horace, prudently changing the pub to a milk bar. 'I had been having an argument with a fellow at the next table,' I concluded, 'and my eloquence so impressed him that he asked me if I would come down to Rosemary Cottage and sell this antique furniture. He has a brother who recently acquired a lot of it.'

'What!'

She sat up in bed, her eyes, though watery, flashing with all the old fire. It was plain that she was about to say something of significance, but before she could speak the door opened and the medicine man appeared, and thinking they were best alone I pushed off and got the books and legged it for the great open spaces.

There was a telephone booth at the end of the road, and I went to it and rang up Percy. These long distance calls run into money, but I felt that he ought to have the good news without delay, no matter what the expense.

It was Horace who answered the phone, and I slipped him the tidings of great joy.

'I've just been seeing my aunt,' I said.

'Oh?' he said.

'She's got a nasty cold,' I said.

'Ah,' he said, and I seemed to detect a note of gratification in his voice, as if he was thinking well of Heaven for having given her a sharp lesson which would teach her to be more careful in future how she went about giving good men the sack.

'But she thinks she'll be all right tomorrow,' I said, 'and the moment the sniffles have ceased and the temperature has returned to normal she's coming down here to inspect our stock. I don't need to tell you what this means. Next to her novels what she loves most in this world is old furniture. It is to her what catnip is to a cat. Confront her with some chair on which nobody could sit with any comfort, and provided it was made by Chippendale, if I've got the name right, the sky's the limit. She's quite likely to buy everything we've got, paying a prince's ransom for each article. I've been with her to sales and with my own eyes have observed her flinging the cash about like a drunken sailor. I know what you're thinking, of course. You feel that after what has passed between you it will be painful for you to meet her again, but you must clench your teeth and stick it like a man. We're all working for the good of the show, so . . . Hullo? Hullo? Are you there?'

He wasn't. He had hung up. Mysterious, I thought, and most disappointing to one who, like myself, had been expecting paeans of joy. However, I was much too bucked to worry about the peculiar behaviour of butlers, and feeling that the occasion called for something in the nature of a celebration I went to the Foreign Office, gave George Tupper his two quid back and took him out to lunch.

It wasn't a very animated lunch, because Tuppy hardly said a word. He seemed dazed. I've noticed the same thing before in fellows to whom I've repaid a small loan. They get a sort of stunned look, as if they had passed through some great spiritual experience. Odd. But it took more than a silent Tuppy to damp my jocund mood, and I was feeling on top of my form when an hour or two later I crossed the threshold of Rosemary Cottage.

'Yoo-hoo!' I cried. 'I'm back.'

I expected shouts of welcome – not, of course, from Erb, but certainly from Horace and Percy. Instead of which, complete silence reigned. They might all have gone for a walk, but that didn't seem likely, because while Percy sometimes enjoyed a little exercise Horace and Erb hadn't set a foot outdoors since we'd been there. And it was as I stood puzzling over this that I noticed that except for a single table – piecrust tables the things are called – all the furniture had gone, too. I don't mind telling you, Corky, that it baffled me. I could make nothing of it, and I was still making nothing of it when I had that feeling you get sometimes that you are not alone, and, turning, I saw that I had company. Standing beside me was a policeman.

There have been times, I will not conceal it from you, when such a spectacle would have chilled me to the marrow, for you never know what may not ensue, once the Force starts popping up, and it just shows how crystal clear my conscience was that I didn't quail but greeted him with a cheery 'Good evening, officer'.

'Good evening, sir,' he responded courteously. 'Is this Rosemary Cottage?'

'Nothing but. Anything I can do for you?'

'I've come on behalf of Miss Julia Ukridge.'

It seemed strange to me that Aunt Julia should have dealings with the police, but aunts notoriously do the weirdest things, so I received the information with a polite 'Oh, really?', adding that she was linked to me by ties of blood, being indeed the sister of my late father, and he said 'Was that so?' and expressed the opinion that it was a small world, a sentiment in which I concurred.

'She was talking of looking me up here,' I said.

'So I understood, sir. But she was unable to come herself, so she sent her maid with the list. She has a nasty cold.'

'Probably caught it from my aunt.'

'Sir?'

'You said the maid had a nasty cold.'

'No, sir, it's Miss Ukridge who has the nasty cold.'

'Ah, now we have got it straight. What did she send the maid for?'

'To bring us the list of the purloined objects.'

I don't know how it is with you, Corky, but the moment anyone starts talking about purloined objects in my presence I get an uneasy feeling. It was with not a little gooseflesh running down my spine that I gazed at the officer.

'Purloined objects?'

'A number of valuable pieces of furniture. Antiques they call them.'

'Oh, my aunt!'

'Yes, sir, they were her property. They were removed from her residence on Wimbledon Common during her absence. She states that she had gone to Brussels to attend one of these conferences where writers assemble, she being a writer, I understand, and she left her butler in charge of the house. When she came back, the valuable pieces of antique furniture weren't there. The butler, questioned, stated that he had taken the afternoon off and gone to the dog races and nobody more surprised than himself when he returned and found the objects had been purloined. He was dismissed, of course, but that didn't help Miss Ukridge's bereavement much. Just locking the stable door after the milk has been spilt, as you might say. And there till this morning the matter rested. But this morning, on information received, the lady was led to suspect that the purloined objects were in this Rosemary Cottage, and she got in touch with the local police, who got in touch with us. She thinks, you see, that the butler did it. Worked in with an accomplice, I mean to say, and the two of them got away with the purloined objects, no doubt in a plain van.'

I believe I once asked you, Corky, if during a political discussion in a pub you had ever suddenly been punched on the nose, and if I remember rightly you replied in the negative. But I have been – twice – and on each occasion I was conscious of feeling dazed and stunned, like George Tupper when I paid him back the two quid he had lent me and took him to lunch. The illusion that the roof had fallen in and landed on top of my head was extraordinarily vivid. Drinking the constable in with a horrified gaze, I seemed to be looking at two constables, both doing the shimmy.

For his words had removed the scales from my eyes, and I saw Horace and Percy no longer as pleasant business associates but as what they were, a wolf in butler's clothing and a bookie who did not know the difference between right and wrong. Yes, yes, as you say, I have sometimes been compelled by circumstances to pinch an occasional trifle like a clock from my aunt, but there is a sharp line drawn between swiping a clock and getting away with a houseful of assorted antique furniture. No doubt they had done it precisely as the constable had said, and it must have been absurdly simple. Nothing to it. No, Corky, you are wrong. I do *not* wish I had thought of it myself. I would have scorned such an action, even though knowing the stuff was fully insured and my aunt would be far better off without it.

'The only thing is,' the officer was proceeding, 'I don't see any antique furniture here. There's that table, but it's not on the list. And if there had been antique furniture here, you'd have noticed it. Looks to me as if they'd sent me to the wrong place,' he said, and with a word of regret that I had been troubled he mounted his bicycle and pedalled off.

He left me, as you can readily imagine, with my mind in a turmoil, and you are probably thinking that what was giving me dark circles under the eyes was the discovery that I had been lured by a specious bookie into selling hot furniture and so rendering myself liable to a sharp sentence as an accessory or whatever they call it, but it wasn't. That was bad enough, but what was worse was the realization that my employer had gone off owing me six weeks' salary. You see, when we had made that gentleman's agreement of ours, he had said that if it was all the same to me, he would prefer to pay me in a lump sum at the end of my term of office instead of week by week, and I had seen no objection. Foolish of me, of course. I cannot impress it on you too strongly, Corky old horse, that if anyone comes offering you money, you should grab it at once and not assent to any suggestion of payment at some later date. Only so can you be certain of trousering the stuff.

So, as I say, I stood there draining the bitter cup, and while I was thus engaged a car stopped in the road outside and a man came up the garden path.

He was a tall man with grey hair and a funny sort of twist to his mouth, as if he had just swallowed a bad oyster and was wishing he hadn't.

'I see you advertise antique furniture,' he said. 'Where do you keep it?'

I was just about to tell him it had all gone, when he spotted the piecrust table.

'This looks a nice piece,' he said, and as he spoke I saw in his eye the unmistakeable antique-furniture-collector's gleam which

I had so often seen in my Aunt Julia's at sales, and I quivered from hair to shoe sole.

You have often commented on my lightning brain and ready resource, Corky ... well, if it wasn't you, it was somebody else ... and I don't suppose I've ever thought quicker than I did then. In a sort of blinding flash it came to me that if I could sell Percy's piecrust table for what he owed me, the thing would be a stand-off and my position stabilized.

'You bet it's a nice piece,' I said, and proceeded to give him the works. I was inspired. I doubt if I have ever, not even when pleading with Flossie that credit was the lifeblood of commerce, talked more persuasively. The golden words simply flowed out, and I could see that I had got him going. It seemed but a moment before he had produced his chequebook and was writing me a cheque for sixty pounds.

'Who shall I make it out to?' he asked, and I said S. F. Ukridge, and he did so and told me where to send the table – somewhere in the Mayfair district of London – and we parted on cordial terms.

And not ten minutes after he had driven off, who should show up but Percy. Yes, Percy in person, the last bloke I had expected to see. I don't think I described him to you, did I, but his general appearance was that of a clean-shaven Santa Claus, and he was looking now more like Santa Claus than ever. Bubbling over with good will and joie de vivre. He couldn't have been chirpier if he had just seen the heavily backed favourite in the big race stub its toe on a fence and come a purler.

'Hullo, cocky,' he said. 'So you got back.'

Well, you might suppose that after what I had heard from the rozzer I would have started right away to reproach him for his criminal activities and to urge him to give his better self a chance to guide him, but I didn't – partly because it's never any use trying to jerk a bookie's better self to the surface, but principally because I wanted to lose no time in putting our financial affairs on a sound basis. First things first has always been my motto.

'You!' I said. 'I thought you had skipped.'

Have you ever seen a bookie cut to the quick? I hadn't till then. He took it big. There's a word my aunt is fond of using in her novels when the hero has said the wrong thing to the heroine and made her hot under the collar. 'She—' – what is it? 'Bridled', that's the word I mean. Percy bridled.

'Who, me?' he said. 'Without paying you your money? What do you think I am – dishonest?'

I apologized. I said that naturally when I returned and found him gone and all the furniture removed it had started a train of thought.

'Well, I had to get the stuff away before your aunt arrived, didn't I? How much do I owe you? Sixty quid, isn't it? Here you are,' he said, pulling out a wallet the size of an elephant. 'What's that you've got there?'

And I'm blowed if in my emotion at seeing him again I hadn't forgotten all about the twisted lip man's cheque. I endorsed it with a hasty fountain pen and pushed it across. He eyed it with some surprise.

'What's this?'

I may have smirked a bit, for I was not a little proud of my recent triumph of salesmanship.

'I just sold the piecrust table to a man who came by in a car.'

'Good boy,' said Percy. 'I knew I hadn't made a mistake in making you vice-president in charge of sales. I've had that table on my hands for months. Took it for a bad debt. How much did you get for it?' He looked at the cheque. 'Sixty quid? Splendid. I only got forty.'

'Eh?'

'From the chap I sold it to this morning.'

'You sold it to somebody this morning?'

'That's right.'

'Then which of them gets it?'

'Why, your chap, of course. He paid more. We've got to do the honest thing.'

'And you'll give your chap his money back?'

'Now don't be silly,' said Percy, and would probably have gone on to reproach me further, but at this moment we had another visitor, a gaunt, lean, spectacled popper-in who looked as if he might be a professor or something on that order.

'I see you advertise antique furniture,' he said. 'I would like to look at ... Ah,' he said, spotting the table. He nuzzled it a good deal and turned it upside down and once or twice looked as if he were going to smell it.

'Beautiful,' he said. 'A lovely bit of work.'

'You can have it for eighty quid,' said Percy.

The professor smiled one of those gentle smiles.

'I fear it is hardly worth that. When I called it beautiful and lovely, I was alluding to Tancy's workmanship. Ike Tancy, possibly the finest forger of old furniture we have today. At a glance I would say that this was an example of his middle period.'

Percy blew a few bubbles.

'You mean it's a fake? But I was told—'

'Whatever you were told, your informant was mistaken. And may I add that if you persist in this policy of yours of advertising and selling forgeries as genuine antiques, you are liable to come into uncomfortable contact with the Law. It would be wise to remove that notice you have at your gate. Good evening, gentlemen, good evening.'

He left behind him what you might call a strained silence, broken after a moment or so by Percy saying 'Cor!'.

'This calls for thought,' he said. 'We've sold that table.'

'Yes.'

'Twice.'

'Yes.'

'And got the money for it.'

'Yes.'

'And it's a fake.'

'Yes.'

'And we passed it off as genuine.'

'Yes.'

'And it seems there's a law against that.'

'Yes.'

'We'd better go to the pub and talk it over.'

'Yes.'

'You be walking on. There's something I want to attend to in the kitchen. By the way, got any matches? I've used all mine.'

I gave him a box and strolled on, deep in thought, and presently he joined me, seeming deep in thought, too. We sat on a stile, both of us plunged in meditation, and then he suddenly uttered an exclamation.

'What a lovely sunset,' he said, 'and how peculiar that the sun's setting in the east. I've never known it to do that before. Why, strike me pink, I believe the cottage is on fire.'

And, Corky, he was perfectly accurate. It was.

* * *

Ukridge broke off his narrative, reached for his wallet and laid it on the table preparatory to summoning the waiter to bring the bill. I ventured a question.

'The cottage was reduced to ashes?'

'It was.'

'The piecrust table, too?'

'Yes, I think it must have burned briskly.'

'A bit of luck for you.'

'Very fortunate. Very fortunate.'

'Percy was probably careless with those matches.'

'One feels he must have been. But he certainly brought about the happy ending. Percy's happy. He's made a good thing out of it. I'm happy. I've made a good thing out of it, too. Aunt Julia has the insurance money, so she also is happy, provided of course that her nasty cold has now yielded to treatment. I doubt if the insurance blokes are happy, but we must always remember that the more cash these insurance firms get taken off them, the better it is for them. It makes them more spiritual.'

'How about the two owners of the table?'

'Oh, they've probably forgotten the whole thing by now. Money means nothing to fellows like that. The fellow I sold it to was driving a Rolls Royce. So looking on the episode from the broad viewpoint ... I beg your pardon?'

'I said "Good afternoon, Mr Ukridge",' said the man who had suddenly appeared at our table, and I saw Ukridge's jaw fall like an express lift going down. And I wasn't surprised, for this was a tall man with grey hair and a curiously twisted mouth. His eyes, as they bored into Ukridge, were bleak.

'I've been looking for you for a long time and hoping to meet you again. I'll trouble you for sixty pounds.'

'I haven't got sixty pounds.'

'Spent some of it, eh? Then let's see what you *have* got,' said the man, turning the contents of the wallet out on the tablecloth and counting it in an efficient manner. 'Fifty-eight pounds, six and threepence. That's near enough.'

'But who's going to pay for my lunch?'

'Ah, that we shall never know,' said the man.

But I knew, and it was with a heavy heart that I reached in my hip pocket for the thin little bundle of pound notes which I had been hoping would last me for another week.

Our Man in America

Crime continues to flourish in and around New York, but what with one thing and another the pickings are not so easy as they used to be. There is a nasty sneaky spirit afoot among those who have anything worth stealing, the principal offenders being banks. There was a time when you could always enrich yourself by getting a gun and going into a bank and asking for money and having it passed to you across the counter, but these idyllic conditions no longer prevail. The other day a marauder, full of optimism, went into a bank and started the correspondence system which has always been in vogue by slipping the cashier a note that said 'Put $25,000 in fives and tens in a paper bag. If you give the alarm, I shall kill you instantly.' And the cashier, instead of obliging, scribbled a reply on a handy piece of paper and pushed it over to him. The message ran: 'Straighten your tie and smile. You're being photographed.'

About the only thing in the crime line that pays off nowadays is forgery. At Ripley, Tennessee, a Mr Howard Lee White, serving a sentence for that crime in the Fort Pillow state prison, was released last Saturday after the necessary papers had been received by the authorities. It turned out – too late – that Mr White had forged these.

'Nothing like this has ever happened here before,' said Warden J. B. Hunt. One gets new experiences.

Nor was this all. Since Mr White left, officials say a man answering his description has left a trail of cheques forged on the prison account all over Tennessee.

*

But while life is all roses and sunshine for Howard Lee White, there are aching hearts up in Washington, where the White House is having a good deal of starling trouble. These birds collect in gangs on the building and in the trees, and it is reported by a source close to the President that the President has been saying that if he never sees another starling in his life, it will be all right with him.

Washington's keenest minds are trying to hit on a way of debirding the premises, and the latest scheme is to make a recording of the cries of a distressed starling and play it where the intruders have assembled, the idea being that when they hear it they will feel that this is no place for them and that they had better leg it while the legging is good.

Sound as far as it goes, but the problem, of course, is how do you distress a starling? It is no good kidding it that the Stock Market has slumped again, because probably it has no shares on margin. You might climb up a tree and pretend to be a cat, hoping that this would draw a sharp shriek of dismay, but in order to do this you would have to look reasonably like a cat, which very few Senators, even when whiskered, do. One wishes one could help out the Administration, but really there seems nothing that one can suggest. Impasse is the word that springs to the lips.

*

According to Howard Gossage, the well-known advertising man, a new and speedier race of humans may be developing as the result of Television commercials, a species that can nip out of the room while the commercial is on, get back when it is over and, as the fellow said, fill the unforgiving minute with sixty seconds' worth of distance run. He instances the case of a twelve-year-old nephew of his, who on May 10 last, just as the commercial was starting went to the kitchen, prepared a peanut butter sandwich, drank half a pint of milk out of the bottle, was rebuked by his mother for this, promised he wouldn't do it again, stroked the cat, patted the dog, and had a fight with his brother, all in 52.3 seconds, returning exactly at the right time for the resumption of the main show.

Interviewed, the child said he had only done what any man would have done. These pioneers are always modest.

*

It has come as something of a shock to New York motorists to learn that the money they have been depositing in parking meters throughout the city all these months has not gone into the pockets of the Transit Authority (whom they love) but into those of a total stranger named Giuseppe Mancini. The thought that they have been supporting Giuseppe to the tune of about $150,000 a year, and that while they have had to rub along on hamburgers he has been tucking into oysters and caviar, is a bitter one.

When a year or so ago Giuseppe got fired from his job as a parking meter maintenance man, he shrewdly stuck like glue to his official key, guaranteed to open five hundred meters in the Third Avenue area, and with its aid he proceeded to clean up, doing a nice $2000-a-night business: and at first sight it would seem that he has provided an answer to the question 'What shall we do with our boys?' Obviously, one would say, get them jobs as parking-meter maintenance men in New York, and let Nature do the rest.

But there is one bad catch in this thing of robbing meters. Parking fees are paid in dimes – ten to the dollar – and while dimes are all right if you can take them or leave them alone, it is embarrassing to have a million five hundred thousand of them about the home, as Giuseppe had. If you pay all your bills in dimes, people begin to ask questions. No doubt it was when he bought a $20,000 house in the country and – presumably – slapped down two hundred thousand dimes on the house-agent's desk that suspicions began to be aroused. At any rate, four gentlemanly detectives jumped on the back of his neck last week as he staggered up Third Avenue with approximately twenty thousand of these coins on his person, and it is very doubtful if he will be with us again until early in the next decade.

*

And here is the latest news from Statesboro, Ga. They have a prison down there, and last Sunday the chaplain was conducting divine service for the inmates.

'Let us now,' he said, 'bow our heads in prayer.'

The prisoners and warders bowed their heads as directed – all except John Patterson (30) and Joseph Gibson (22), who slipped out and went off in a lorry and have not been heard from since.

As Bingo Little left the offices of *Wee Tots*, the weekly journal which has done so much to mould thought in the nurseries of Great Britain, his brow was furrowed and his heart heavy. The evening was one of those fine evenings which come to London perhaps twice in the course of an English summer, but its beauty struck no answering chord in his soul. The skies were blue, but he was bluer. The sun was smiling, but he could not raise so much as a simper.

When his wife and helpmeet, Rosie M. Banks the popular novelist, had exerted her pull and secured for him the *Wee Tots* editorship, she had said it would be best not to haggle about salary but to take what Henry Cuthbert Purkiss, its proprietor, offered, and he had done so, glad to have even the smallest bit of loose change to rattle in his pocket. But recently there had been unforeseen demands on his purse. Misled by a dream in which he had seen his Aunt Myrtle (relict of the late J. G. Beenstock) dancing the Twist in a bikini bathing suit outside Buckingham Palace, he had planked his month's stipend on Merry Widow for the two-thirty at Catterick Bridge, and it had come in fifth in a field of seven. This disaster had left him with a capital of four shillings and threepence, so he had gone to Mr Purkiss and asked for a raise, and Mr Purkiss had stared at him incredulously.

'A *what*?' he cried, wincing as if some unfriendly tooth had bitten him in the fleshy part of the leg.

'Just to show your confidence in me and encourage me to rise to new heights of achievement,' said Bingo. 'It would be money well spent,' he pointed out, tenderly picking a piece of fluff off Mr Purkiss's coat sleeve, for everything helps on these occasions.

No business resulted. There were, it seemed, many reasons why Mr Purkiss found himself unable to accede to the request. He placed these one by one before his right-hand man, and an hour or so later, his daily task completed, the right-hand man went on his way, feeling like a left-hand man.

He told himself that he had not really hoped, for Mr Purkiss notoriously belonged to – indeed, was the perpetual president of – the slow-with-a-buck school of thought and no one had ever found it easy to induce him to loosen up, but nevertheless the disappointment was substantial. And what put the seal on his depression was that Mrs Bingo was not available to console him. In normal circumstances he would have hastened to her and cried on her shoulder, but she was unfortunately not among those present. She had gone with Mrs Purkiss to attend the Founder's Day celebrations at the Brighton seminary where they had been educated and would not be back till tomorrow.

It looked like being a bleak evening. He was in no mood for revelry, but even if he had been, he would have found small scope for it on four shillings and threepence. It seemed to him that his only course was to go to the Drones for a bite of dinner and then return to his lonely home and so to bed, and he was passing through Trafalgar Square en route for Dover Street, where the club was situated, when a sharp exclamation or cry at his side caused him to halt, and looking up he saw that what had interrupted his reverie was a red-haired girl of singular beauty who had that indefinable air of being ready to start something at the drop of a hat which red-haired girls in these disturbed times so often have.

'Oh, hullo,' he said, speaking with the touch of awkwardness customary in young husbands accosted by beautiful girls when their wives are away. He had had no difficulty in recognizing her. Her name was Mabel Murgatroyd, and they had met during a police raid on the gambling club they were attending in the days before modern enlightened thought made these resorts legal, and had subsequently spent an agreeable half-hour together in a water barrel in somebody's garden. He had not forgotten the incident, and it was plain that it remained green in Miss Murgatroyd's memory also, for she said:

'Well, lord love a duck, if it isn't my old room mate Bingo Little! Fancy meeting you again. How's tricks? Been in any interesting water barrels lately?'

Bingo said No, not lately.

'Nor me. I don't know how it is with you, but I've sort of lost my taste for them. The zest has gone. When you've seen one, I often say, you've seen them all. But there's always something to fill the long hours. I'm going in more for politics these days.'

'What, standing for Parliament?'

'No, banning the bomb and all that.'

'What bomb would that be?'

'The one that's going to blow us all cross-eyed unless steps are taken through the proper channels.'

'Ah yes, I know the bomb you mean. No good to man or beast.'

'That's what we feel. When I say "we", I allude to certain of the younger set, of whom I am one. We're protesting against it. Every now and then we march from Aldermaston, protesting like a ton of bricks.'

'Hard on the feet.'

'But very satisfying to the soul. And then we sit a good deal.'

'Sit?'

'That's right.'

'Sit where?'

'Wherever we happen to be. Here, to take an instance at random.'

'What, in the middle of Trafalgar Square? Don't the gendarmerie object?'

'You bet they do. They scoop us up in handfuls.'

'Is that good?'

'Couldn't be better. The papers feature it next morning, and that helps the cause. Ah, here comes a rozzer now, just when we need him. Down with you,' said Mabel Murgatroyd, and seizing Bingo by the wrist she drew him with her to the ground, causing sixteen taxi cabs, three omnibuses and eleven private cars to halt in their tracks, their drivers what-the-helling in no uncertain terms.

It was a moment fraught with discomfort for Bingo. Apart from the fact that all this was doing his trousers no good, he had the feeling that he was making himself conspicuous, a thing he particularly disliked, and in this assumption he was perfectly correct. The suddenness of his descent, too, had made him bite his tongue rather painfully.

But these were, after all, minor inconveniences. What was really disturbing him was the approach of the Government employee to whom his companion had alluded. He was coming alongside at the rate of knots, and his aspect was intimidating to the last degree. His height Bingo estimated at about eight feet seven, and his mood was plainly not sunny.

Nor was this a thing to occasion surprise. For weeks he had been straining the muscles of his back lifting debutantes off London's roadways, and the routine had long since begun to afflict him with ennui. His hearty dislike of debutantes was equalled only by his distaste for their escorts. So now without even saying 'Ho' or 'What's all this?' he attached himself to the persons of Bingo and Miss Murgatroyd and led them from the scene. And in next to no time Bingo found himself in one of Bosher Street's cosy prison cells, due to face the awful majesty of the law on the following morning.

It was not, of course, an entirely novel experience for him. In his bachelor days he had generally found himself in custody on Boat Race night. But he was now a respectable married man and had said goodbye to all that, and it is not too much to say that he burned with shame and remorse. He was also extremely apprehensive. He knew the drill on these occasions. If you wished to escape seven days in the jug, you had to pay a fine of five pounds, and he doubted very much if the M.C. next morning would be satisfied with four shillings and threepence down and an I.O.U. for the remainder. And what Mrs Bingo would have to say when informed on her return that he was in stir, he did not care to contemplate. She would unquestionably explode with as loud a report as the bomb which he had been engaged in banning.

It was consequently with a surge of relief that nearly caused him to swoon that on facing the magistrate at Bosher Street Police Court he found him to be one of those likeable magistrates who know how to temper justice with mercy. Possibly because it was his birthday but more probably because he was influenced by Miss Murgatroyd's radiant beauty, he contented himself with a mere reprimand, and the erring couple were allowed to depart without undergoing the extreme penalty of the law.

Joy, in short, had come in the morning, precisely as the psalmist said it always did, and it surprised Bingo that his fellow-lag seemed not to be elated. Her lovely face was pensive, as if there was something on her mind. In answer to his query as to why she was not skipping like the high hills she explained that she was thinking of her white-haired old father, George Francis Augustus Delamere, fifth Earl of Ippleton, whose existence at the time when she was making her Trafalgar Square protest had temporarily slipped her mind.

'When he learns of this, he'll be fit to be tied,' she said.

'But why should he learn of it?'

'He learns of everything. It's a sort of sixth sense. Have you any loved ones who will have criticisms to make?'

'Only my wife, and she's away.'

'You're in luck,' said Mabel Murgatroyd.

Bingo could not have agreed with her more wholeheartedly. He and Mrs Bingo had always conducted their domestic life on strictly turtle dove lines, but he was a shrewd enough student of the sex to know that you can push a turtle dove just so far. Rosie was the sweetest girl in a world where sweet girls are rather rare, but experience had taught him that, given the right conditions, she was capable of making her presence felt as perceptibly as one of those hurricanes which become so emotional on reaching Cape Hatteras. It was agreeable to think that there was no chance of her discovering that in her absence he had been hobnobbing in the dock at Bosher Street Police Court with red-haired girls of singular beauty.

It was, accordingly, with the feeling that if this was not the best of all possible worlds, it would do till another came along that he made his way to the office of *Wee Tots* and lowered his trouser-seat into the editorial chair. He had slept only fitfully on the plank bed with which the authorities had provided him and he had had practically no breakfast, but he felt that the vicissitudes through which he had passed had made him a deeper, graver man, which is always a good thing. With a light heart he addressed himself to the morning's correspondence, collecting material for the Uncle Joe To His Chickabiddies page which was such a popular feature of the paper, and he was reading a communication from Tommy Bootle (aged twelve) about his angora rabbit Kenneth, when the telephone rang and Mrs Bingo's voice floated over the wire.

'Bingo?'

'Oh, hullo, light of my life. When did you get back?'

'Just now.'

'How did everything go?'

'Quite satisfactorily.'

'Did Ma Purkiss make a speech?'

'Yes, Mrs Purkiss spoke.'

'Lots of the old college chums there, I suppose?'

'Quite a number.'

'Must have been nice for you meeting them. No doubt you got together and swopped reminiscences of midnight feeds in the dormitory and what the Games Mistress said when she found Maud and Angela smoking cigars behind the gymnasium.'

'Quite. Bingo, have you seen the *Mirror* this morning?'

'I have it on my desk, but I haven't looked at it yet.'

'Turn to Page Eight,' said Mrs Bingo, and there was a click as she rang off.

Bingo did as directed, somewhat puzzled by her anxiety to have him catch up with his reading and also by a certain oddness he had seemed to detect in her voice. Usually it was soft and melodious, easily mistaken for silver bells ringing across a sunlit meadow in Springtime, but in the recent exchanges he thought he had sensed in it a metallic note, and it perplexed him.

But not for long. Scarcely had his eyes rested on the page she had indicated when all was made clear to him and the offices of *Wee Tots* did one of those *entrechats* which Nijinsky used to do in the Russian ballet. It was as if the bomb Miss Murgatroyd disliked so much had been touched off beneath his swivel chair.

Page Eight was mostly pictures. There was one of the Prime Minister opening a bazaar, another of a resident of Chipping Norton who had just celebrated his hundredth birthday, a third of students rioting in Pernambuco or Mozambique or somewhere. But the one that interested him was the one at the foot of the page. It depicted a large policeman with a girl of singular beauty in one hand and in the other a young man whose features, though somewhat distorted, he was immediately able to recognize. Newspaper photographs tend occasionally to be blurred, but this one was a credit to the artist behind the camera.

It was captioned

THE HON. MABEL MURGATROYD AND FRIENDS

and he sat gazing at it with his eyes protruding in the manner popularized by snails, looking like something stuffed by a taxidermist who had learned his job from a correspondence course and had only got as far as Lesson Three. He had had nasty jars before in his time, for he was one of those unfortunate young men whom Fate seems to enjoy kicking in the seat of the pants, but never one so devastating as this.

Eventually life returned to the rigid limbs, and there swept over him an intense desire for a couple of quick ones. He had got, he realized, to do some very quick thinking and he had long ago learned the lesson that nothing so stimulates the thought processes as a drop of the right stuff. To grab his hat and hasten to the Drones Club was with him the work of an instant. It was not that the stuff was any righter at the Drones than at a dozen other resorts that sprang to the mind, but at these ready money had to pass from hand to hand before the pouring started and at the Drones there were no such tedious formalities. You just signed your name.

It occurred to him, moreover, that at the Drones he might find someone who would have something to suggest. And as luck would have it the first person he ran into in the bar was Freddie Widgeon, not only one of the finest minds in the club but a man who all his adult life had been thinking up ingenious ways of getting himself out of trouble with the other sex.

He related his story, and Freddie, listening sympathetically, said he had frequently been in the same sort of jam himself. There was, he said, only one thing to do, and Bingo said that one would be ample.

'I am assuming,' said Freddie, 'that you haven't the nerve to come the heavy he-man over the little woman?'

'The what?'

'You know. Looking her in the eye and making her wilt. Shoving your chin out and saying "Oh, yeah?" and "So what?".'

Bingo assured him that he was not in error. The suggested procedure was not within the range of practical politics.

'I thought not,' said Freddie. 'I have seldom been able to function along those lines myself. It's never easy for the man of sensibility and refinement. Then what you must do is have an accident.'

Bingo said he did not grasp the gist, and Freddie explained.

'You know the old gag about women being tough babies in the ordinary run of things but becoming ministering angels when pain and anguish wring the brow. There's a lot in it. Arrange a meeting with Mrs Bingo in your normal robust state with not even a cold in the head to help you out, and she will unquestionably reduce you to a spot of grease. But go to her all bunged up with splints and bandages, and her heart will melt. All will be forgiven and forgotten. She will cry "Oh, Bingo darling!" and weep buckets.'

Bingo passed a thoughtful finger over his chin.

'Splints?'

'That's right.'

'Bandages?'

'Bandages is correct. If possible, bloodstained. The best thing to do would be to go and get knocked over by a taxi cab.'

'What's the next best thing?'

'I have sometimes obtained excellent results by falling down a coal hole and spraining an ankle, but it's not easy to find a good coal hole these days, so I think you should settle for the taxi.'

'I'm not sure I like the idea of being knocked over by a taxi.'

'You would prefer a lorry?'

'A lorry would be worse.'

'Then I'll tell you what. Go back to the office and drop a typewriter on your foot.'

'But I should break a toe.'

'Exactly. You couldn't do better. Break two or even three. No sense in spoiling the ship for a ha'porth of tar.'

A shudder passed through Bingo.

'I couldn't do it, Freddie old man,' he said, and Freddie clicked his tongue censoriously.

'You're a difficult fellow to help. Then the only thing I can suggest is that you have a double.'

'I've already had one.'

'I don't mean that sort of double. Tell Mrs Bingo that there must be someone going about the place so like you that the keenest eye is deceived.'

Bingo blossomed like a flower in June. Almost anything that did not involve getting mixed up with taxi cabs and typewriters would have seemed good to him, and this seemed particularly good.

'This business of doubles,' Freddie continued, 'is happening every day. You read books about it. I remember one by Phillips Oppenheim where there was an English bloke who looked just like a German bloke, and the English bloke posed as the German bloke or vice versa, I've forgotten which.'

'And got away with it?'

'With his hair in a braid.'

'Freddie,' said Bingo, 'I believe you've hit it. Gosh, it was a stroke of luck for me running into you.'

But, back at the office, he found his enthusiasm waning. Doubts began to creep in, and what he had supposed to be the scheme of a lifetime lost some of its pristine attractiveness. Mrs Bingo wrote stories about girls who wanted to be loved for themselves alone and strong silent men who went out into the sunset with stiff upper lips, but she was not without a certain rude intelligence and it was more than possible, he felt, that she might fail to swallow an explanation which he could now see was difficult of ingestion. In its broad general principles Freddie's idea was good, but his story, he could see, would need propping up. It wanted someone to stiffen it with a bit of verisimilitude, and who better for this purpose than Miss Murgatroyd? Her word would be believed. If he could induce her to go to Mrs Bingo and tell her that she had never set eyes on him in her life and that her Trafalgar Square crony was a cousin of hers of the name – say – of Ernest Maltravers or Eustace Finch-Finch – he was not fussy about details – the home might yet be saved from the melting pot. He looked up George Francis Augustus Delamere, fifth Earl of Ippleton, in the telephone book and was presently in communication with him.

'Lord Ippleton?'

'Speaking.'

'Good morning.'

'Who says so?'

'My name is Little.'

'And mine,' said the peer, who seemed to be deeply moved, 'is mud.'

'I beg your pardon?'

'Mud.'

'Mud?'

'Yes, mud, after what that ass of a daughter of mine got up to yesterday. I shan't be able to show my face at the club. The boys at the Athenaeum will kid the pants off me. Sitting on her fanny in the middle of Trafalgar Square and getting hauled in by the flatties. I don't know what girls are coming to these days. If my mother had behaved like that, my old governor would have spanked her with the butt end of a slipper, and that's what some responsible person ought to do to young Mabel. "See what you've done, you blighted female," I said to her when she rolled in from the police court. "Blotted the escutcheon, that's what you've done. There hasn't been such a scandal in the family since our ancestress Lady Evangeline forgot to say No to Charles the Second!" I let her have it straight from the shoulder.'

'Girls will be girls,' said Bingo, hoping to soothe.

'Not while I have my health and strength they won't,' said Lord Ippleton.

Bingo saw that nothing was to be gained by pursuing this line of thought. Mabel Murgatroyd's parent was plainly in no mood for abstract discussion of the modern girl. Even at this distance he could hear him gnashing his teeth. Unless it was an electric drill working in the street. He changed the subject.

'I wonder if I could speak to Miss Murgatroyd?'

'Stop wondering.'

'I can't.'

'No.'

'Why not?'

'Because I've shipped her off to her aunt in Edinburgh with strict instructions to stay there till she's got some sense into her fat little head.'

'Oh, gosh!'

'Oh what?'

'Gosh.'

'Why do you say "Gosh"?'

'I couldn't help it.'

'Don't be an ass. Anybody can help saying "Gosh." It only requires will-power. What are you, a reporter?'

'No, just a friend.'

Bingo had never heard the howl of a timber wolf which had stubbed its toe on a rock while hurrying through a Canadian forest, but he thought it must closely resemble the sound that nearly cracked his ear drum.

'A friend, eh? You are, are you? No doubt one of the friends who have led the ivory-skulled little moron astray and started her off on all this escutcheon-blotting. I'd like to skin the lot of you with a blunt knife and dance on your remains. Bounders with beards! You have a beard, of course?'

'No, no beard.'

'Don't try to fool me. All you ghastly outsiders are festooned with the fungus. You flaunt it. Why the devil don't you shave?'

'I shave every day.'

'Is that so? Did you shave today?'

'As a matter of fact, no. I hadn't time. I had rather a busy morning.'

'Then will you do me a personal favour?'

'Certainly, certainly.'

'Go back to whatever germ-ridden den you inhabit and do it now. And don't use a safety razor, use one of the old-fashioned kind, because then there's a sporting chance that you may sever your carotid artery, which would be what some writer fellow whose name I can't recall described as a consummation devoutly to be wished. Goodbye.'

It was in thoughtful mood that Bingo replaced the receiver. He fancied that he had noticed an animosity in Lord Ippleton's manner – guarded, perhaps, but nevertheless unmistakeably animosity – and he was conscious of that feeling of frustration which comes to those who have failed to make friends and influence people. But this was not the main cause of his despondency. What really made the iron enter into his soul was the realization that with Mabel Murgatroyd in Edinburgh, not to return till the distant date when she had got some sense into her fat little head, he had lost his only chance of putting across that double thing and making it stick. It was, he now saw more clearly than ever, not at all the sort of story a young husband could hope to make convincing without the co-operation of a strong supporting cast. Phillips Oppenheim might have got away with it, but that sort of luck does not happen twice.

It really began to seem as if Freddie Widgeon's typewriter-on-toe sequence was his only resource, and he stood for some time eyeing the substantial machine on which he was wont to turn out wholesome reading matter for the chicks. He even lifted it and held it for a moment poised. But he could not bring himself to let it fall. He hesitated and delayed. If Shakespeare had happened to come by with Ben Jonson, he would have nudged the latter in the ribs and whispered 'See that fellow, rare Ben? He illustrates exactly what I was driving at when I wrote that stuff about letting "I dare not" wait upon "I would" like the poor cat in the adage.'

Finally he gave up the struggle. Replacing the machine, he flung himself into his chair and with his head in his hands uttered a hollow groan. And as he did so, he got the impression that there was a curious echo in the room, but looking up he saw that he had been in error in attributing this to the acoustics. There had been two groans in all, and the second one had proceeded from the lips of H. C. Purkiss. The proprietor of *Wee Tots* was standing in the doorway of his private office, propping himself against the woodwork with an outstretched hand, and it was obvious at a glance that he was not the suave dapper H. C. Purkiss of yesterday. There were dark circles under his eyes, and those eyes could have stepped straight on to any breakfast plate and passed without comment as poached eggs. His nervous system, too, was plainly far from being in midseason form, for when one of the local sparrows, perching on the window sill, uttered a sudden *cheep*, he quivered in every limb and made what looked to Bingo like a spirited attempt to lower the European record for the standing high jump.

'Ah, Mr Little,' he said huskily. 'Busy at work, I see. Good, good. Is there anything of interest in the morning post bag?'

'Mostly the usual gibbering,' said Bingo. 'Amazing how many of our young subscribers seem to have softening of the brain. There is a letter from Wilfred Waterson (aged seven) about his parrot Percy which would serve him as a passport into any but the most choosy lunatic asylum. He seems to think it miraculous that the bird should invite visitors to have a nut, as if that wasn't the first conversational opening every parrot makes.'

Mr Purkiss took a more tolerant view.

'I see your point, Mr Little, but we must not expect old heads on young shoulders. And speaking of heads,' he went on, quivering like an Ouled Nail stomach dancer, 'I wonder if you could oblige me with a couple of aspirins? Or a glass of tomato juice with a drop of Worcester sauce in it would do. You have none? Too bad. It might have brought a certain relief.'

Illumination flashed upon Bingo. If an editor's respect for his proprietor had been less firmly established, it might have flashed sooner.

'Good Lord!' he cried. 'Were you on a toot last night?'

Mr Purkiss waved a deprecating hand, nearly overbalancing in the process.

'Toot is a harsh word, Mr Little. I confess that in Mrs Purkiss's absence I attempted to alleviate my loneliness by joining a group of friends who wished to play poker. It was a lengthy session, concluding only an hour ago, and it is possible that in the course of the evening I may have exceeded – slightly – my customary intake of alcoholic refreshment. It seemed to be expected of me, and I did not like to refuse. But when you use the word "toot" . . .'

Bingo had no wish to be severe, but except when throwing together stories to tell Mrs Bingo he liked accuracy.

'It sounds like a toot to me,' he said. 'The facts all go to show that . . .'

He broke off. An idea of amazing brilliance had struck him. Twenty-four hours ago he would never have had the moral courage to suggest such a thing, but now that H. C. Purkiss had shown himself to be one of the boys – poker parties in the home and all that – he was convinced that if he, Bingo, begged him, Purkiss, to say that he, Bingo, had been with him, Purkiss, last night, he, Purkiss, would not have the inhumanity to deny him, Bingo, a little favour which would cost him, Purkiss, nothing and would put him, Bingo, on velvet. For Mrs Bingo would not dream of disbelieving a statement from such a source. And he had just opened his lips to speak, when Mr Purkiss resumed his remarks.

'Perhaps you are right, Mr Little. Quite possibly toot may be the *mot juste*. But however we describe the episode, one thing is certain, it has placed me in a position of the gravest peril. The party – party is surely a nicer word – took place at the house of one of the friends I was mentioning, and I am informed by my maidservant that Mrs Purkiss made no fewer than five attempts to reach me on the telephone last night – at 10.30 p.m., at 11.15 p.m., shortly after midnight, at 2 a.m. and again at 4.20 a.m., and I greatly fear . . .'

'You mean you were away from home all *night*?'

'Alas, Mr Little, I was.'

Bingo's heart sank. He would have reeled beneath the shock, had he not been seated. This was the end. This put the frosting on the cake. Impossible now to assure Mrs Bingo that he had been with Mr Purkiss during the hours he had spent in his Bosher Street cell. So poignant was his anguish that he uttered a piercing cry, and Mr Purkiss rose into the air, dislodging some plaster from the ceiling with the top of his head.

'So,' the stricken man went on, having returned to terra firma, 'I should be infinitely grateful to you, Mr Little, if you would vouch for it that I was with you till an advanced hour at your home. It would, indeed, do no harm if you were to tell Mrs Purkiss that we sat up so long discussing matters of office policy that you allowed me to spend the night in your spare room.'

Bingo drew a deep breath. It has been sufficiently established that the proprietor of *Wee Tots* was not as of even date easy on the eye, but to him he seemed a lovely spectacle. He could not have gazed on him with more appreciation if he had been the Taj Mahal by moonlight.

His manner, however, was austere. A voice had seemed to whisper in his ear that this was where, if he played his cards right, he could do himself a bit of good. There was, so he had learned from a reliable source, a tide in the affairs of men which, taken at the flood, leads on to fortune.

He frowned, at the same time pursing his lips.

'Am I to understand, Purkiss, that you are asking me to tell a deliberate falsehood?'

'You would be doing me a great kindness.'

In order to speak, Bingo had been obliged to unpurse his lips, but he still frowned.

'I'm not sure,' he said coldly, 'that I feel like doing you kind-nesses. Yesterday I asked you for a raise of salary and you curtly refused.'

'Not curtly. Surely not curtly, Mr Little.'

'Well, fairly curtly.'

'Yes, I remember. But I have given the matter thought, and I am now prepared to increase your stipend by – shall we say ten pounds a month?'

'Make it fifty.'

'Fifty!'

'Well, call it forty.'

'You would not consider thirty?'

'Certainly not.'

'Very well.'

'You agree?'

'I do.'

The telephone rang.

'Ah,' said Bingo. 'That is probably my wife again. Hullo?'

'Bingo?'

'Oh, hullo, moon of my delight. What became of you when we were talking before? Why did you buzz off like a jack rabbit?'

'I had to go and look after Mrs Purkiss.'

'Something wrong with her?'

'She was distracted because Mr Purkiss was not at home all night.'

Bingo laughed a jolly laugh.

'Of course he wasn't. He was with me.'

'What!'

'Certainly. We had office matters to discuss, and I took him home with me. We sat up so long that I put him up in the spare room. He spent the night there.'

There was a long silence at the other end of the wire. Then Mrs Bingo spoke.

'But that photograph!'

'Which photograph? Oh, you mean the one in the paper, and

I think I know what's in your mind. It looked rather like me, didn't it? I was quite surprised. I've often heard of this thing of fellows having doubles, but I've never come across an instance of it before. Except in books, of course. I remember one by Phillips Oppenheim where there was an English bloke who looked just like a German bloke, and the English bloke posed with complete success as the German bloke or vice versa, I've forgotten which. I believe it caused quite a bit of confusion. But, getting back to that photograph, obviously if I spent the night with Mr Purkiss I couldn't have spent it in a dungeon cell, as my double presumably did. But perhaps you would care to have a word with Mr Purkiss, who is here at my side. For you, Purkiss,' said Bingo, handing him the telephone.

Our Man in America

One seems to be writing a good deal about criminals these days, but owing to the eccentricity of their methods the subject is really too fascinating to leave. A gang – probably international – operating in Gold Hill, North Carolina, have just pulled off a big coup, but not having thought the thing out properly beforehand are finding themselves in a rather aggravating position, unable to establish connection with a fence willing to handle the swag. They got their booty all right, but what is holding everything up is that there seems no way of cashing in on it. There they are, all loaded up with church pews and no market in sight.

The pews in question were those in St John's Lutheran church of Gold Hill. The gang got away with ten of them the first time, and in a second and more successful raid collected twenty-five, plus the pulpit. And now – too late – they are beginning to realize that there is no real money in this branch of industry. It is no good lurking in dark street corners and popping out on passers-by with a whispered 'Psst! Want a pulpit?'. Business almost never results. Even if you shade the price a bit to suit all purses it is only a very occasional customer who is tempted by the offer of a hot pulpit. And the same thing applies to hot pews.

*

In Newark, N.J., the authorities have been doing some rather interesting research work. Superior Court Judge Mark A. Sullivan wanted the other day to find out how much alcohol a motorist had to absorb to be incapable of driving, so he rounded up a bunch of human guinea pigs and in the words of the *N.Y. Herald-Tribune* 'turned the bar of justice into a plain ordinary drinking bar'. (No, sorry, I wronged Judge Sullivan. He was on vacation, and the host at the party was Essex County Prosecutor Charles V. Webb.)

Well, sir, you'd oughta been there. In next to no time the court-room was just a shambles of potato chips, olive pips, empty bottles and popcorn. Five citizens submitted themselves to the test, and it was not long before additional Scotch and rye had to be sent for to keep up with their capacities. And of course all five of them singing Sweet Adeline in close harmony and telling the County Prosecutor (a) that their wives did not understand them and (b) that they could lick any man in the room. And the horrible thing is that all this started at ten in the morning. Really, Charles Webb, I am as broadminded as the next man, but I do feel there are limits.

And how, you ask, did it all come out? Well, as far as the Drunk-O-Meter could gather, it is unwise to drive your car in anything approaching heavy traffic after you have imbibed fourteen ounces of Scotch. Unless you happen to be an undertaker's assistant. That is how one of the five earns his living, and he got up to nineteen ounces before the Drunk-O-Meter blew the whistle on him.

(I was so busy shaking my head and pursing my lips over the above orgy that I forgot to mention that one of the experimenters drank his whisky with orange soda. It has haunted me in my dreams ever since.)

*

The impression left on the mind when one reads in the papers of the local rules and regulations in force all over the country is that life in America can be very difficult. Almost every avenue to wholesome fun seems to be barred. In Rumford, Maine, for instance, it is illegal for a tenant to bite his landlord, while in Youngstown, Ohio, stiff sentences are passed on those who tie giraffes to light standards. In Nogales, Arizona, there is an ordinance prohibiting the wearing of braces; in San Francisco one which won't let you shoot jack rabbits from cable cars; and in Dunn, South Carolina, unless you have the permission of the headmistress, a permission very sparingly granted, it is unlawful to 'act in an obnoxious manner on the campus of a girls' school'.

You hardly know where to live in America these days, especially if you are a woman. Go to Owensboro, Kentucky, and you get arrested for buying a new hat without having your husband try it on first, while if you decide on Carmel, California, you find you are not allowed to take a bath in a business office, the one thing all women want to do on settling down in a new community. For men probably the spot to be avoided with the greatest care is Norton, Virginia, where 'it is illegal to tickle a girl'.

*

A recently published history of Macy's department store contains many arresting anecdotes of the late Jacob Strauss, one of the partners. The one which touched me most was of the occasion when Mr Strauss came upon a lad, who described himself as a stock boy, playing with an electric train in the toy department and dismissed him instantly with a week's salary and two weeks' severance pay. It was not until the money had changed hands and the child had departed that Mr Strauss discovered that his young friend, though unquestionably a stock boy, was a stock boy not at Macy's, but at Gimbel's down the street.

'Ah, there you are, Mr Little,' said H. C. Purkiss. 'Are you engaged for dinner tonight?'

Bingo replied...

But before recording Bingo's reply it is necessary to go back a step or two and do what is known to lawyers as laying the proper foundation.

It was the practice of H. C. Purkiss, proprietor of *Wee Tots*, the journal for the nursery and the home, to take his annual holiday in July. This meant that Bingo, the paper's up-and-coming young editor, had to take his in June or August. This year, as in the previous year, he had done so towards the middle of the former month, and he rejoined the human herd, looking bronzed and fit, a few days before the Eton and Harrow match. And he was strolling along Piccadilly, thinking of this and that, when he ran into his fellow clubman Catsmeat Potter-Pirbright (Claude Cattermole, the popular actor of juvenile roles) and after a conversation of great brilliance but too long to be given in detail Catsmeat asked him if he would care to have a couple of seats next week for the dramatic entertainment in which he was appearing. And Bingo, enchanted at the prospect of getting into a theatre on the nod, jumped at the offer like a rising trout. He looked forward with bright enthusiasm to seeing Catsmeat bound on with a racquet at the beginning of act one shouting 'Tennis, anyone?' as he presumed he would do.

There remained the problem of choosing a partner for the round of pleasure. His wife, Rosie M. Banks, the widely read author of novels of sentiment, was at Droitwich with her mother and Algernon Aubrey, the bouncing baby who had recently appeared on the London scene. He thought of Mr Purkiss, but rejected the idea. Eventually he decided to go and ask his Aunt Myrtle, Mrs J. G. Beenstock, if she would like to come along. It would mean an uncomfortable evening. She would overflow into his seat, for she was as stout a woman as ever paled at the sight of a diet sheet and, had she been in Parliament, would have counted two on a division, but she was a lonely, or fairly lonely, widow and he felt it would be a kindly act to bring a little sunshine into her life. He ankled round, accordingly, to her house and his ring at the bell was answered by Wilberforce, her butler, who regretted to say that Madam was not in residence, being on one of those Mediterranean cruises. He was anticipating her return, said Wilberforce, either tomorrow or the day after, and Bingo was about to push off when the butler, putting a hand over his mouth and speaking from the side of it, said in a hushed whisper:

'Do you want to make a packet, Mr Richard?'

A packet being what above all things Bingo was always desirous of making, his reply in the affirmative was both immediate and eager.

'Put your shirt on Whistler's Mother for the two o'clock at Hurst Park tomorrow,' whispered Wilberforce, and having added that prompt action would enable him to get odds of eight to one he went about his butlerine duties, leaving Bingo in a frame of mind which someone like the late Gustave Flaubert, who was fussy about the right word, would have described as chaotic.

What to do, what to do, he was asking himself, this way and that dividing the swift mind. On the one hand, Wilberforce was a knowledgeable man who enjoyed a wide acquaintance with jockeys, race course touts, stable cats and others who knew a bit. His judgment of form could surely be trusted. On the other hand, Mrs Bingo, who like so many wives was deficient in sporting blood, had specifically forbidden him to wager on racehorses, and he shrank from the scene which must inevitably ensue, should the good thing come unstuck and she found out about it. The situation was unquestionably one that provided food for thought.

And then he realized that his problem was after all only an academic one, for he was down to his last five bob with nothing coming in till pay day, and with bookies money has to change hands before a deal can be consummated. If a dozen Whistler's Mothers were entered for a dozen two o'clock races, he was in no position to do anything about it.

It was quite a relief really to have the thing settled for him, and he was in excellent spirits when he got home. He took off his shoes, mixed himself a mild gin and tonic, and was about to curl up on the sofa with a good book, when the telephone rang.

A well-remembered voice came over the wire.

'Sweetie?'

'Oh, hullo, sweetie.'

'When did you get back?'

'Just clocked in.'

'How are you?'

'I'm fine, though missing you sorely. And you?'

'I'm fine.'

'And Algy?'

'He's fine.'

'And your mother?'

'Only pretty good. She swallowed some water at the brine baths this morning. She's better now, but she still makes a funny whistling sound when she breathes.'

The receiver shook in Bingo's right hand. The good book with which he had been about to curl up fell limply from his left. He had always been a great believer in signs and omens, and if this wasn't a sign and omen he didn't know a sign and omen when he saw one.

'Did you say your mother was a Whistler's – or rather a whistling mother?' he gasped at length.

'Yes, it sounds just like gas escaping from a pipe.'

Bingo tottered to a chair, taking the telephone with him. He was feeling bitter, and he had every excuse for feeling bitter. Here he was with a sure thing at his disposal, barred from cashing in on it for lack of funds. Affluence had been offered to him on a plate with watercress round it, and he must let it go because he did not possess the necessary entrance fee. He could not have had a more vivid appreciation of the irony of life if he had been Thomas Hardy.

'Oh, by the way,' said Mrs Bingo, 'what I really rang up about. You know it's Algy's birthday next week. I've bought him a rattle and some sort of woolly animal, but I think we ought to put something in his little wee bank account, as we did last year. So I'm sending you ten pounds. Goodbye, sweetie, I must rush. I'm having a perm and I'm late already.'

* * *

She rang off, and Bingo sat tingling in every limb. He continued to tingle not only till bedtime but later. Far into the silent night he tossed on his pillow, a prey to the hopes and fears he had experienced when Wilberforce had mooted the idea of his making a packet. Once more the question 'What to do?' raced through his fevered mind. It was not qualms about touching his offspring for a temporary loan that made him waver and hesitate. That end of it was all right. Any son of his, he knew, would be only too glad to finance a father's sporting venture, particularly when that sporting venture was in the deepest and fullest sense of the words money for jam. And he did not need to tell the child that when the bookie brassed up on settling day he would get his cut and find his little wee bank account augmented not by one tenner but by two.

No, it was the thought of Mrs Bingo that made him irresolute. Wilberforce was confident that Whistler's Mother would defy all competition, giving the impression that having a bit on her was virtually tantamount to finding money in the street, but these good things sometimes go wrong. The poet Burns has pointed this out to his public. 'Gang agley' was how he put it, for he did not spell very well, but it meant the same thing. And if this one went agley, what would the harvest be? He fell asleep still wondering if he dared risk it.

But the next morning he was his courageous self again. The luncheon hour found him in the offices of Charles ('Charlie Always Pays') Pikelet, the well-known turf accountant, handing over the cash, and at 2.13 sharp he was in a chair in the Drones Club smoking-room with his face buried in his hands. The result of the two o'clock race at Hurst Park had just come over the tape, and the following horses had reached journey's end ahead of Whistler's Mother – Harbour Lights, Sweet Pea, Scotch

Mist, Parson's Pleasure, Brian Boru, Ariadne and Christopher Columbus. Eight ran. Unlike Wilberforce, the poet Burns had known what he was talking about.

How long he sat there, a broken man, he could not have said. When he did emerge from his coma, it was to become aware that a good deal of activity was in progress in the smoking-room. A Crumpet was sitting at a table near the door with a pencil in his hand and a sheet of paper before him, and there was a constant flowing of members to this table. He could make nothing of it, and he turned for an explanation to Catsmeat Potter-Pirbright, who had just taken the chair next to him.

'What's going on?' he asked.

'It was the Fat Uncles Sweep,' Catsmeat said.

'The what?'

Catsmeat was amazed.

'Do you mean to say you don't know about the Fat Uncles Sweep? Weren't you here last year when it started?'

'I must have been away.'

'The race is run on the first day of the Eton and Harrow match.'

'Ah, then I was away. I always have to take my holiday early, and don't get back for the Eton and Harrow match. I did this time, but not as a rule. What is it?'

Catsmeat explained. An intelligent Drone, he said, himself the possessor of one of the fattest uncles in London, had noticed how many of his fellow members had fat uncles, too, and had felt it a waste of good material not to make these the basis of a sporting contest similar, though on a smaller scale, to those in operation in Ireland and Calcutta. The mechanics of the thing were simple. You entered your uncle, others entered theirs, the names were shaken up in a hat and the judging was done by McGarry, the club bartender, who had the uncanny gift of being able to estimate to an ounce the weight of anything, from a Pekinese to a Covent Garden soprano, just by looking at it.

'And the fellow who draws the winning ticket,' Catsmeat concluded, 'scoops the jackpot. Except, of course, for the fifty pounds allotted to the winning uncle's owner as prize money.'

A loud gasp escaped Bingo. A passer-by would have noticed that his eyes were shining with a strange light.

'Fifty pounds?'

'That's right.'

Bingo shot from his chair and gazed wildly about the room.

'Where's Oofy?' he cried, alluding to Oofy Prosser, the club's millionaire.

'In the bar, I believe. What do you want him for?'

'I want to enter my Aunt Myrtle and sell him a piece of her to enable me to meet current expenses.'

'But—'

'Don't sit there saying "But". When's the drawing?'

'Three days from now.'

'Plenty of time. I'll approach him at once.'

'But—'

'That word again! What's bothering you? If you think Oofy won't make a deal, you're wrong. He's a business man. He'll know he'll be on a sure thing. You've seen my Aunt Myrtle and you can testify to her stoutness. There can't possibly be an uncle fatter than her. Let's go and find Oofy now and have him draw up an agreement.'

'But aunts aren't eligible. Only uncles.'

Bingo stared at him, aghast.

'What . . . what did you say?'

Catsmeat repeated his statement, and Bingo quivered in every limb.

'You mean to tell me that if a man has the stoutest aunt in the West End of London, an aunt who, if she were not independently wealthy, could be making a good living as the Fat Woman in a circus, he can't cash in on her?'

'I'm afraid not.'

'What a monstrous thing! Are you sure?'

'Quite sure. It's all in the book of rules.'

It was a Bingo with heart bowed down and feeling more like a toad beneath a harrow than the editor of a journal for the nursery and the home who returned to the offices of *Wee Tots* and endeavoured to concentrate on the letters which had come in from subscribers for the Correspondence page. He took up a communication from Edwin Waters (aged seven) about his Siamese cat Miggles, but he found his attention wandering. He found the same difficulty in becoming engrossed in four pages from Alexander Allbright (aged six) about his tortoise Shelley, and he had started on a lengthy screed from Anita Ellsworth (aged eight) which seemed to have to do with a canary of the name of Birdie, when the door of the inner office opened and Mr Purkiss appeared.

'Ah, there you are, Mr Little,' said H. C. Purkiss. 'Are you engaged for dinner tonight?'

Which, if you remember, is where we came in.

Bingo replied hollowly that he was not, and might have added that if his employer was about to invite him to share the evening meal, he was prepared to defend himself with tooth and claw.

'I thought that Mrs Little might be having guests.'

'She's at Droitwich with her mother. Her mother is taking the brine baths. She has rheumatism.'

'Splendid. Excellent. Capital,' said Mr Purkiss, hastening to explain that it was not the fact of Bingo's mother-in-law having trouble with her joints that exhilarated him. 'Then you are free. I am delighted to hear it. Tell me, Mr Little, are you familiar with the work of an American author of juvenile fiction named Kirk Rockaway? No? I am not surprised. He is almost unknown on this side of the Atlantic, but his Peter the Pup, Kootchy the Kitten and Hilda the Hen are, I understand, required reading for the children of his native country. I have glanced at some of his works and they are superb. He is just the circulation-builder *Wee Tots* needs. He is here in London on a visit.'

Bingo was a conscientious editor. His personal affairs might be in a state of extreme disorder, but he was always able to shelve his private worries when it was a matter of doing his paper a bit of good.

'We'd better go after him before those blighters at *Small Fry* get ahead of us,' he said.

Mr Purkiss smiled triumphantly.

'I have already done so. I met him at a tea party given in his honour yesterday, and he has accepted an invitation to dine with me tonight at Barribault's Hotel.'

'That's good.'

'And this,' said Mr Purkiss, 'is better. At that tea party a most significant thing happened. Somebody mentioned Mrs Little's books, and he turned out to be a warm admirer of them. He spoke of them with unbounded enthusiasm. You see what I am about to say, Mr Little?'

'He wants her autograph?'

'That, of course, and I assured him that he could rely on her.

But obviously tonight's arrangements must be changed. You, not I, must be his host. As Mrs Little's husband, you are the one he will want to meet. I will ring him up now.'

Mr Purkiss went back to his room, to return a few moments later, beaming.

'All is settled, Mr Little. I had, I am afraid, to stoop to a slight prevarication. I told him I was subject to a bronchial affection which rendered it inadvisable for me to venture out at night, but that my editor, the husband of Rosie M. Banks, would be there in my place. He was all enthusiasm and is looking forward keenly to meeting you. I will, of course, defray your expenses. Here are ten pounds. That will amply cover the cost of dinner, for Mrs Rockaway tells me he is a lifelong teetotaller, so there will be no wine bill. You can bring me the change tomorrow.'

To say that Bingo was elated at the prospect of an evening out with a man who wrote about hens and kittens and drank only lemonade would be incorrect. Nor did he fail to writhe at the thought that Life had sprung another of its ironies on him by putting ten pounds in his trouser pocket but making it impossible for him to divert the sum into Algernon Aubrey's little wee bank account. For one mad moment he toyed with the idea of not giving Kirk Rockaway dinner and holding on to Mr Purkiss's tenner, but he discarded it. If he stood Kirk Rockaway up, the hen and kitten specialist would be bound to contact Mr Purkiss and ask him what the hell, and Mr Purkiss, informed of the circumstances, would instantly relieve his young assistant of his editorial post. And if he suddenly ceased to occupy the editorial chair, Mrs Bingo would want to know why, and ... but here Bingo preferred to abandon this train of thought. Shortly before eight o'clock he was in the lobby of Barribault's Hotel, and in due course Kirk Rockaway appeared.

One says 'appeared', but the word would not have satisfied Gustave Flaubert. He would have suggested some such alternative as 'loomed up' or 'came waddling along' as being more exact, for the author of Kootchy the Kitten and Peter the Pup was one of the fattest men that ever broke a try-your-weight machine. He looked as if he had been eating nothing but starchy foods since early boyhood, and it saddened Bingo to think of all this wonderful material going to waste. If only this man could have been his uncle, he felt wistfully. Oofy Prosser would have paid twenty pounds for a mere third of him.

'Mr Little?' said this human hippopotamus. He grasped Bingo's hand and subjected him to a pop-eyed but reverent gaze. 'Well, well, well!' he said. 'This is certainly a great moment for me. Mrs Little's books have been an inspiration to me for years. I read them incessantly and I am not ashamed to say with tears in my eyes. She seems to make the world a better, sweeter place. I am looking forward to having the privilege of meeting her. How is she? Well, I hope?'

'Oh, fine.'

'That's good,' said Kirk Rockaway, and then he uttered these astounding words: 'Let's get one thing straight, Mr Little. The money of Rosie M. Banks's husband is no good in this hotel. Dismiss all thought of picking up the tab tonight. This dinner is on me.'

'What!'

'Yes, sir. I wouldn't be able to look Mrs Little in the face if I let you pay for it.'

The lobby of Barribault's Hotel is solidly constructed and the last thing in the world to break suddenly into the old-fashioned buck-and-wing dance, but to Bingo it seemed that it was forgetting itself in this manner. There were two pillars in its centre, and he distinctly saw them do a kick upwards and another kick sideways. Ecstasy for a moment kept him dumb. Then he was able to murmur that this was awfully kind of Mr Rockaway.

'Don't give it a thought,' said Kirk Rockaway. 'Let's go in, shall we?'

Over the smoked salmon what conversation took place was confined to Bingo's host. Bingo himself still felt incapable of speech. The realization that by this miracle at the eleventh hour he had been saved from the fate that is worse than death – viz. having to confess the awful truth to Mrs Bingo and listen to her comments on his recent activities, seemed to have paralysed his vocal cords. He was still dazed and silent when the soup arrived.

The evening was warm and it had been quite a walk through the lobby and into the restaurant and across the restaurant to their table, and Kirk Rockaway, evidently unused to exercise, had felt the strain. By the time the soup came, beads of perspiration had begun to form on his forehead, and after about the fifth spoonful he reached in his breast pocket for a handkerchief. He pulled it out and with it came a cabinet-size photograph which shot through the air and fell into Bingo's plate. And as Bingo fished it from the purée and started to dry it with his napkin, something familiar about it struck his attention. It portrayed a woman of ample dimensions looking over her shoulder in an arch sort of way, and with a good deal of surprise he recognized her as Mrs J. G. Beenstock, the last person he would have expected to find in his soup.

'Well, well,' he said. 'So you know my aunt?'

'Your what?'

'My aunt.'

Kirk Rockaway stared at him, astounded.

'Is that divine woman your aunt?'

'That's just what she is.'

'You amaze me!'

'I'm amazed, too. What are you doing going about with her photograph next to your heart?'

Kirk Rockaway hesitated for a moment. He seemed to be blushing, though it was hard to say for certain, his face from the start having been tomatoesque. Finally he spoke.

'Shall I tell you something?' he said.

'Do.'

'I've come all the way from Oakland, San Francisco, to marry her.'

It was Bingo's turn to stare, astounded.

'You mean you and Aunt Myrtle are engaged?'

So great was his emotion that he could hardly frame the words. It seemed to him too good to be true, too like a beautiful dream, that this obese bimbo was about to become his uncle and so eligible for the Drones Club contest.

An embarrassed look had come into Kirk Rockaway's face. Again he hesitated before he spoke.

'No, we're not engaged.'

'You aren't?'

'Not yet. It's like this. She came to San Francisco a year or so ago.'

'Yes, I remember she went over to America. She's very fond of travelling.'

'We met at a dinner party. It was a Thanksgiving dinner with turkey, sweet potatoes, mince pie – the customary Thanksgiving menu. She sat opposite me, and the way she sailed into the turkey – enjoying it, *understanding* it, not pecking at it as the other women were doing – hit me right here,' said Kirk Rockaway, touching the left side of his bulging waistcoat. 'And when I watched her handle the mince pie, I knew my fate was sealed. But I haven't actually proposed yet.'

'Why not?'

'I haven't the nerve.'

'What!'

'No, sir, I haven't the nerve.'

'Why not?'

'I don't know. I just haven't.'

A blinding light flashed upon Bingo. Mr Purkiss's words rang in his ears. 'He is a lifelong teetotaller' Mr Purkiss had said, and the whole thing became clear to him.

'Have you tried having a drink?' he asked.

'I've drunk a good deal of barley water.'

'Barley water!'

'But it seems to have no effect.'

'I'm not surprised. Barley water!' Bingo's voice was vibrant with scorn. 'What on earth's the good of barley water? How can you expect to be the masterful wooer on stuff like that? I should be a bachelor today if I hadn't had the prudence to fill myself to the brim with about a quart of mixed champagne and stout before asking Rosie to come registrar's-officing with me. That's what you want, champagne and stout. It'll make a new man of you.'

Kirk Rockaway looked dubious.

'But that's alcohol, and I promised my late mother I would never drink alcohol.'

'Well, I think if you could get in touch with her on the ouija board and explain the situation, making it clear that you needed the stuff for a good cause, she would skip the red tape and tell you to go to it. But that would take time. It might be hours before you got a connection. What you want is a noggin of it now, and then when you are nicely primed, we will go and drop in on my aunt. She has been away on a Mediterranean cruise, but she may be back by now. Waiter, bring us a bottle of Bollinger and all the stout you can carry.'

It was some half-hour later that Kirk Rockaway looked across the table with a new light in his eyes. They had become reddish in colour and bulged a good deal. His diction, when he spoke, was a little slurred.

'Old man,' he said, 'I like your face.'

'Do you, old man?' said Bingo.

'Yes, old man, I do. And do you know why I like your face?'

'No, old man, I don't. Why do you like my face?'

'Because it is so different in every respect from Mortimer Frisby's.'

'Who is Mortimer Frisby?'

'You may well ask. He conducts the Children's Page on the *San Francisco Herald*, and calls himself a critic. Do you know what he said about my last book, old man?'

'No, what did he say, old man?'

'I'll tell you what he said. His words are graven on my heart and I quote verbatim. "We think," he said, "that Mr Rockaway should not too lightly assume that all the children he writes for have water on the brain." How about that?'

'Monstrous!'

'Monstrous is right.'

'Abominable!'

'Abominable is correct.'

'The man must be mad.'

'Of course he is. But if he thinks he'll get off on a plea of insanity, he's very much mistaken. I propose to poke him in the snoot. We'll have just one more bottle for the road, and then I'll go and attend to it.'

'Where is he?'

'San Francisco.'

'You can't go to San Francisco.'

'Why not? I believe,' said Kirk Rockaway a little stiffly, 'that San Francisco is open for being gone to at about this time.'

'But it's such a long way. Besides, you were going to propose to my aunt.'

'Was I? Yes, by jove, you're right. It had slipped my mind.'

'Do it now. If you're feeling up to it.'

'I'm feeling great. I'm feeling strong, forceful, dominant. Do you know what I shall do to that woman?'

'Bend her to your will?'

'Precisely. I shall stand no nonsense from her. Women are apt to want long engagements and wedding services with full choral effects, but none of that for me. We shall be married . . . where was it you said you were married?'

'At the registrar's.'

'They give you quick service there?'

'Very quick. Over in a flash.'

'Then that's the place that gets my custom. And if I hear a yip out of her to the contrary, I shall poke her in the snoot. Come on, pay the check and let's go.'

Bingo's jaw fell.

'You mean pay the bill?'

'If that's what you like to call it.'

'But I thought you were standing me this dinner.'

'What ever gave you that silly idea?'

'You said you would because I was Rosie M. Banks's husband.'

'Whose husband?'

'Rosie M. Banks's.'

'Never heard of her,' said Kirk Rockaway. 'It's your treat, so come across. Or would you prefer that I gave you a poke in the snoot?'

And his physique was so robust and his manner so intimidating that it seemed to Bingo that he had no alternative. With a groan that came up from the soles of his feet he felt in his pocket for Mr Purkiss's ten pounds and with trembling finger beckoned to the waiter.

Bingo's aunt's house was in the Kensington neighbourhood, and thither they repaired in a taxi cab. It was a longish journey, but Kirk Rockaway enlivened it with college yells remembered from earlier days. As they alighted, he was in the middle of one and he finished it while ringing the door bell.

The door opened. Willoughby appeared. Kirk Rockaway tapped him authoritatively on the chest and said:

'Take me to your leader!'

'Sir!'

'The Beenstock broad. I want a word with her.'

'Mrs Beenstock is not at home, and I would be greatly obliged, sir, if you would pop off.'

'I will not pop off. I demand to see the woman I love instantly,' thundered Kirk Rockaway, continuing to tap the butler like a woodpecker. 'There is a plot to keep her from me, and I may mention that I happen to know the ringleaders. If you do not immediately—'

He broke off, not because he had said his say but because he overbalanced and fell down the steps. Bingo, who had entered the hall, thought he saw him bounce twice, but he was in a state of great mental perturbation and may have been mistaken. Willoughby closed the front door, and Bingo wiped his forehead. His own forehead, not Willoughby's.

'Isn't my aunt at home?'

'No, sir. She returns tomorrow.'

'Why didn't you tell the gentleman that?'

'The gentleman was pie-eyed, Mr Richard. Hark at him now.'

He was alluding to the fact that Kirk Rockaway was now banging on the door with the knocker, at the same time shouting in a stentorian voice that the woman he loved was being held incommunicado by a gang in the pay of Mortimer Frisby. Then abruptly the noise ceased and Bingo, peering through the little window at the side of the door, saw that the sweet singer of Oakland, San Francisco, was in conversation with a member of the police force. He was too far away to catch the gist of their talk, but it must have been acrimonious, for it had been in progress only a few moments when Kirk Rockaway, substituting action for words, hit the constable on the tip of the nose. The hand of the law then attached itself to his elbow and he was led away into the night.

The magistrate at Bow Street next morning took a serious view of the case. The tidal wave of lawlessness which was engulfing London, he said, must be checked and those who added fuel to its flames by punching policemen must be taught that they could not escape the penalty of their misdeeds.

'Fourteen days,' he said, coming to the point, and Bingo, who had attended the proceedings, tottered from the court feeling that this was the end. No hope now of that well-nourished man marrying his Aunt Myrtle in time to be entered for the Fat Uncles stakes. When the judging was done, he would still be in his prison cell – gnawed, Bingo hoped, for he was in bitter mood, by rats. The future looked dark to him. He recalled a poem in which there had occurred the line 'The night that covers me, black as the Pit from pole to pole', and he felt that if he had been asked to describe his general position at the moment, he could not have put the thing better himself. The words fitted his situation like the paper on the wall.

Only one ray of hope, and that a faint one, lightened his darkness. Willoughby had said that his aunt would be back from her Mediterranean cruise today, and he had sometimes found her responsive to the touch, if tactfully approached. It was a chance which Charles ('Charlie Always Pays') Pikelet would have estimated at perhaps 100 to 8, but it was a chance. He hastened to her house and pressed the front door bell.

'Good morning, Willoughby.'

'Good morning, Mr Richard.'

'You and your Whistler's Mothers!'

'I would prefer not to dwell on that topic, sir.'

'So would I. Is my aunt in?'

'No, sir. They have gone out to do some shopping.'

'They?' said Bingo, surprised that the butler should have spoken of his employer, stout though she was, in the plural.

'Madam and Sir Hercules, Mr Richard.'

'Who on earth is Sir Hercules?'

'Madam's husband, sir. Sir Hercules Foliot-Foljambe.'

'What!'

'Yes, sir. It appears that they were shipmates on the cruise from which Madam has just returned. I understand that the wedding took place in Naples.'

'Well, I'll be blowed. You never know what's going to happen next in these disturbed times, do you?'

'No, sir.'

'Of all the bizarre occurrences! What sort of a chap is he?'

'Bald, about the colour of tomato ketchup, and stout.'

Bingo started.

'Stout?'

'Yes, sir.'

'How stout?'

'There is a photograph of the gentleman in Madam's boudoir, if you care to see it.'

'Let's go,' said Bingo. He was conscious a strange thrill, but at the same time he was telling himself that he must not raise his hopes too high. Probably, judged by Drones standards, this new uncle of his would prove to be nothing special.

A minute later, he had reeled and a sharp cry had escaped his lips. He was looking, spellbound, at the photograph of a man so vast, so like a captive balloon, that Kirk Rockaway seemed merely pleasantly plump in comparison. A woman, he felt, even one as globular as his Aunt Myrtle, would have been well advised before linking her lot with his to consult her legal adviser to make sure that she was not committing bigamy.

A long sigh of ecstasy proceeded from him.

'Up from the depths!' he murmured. 'Up from the depths!'

'Sir?'

'Nothing, nothing. Just a random thought. I'm going to borrow this photograph, Willoughby.'

'Madam may be annoyed on discovering its absence.'

'Tell her she'll have it back this afternoon. I only want to show it to a man at the Drones,' said Bingo.

He was thinking of his coming interview with Oofy Prosser. If Oofy was prepared to meet his terms, he would let him have – say – twenty per cent of this certain winner, but he meant to drive a hard bargain.

This has not been a good theatrical season. Except for two or three musicals no Broadway production, as far as can be ascertained, has made a profit, and, as always, no contribution has been made to the takings by the Second Act Club.

The Second Act Club consists of young fellows who are fond of the theatre but dislike paying for tickets, and the way you get round this formality is as follows. What you do is go to a bar across from the theatre and check your hat and coat. Then when the people come out at the first act intermission you stroll across the street and mingle with them till the buzzer sounds for Act Two, when you accompany them back into the theatre and select your seat. Unless the thing is a sell-out, there are sure to be some empties.

Closely linked with the Second Act Club is the Opening Night Party Association, though this, owing to its more testing demands on the nervous system, has fewer practising members. A comparative weakling can sneak into second acts, but in order to attend an opening night party to which you have not been invited you need presence and aplomb, not to mention a dinner jacket and a clean shirt, both well beyond the scope of the average Second Acter.

The theory is that nobody knows who anybody else is at an

opening night party, so you hang around Sardi's or wherever it may be till the guests begin to arrive and then join them at their table. It is seldom that anyone likes to question anybody's bona fides, as the questionee may turn out to be the producer's wife's favourite brother, so there is really very little risk except that you may be kissed by the female star when you tell her how wonderful she was. We would strongly advise any young man starting out in life to become an opening night banqueter rather than a Second Acter, for even the second act of the sort of play they are putting on nowadays is best avoided, and though you may sometimes strike a bad patch and get thrown out of an opening night party, it will probably not be till you are well ahead of the game in the matter of lobster Newburg and champagne.

*

No news from Philadelphia at the moment of going to press except a rather unpleasant episode in the life of Robert Gilpin, a gatekeeper at the local Zoo. Seems he was standing at his post, when a young man approached him carrying a red-bellied turtle.

'Ah,' said Mr Gilpin. 'A red-bellied turtle, eh? Just what we happen to be short of. Come in and let me have it.'

The young man came in and let him have it on the base of the skull. Then, stepping over his prostrate body, he took a hundred dollars from the gatehouse cash register and withdrew. Asked by reporters how it felt to be beaned with a red-bellied turtle, Mr Gilpin replied that it was about the same as being beaned with any other kind of turtle. Nothing much in it either way, he said.

*

The wise guys who understand national finance have been telling us that we are in for a bad time unless something is done to curb the Administration's 'reckless spending programme', giving the impression that they think our money is being unwisely handled by the men up top. I am sure very few of us will agree with this. One of the reasons why our faces light up when the time comes to hand over four-fifths of our last year's income to the government is that we know that the lolly will be employed to some good end.

Only the other day the government started a project for studying the diving reflex and volume receptors of seals, which is a thing I can hardly wait to find out about, and now they are touching me for a bit more because they want to take a census of fish. Four hundred skin-divers are diving daily into the Atlantic and Pacific oceans in order to 'determine the distribution of the fish that inhabit American waters', and that sort of thing comes high. You know what skin-divers are like. They want theirs. By the time I have paid this bunch their salaries, it is very doubtful if I shall be able to afford the one meat meal a week to which I had been looking forward.

But I can quite see how it would jeopardize America's safety not to count these fish, so I shall make do quite happily on biscuits and cheese, and of course there is always the chance that a kindly skin-diver, grateful for my patronage, will slip me a halibut or something on the side.

*

Talking of dogs – not that we were, but suppose we had been – there is a Television writer in these parts who never wants to hear the word mentioned again. They told him the other day to do a story featuring a cocker spaniel which was on the pay roll, and he wrote one of those charming little domestic comedies which, after the usual complications and misunderstandings, ended with the family going out to dinner at a restaurant accompanied by the dog.

So far, so good. But he had not reckoned with the thoroughness with which TV organizations go into these things. The assistant director said to the director 'Do you think it's all right to have a cocker spaniel dining at a restaurant?'. The director did not feel equal to deciding an important point like that, and put it up to the producer. The producer, not liking to commit himself, passed the buck to the executive producer, who handed it on to the advertising agency, who after a good deal of thought felt that the only safe course was to apply directly to the sponsor. The sponsor was on a yacht cruise, but after three days they managed to locate him.

'Is it okay,' they asked, 'for a cocker spaniel to go out to dinner with the family?'

'Sure,' said the sponsor. 'Why not?'

So everybody was happy except the writer, who got properly ticked off for costing the management four days' shooting.

'In future,' they told him, 'lay off the controversial stuff.'

*

A funny thing happened to Garry Moore, the Television comedian, on his way to the studio the other night. His face being so familiar to the viewing public, he is always being stopped in the street and asked for his autograph, and as he is a kindly man who believes in keeping in with the fans, he never fails to oblige. On this occasion he was coming along Sixth Avenue to attend a late-night rehearsal, when, as he passed the mouth of a dark alley, a man emerged and said something in a low voice.

'Why, certainly, certainly,' said Mr Moore heartily. 'Only too pleased,' and he took an old envelope from his pocket, scribbled his name on it and went his way. It was a few minutes later that he suddenly realized that what the member of his public had whispered in his ear was 'This is a stick-up.'

The little group of serious thinkers in the bar parlour of the Angler's Rest were talking about twins. A Gin and Tonic had brought the subject up, a cousin of his having recently acquired a couple, and the discussion had not proceeded far when it was seen that Mr Mulliner, the Sage of the bar parlour, was smiling as if amused by some memory.

'I was thinking of my brother's sons, George and Alfred,' he explained. 'They were twins.'

'Identical?' asked a Scotch on the Rocks.

'In every respect.'

'Always getting mistaken for each other, I suppose?'

'They would have been, no doubt, if they had moved in the same circles, but their walks in life kept them widely separated. Alfred was a professional conjuror and spent most of his time in London, while George some years previously had gone to seek his fortune in Hollywood, where after various vicissitudes he had become a writer of additional dialogue on the staff of Jacob Schnellenhamer of the Colossal-Exquisite corporation.

The lot of a writer of additional dialogue in a Hollywood studio is not an exalted one – he ranks, I believe, just above a script girl and just below the man who works the wind machine – but any pity I might have felt for George for being one of the dregs was mitigated by the fact that I knew his position was only temporary, for on his thirtieth birthday, which would be occurring very shortly, he would be coming into possession of a large fortune left to him in trust by his godmother.

It was on Mr Schnellenhamer's yacht that I met George again after an interval of several years. I had become friendly with Mr Schnellenhamer on one of his previous visits to England, and when I ran into him one day in Piccadilly he told me he was just off to Monte Carlo to discuss some business matters with Sam Glutz of the Perfecto-Wonderful, who was wintering there, and asked me if I would care to come along. I accepted the invitation gratefully, and the first person I saw when I came on board was George.

I found him in excellent spirits, and I was not surprised, for he said he had reached the age of thirty a few days ago and would be collecting his legacy directly we arrived in Monaco.

'Your trustee is meeting you there?'

'He lives there. An old boy of the name of Bassinger.'

'Well, I certainly congratulate you, George. Have you made any plans?'

'Plenty. And the first is to stop being a Yes man.'

'I thought you were a writer of additional dialogue.'

'It's the same thing. I've been saying Yes to Schnellenhamer for three years, but no longer. A radical change of policy there's going to be. In the privacy of my chamber I've been practising saying No for days. No, Mr Schnellenhamer!' said George. 'No, no, no! You're wrong, Mr Schnellenhamer. You're quite mistaken, Mr Schnellenhamer. You're talking through your hat, Mr Schnellenhamer. Would it be going too far if I told him he ought to have his head examined?'

'A little, I think.'

'Perhaps you're right.'

'You don't want to hurt his feelings.'

'I don't think he has any. Still, I see what you mean.'

We arrived in Monte Carlo after a pleasant voyage, and as soon as we had anchored in Monaco harbour I went ashore to see the sights and buy the papers, and I was thinking of returning to the yacht, when I saw George coming along, seeming to be in a hurry. I hailed him, and to my astonishment he turned out to be not George but Alfred, the last person I would have expected to find in Monte Carlo. I had always supposed that conjurors never left London except to appear at children's parties in the provinces.

He was delighted to see me. We had always been very close to one another. Many a time as a boy he had borrowed my top hat in order to take rabbits out of it, for even then he was acquiring the rudiments of his art and the skill which had enabled him to bill himself as The Great Alfredo. There was genuine affection in his manner as he now produced a hardboiled egg from my breast pocket.

'But how in the world do you come to be here, Alfred?' I asked.

His explanation was simple.

'I'm appearing at the Casino. I have a couple of spots in the revue there, and I don't mind telling you that I'm rolling the customers in the aisles nightly,' he said, and I recalled that he had always interspersed his feats with humorous dialogue. 'How do you happen to be in Monte Carlo? Not on a gambling caper, I trust?'

'I am a guest on Mr Schnellenhamer's yacht.'

He started at the mention of the name.

'Schnellenhamer? The movie man? The one who's doing the great Bible epic *Solomon And The Queen Of Sheba*?'

'Yes. We are anchored in the harbour.'

'Well, well,' said Alfred. His air was pensive. My words had apparently started a train of thought. Then he looked at his watch and uttered an exclamation. 'Good Lord,' he said, 'I must rush, or I'll be late for rehearsal.'

And before I could tell him that his brother George was also on Mr Schnellenhamer's yacht he had bounded off.

Mr Schnellenhamer was on the deck when I reached the yacht, concluding a conversation with a young man whom I presumed to be a reporter, come to interview him. The young man left, and Mr Schnellenhamer jerked a thumb at his retreating back.

'Listen,' he said. 'Do you know what that fellow's been telling me? You remember I was coming here to meet Sam Glutz? Well, it seems that somebody mugged Sam last night.'

'You don't say!'

'Yessir, laid him out cold. Are those the papers you've got there? Lemme look. It's probably on the front page.'

He was perfectly correct. Even George would have had to say 'Yes, Mr Schnellenhamer'. The story was there under big headlines. On the previous night, it appeared, Mr Glutz had been returning from the Casino to his hotel, when some person unknown had waylaid him and left him lying in the street in a considerably battered condition. He had been found by a passer-by and taken to the hospital to be stitched together.

'And not a hope of catching the fellow,' said Mr Schnellenhamer.

I pointed out that the paper said that the police had a clue, and he snorted contemptuously.

'Police!'

'At your service,' said a voice, and turning I saw what I thought for a moment was General De Gaulle. Then I realized that he was some inches shorter than the General and had a yard or so less nose. But not even General De Gaulle could have looked sterner and more intimidating. 'Sergeant Brichoux of the Monaco police force,' he said. 'I have come to see a Mr Mulliner, who I understand is a member of your entourage.'

This surprised me. I was also surprised that he should be speaking English so fluently, but the explanation soon occurred to me. A sergeant of police in a place like Monte Carlo, constantly having to question international spies, heavily veiled adventuresses and the like, would soon pick it up.

'I am Mr Mulliner,' I said.

'Mr George Mulliner?'

'Oh, George? No, he is my nephew. You want to see him?'

'I do.'

'Why?' asked Mr Schnellenhamer.

'In connection with last night's assault on Mr Glutz. The police have reason to believe that he can assist them in their enquiries.'

'How?'

'They would like him to explain how his wallet came to be lying on the spot where Mr Glutz was attacked. One feels, does one not, that the fact is significant. Can I see him, if you please?' said Sergeant Brichoux, and a sailor was despatched to find George. He returned with the information that he did not appear to be on board.

'Probably gone for a stroll ashore,' said Mr Schnellenhamer.

'Then with your permission,' said the sergeant, looking more sinister than ever, 'I will await his return.'

'And I'll go and look for him,' I said.

It was imperative, I felt, that George be intercepted and

warned of what was waiting for him on the yacht. It was, of course, absurd to suppose that he had been associated in any way with last night's outrage, but if his wallet had been discovered on the scene of the crime, it was obvious that he would have a good deal of explaining to do. As I saw it, he was in the position the hero is always getting into in novels of suspense – forced by circumstances, though innocent, into the role of Suspect Number One and having a thoroughly sticky time till everything comes right in the last chapter.

It was on a bench near the harbour that I found him. He was sitting with his head between his hands, probably feeling that if he let go of it it would come in half, for when I spoke his name and he looked up, it was plain to see that he was in the grip of a severe hangover. I am told by those who know that there are six varieties of hangover – the Broken Compass, the Sewing Machine, the Comet, the Atomic, the Cement Mixer and the Gremlin Boogie, and his aspect suggested that he had got them all.

I was not really surprised. He had told me after dinner on the previous night that he was just off to call on his trustee and collect his inheritance, and it was natural to suppose that after doing so he would celebrate. But when I asked him if this was so, he uttered one of those hollow rasping laughs that are so unpleasant.

'Celebrate!' he said. 'No, I wasn't celebrating. Shall I tell you what happened last night? I went to Bassinger's hotel and gave my name and asked if he was in, and they told me he had checked out a week or two ago and had left a letter for me. I took the letter. I opened it. I read it. And having read it . . . Have you ever been slapped in the eye with a wet fish?'

'Oddly enough, no.'

'I was once when I got into an argument with an angler down at Santa Monica, and the sensation now was very similar. For this letter, this *billet doux* from that offspring of unmarried parents P. P. Bassinger, informed me that he had been gambling for years with the trust money and was deeply sorry to say that there was now no trust. It had gone. So, he added, had he. By the time I read this, he said, he would be in one of those broadminded South American countries where they don't believe in extradition. He apologized profusely, but places the blame on some man he had met in a bar who had given him an infallible system for winning at the tables. And why my godmother gave the trusteeship to someone living in Monte Carlo within easy walking distance of the Casino we shall never know. Just asking for it is the way it looks to me.'

My heart bled for him. By no stretch of optimism could I regard this as his lucky day. All this and Sergeant Brichoux, too. There was a quaver in my voice as I spoke.

'My poor boy!'

'Poor is right.'

'It must have been a terrible shock.'

'It was.'

'What did you do?'

'What would you have done? I went out and got pie-eyed. And here's a funny thing. I had the most extraordinary nightmare. Do you ever have nightmares?'

'Sometimes.'

'Bad ones?'

'Occasionally.'

'I'll bet they aren't as bad as the one I had. I dreamed that I had done a murder. And that dream is still lingering with me. I keep seeing myself engaged in a terrific brawl with someone and laying him out. It's a most unpleasant sensation. Why are you looking at me like a sheep with something on its mind?'

I had to tell him.

'It wasn't a nightmare, George.'

He seemed annoyed.

'Don't be an ass. Do you think I don't know a nightmare when I see one?'

'I repeat, it was no nightmare.'

He looked at me incredulously, his jaw beginning to droop like a badly set soufflé.

'You don't mean it actually happened?'

'I fear so. The papers have featured it.'

'I really slugged somebody?'

'Not just somebody. The president of a motion picture corporation, which makes your offence virtually *lèse majesté*.'

'Then how very fortunate,' said George, looking on the bright side after a moment of intense thought, 'that nobody can possibly know it was me. That certainly takes a weight off my mind. You're still goggling at me like a careworn sheep. Why is that?'

'I was thinking what a pity it was that you should have dropped your wallet – containing your name and address – on the spot of the crime.'

'Did I do that?'

'You did.'

'Hell's bells!'

'Hell's bells is correct. There's a sergeant of police on board the yacht now, waiting for your return. He has reason to believe that you can assist him in his enquiries.'

'Death and despair!'

'You may well say so. There is only one thing to be done.

You must escape while there is yet time. Get over the frontier into Italy.'

'But my passport's on the yacht.'

'I could bring it to you.'

'You'd never find it.'

'Then I don't know what to suggest. Of course, you might—'

'That's no good.'

'Or you could—'

'That's no good, either. No,' said George, 'this is the end. I'm a rat in a trap. I'm for it. Well-meaning, not to be blamed, the victim of the sort of accident that might have happened to anyone when lit up as I was lit, but nevertheless for it. That's Life. You come to Monte Carlo to collect a large fortune, all pepped up with the thought that at last you're going to be able to say No to old Schnellenhamer, and what do you get? No fortune, a headache, and to top it all off the guillotine or whatever they have in these parts. That's Life, I repeat. Just a bowl of cherries. You can't win.'

Twin! I uttered a cry, electrified.

'I have it, George!'

'Well?'

'You want to get on the yacht.'

'Well?'

'To secure your passport.'

'Well?'

'Then go there.'

He gave me a reproachful look.

'If,' he said, 'you think this is the sort of stuff to spring on a man with a morning head who is extremely worried because the bloodhounds of the law are sniffing on his trail and he's liable to be guillotined at any moment, I am afraid I cannot agree with you. On your own showing that yacht is congested with sergeants of police, polishing the handcuffs and waiting eagerly for my return. I'd look pretty silly sauntering in and saying "Well, boys, here I am". Or don't you think so?'

'I omitted to mention that you would say you were Alfred.'

He blinked.

'Alfred?'

'Yes.'

'My brother Alfred?'

'Your twin brother Alfred,' I said, emphasizing the second word in the sentence, and I saw the light of intelligence creep slowly into his haggard face. 'I will go there ahead of you and sow the good seed by telling them that you have a twin brother who is your exact double. Then you make your appearance. Have no fear that your story will not be believed. Alfred is at this moment in Monte Carlo, performing nightly in the revue at the Casino and is, I imagine, a familiar figure in local circles. He is probably known to the police – not, I need scarcely say, in any derogatory sense but because they have caught his act and may even have been asked by him to take a card – *any* card – and memorize it before returning it to the pack, his aim being to produce it later from the inside of a lemon. There will be no question of the innocent deception failing to succeed. Once on board it will be a simple matter to make some excuse to go below. An urgent need for bicarbonate of soda suggests itself. And once below you can find your passport, say a few graceful words of farewell and leave.'

'But suppose Schnellenhamer asks me to do conjuring tricks?'

'Most unlikely. He is not one of those men who are avid for entertainment. It is his aim in life to avoid it. He has told me that it is the motion picture magnate's cross that everybody he meets starts acting at him in the hope of getting on the payroll. He says that on a good morning in Hollywood he has sometimes been acted at by a secretary, two book agents, a life insurance man, a masseur, the man with the benzedrine, the studio watchman, a shoe shine boy and a barber, all before lunch. No need to worry about him wanting you to entertain him.'

'But what would be Alfred's reason for coming aboard?'

'Simple. He has heard that Mr Schnellenhamer has arrived. It would be in the Society Jottings column. He knows that I am with Mr Schnellenhamer—'

'How?'

'I told him so when I met him yesterday. So he has come to see me.'

The light of intelligence had now spread over George's face from ear to ear. He chuckled hoarsely.

'Do you know, I really believe it would work.'

'Of course it will work. It can't fail. I'll go now and start paving the way. And as your raiment is somewhat disordered, you had better get a change of clothes, and a shave and a wash and brush-up would not hurt. Here is some money,' I said, and with an encouraging pat on the back I left him.

Brichoux was still at his post when I reached the yacht, inflexible determination written on every line of his unattractive face. Mr Schnellenhamer sat beside him looking as if he were feeling that what the world needed to make it a sweeter and better place was a complete absence of police sergeants. He had never been fond of policemen since one of them, while giving him a parking ticket, had recited Hamlet's To be or not to be speech to give him some idea of what he could do in a dramatic role. I proceeded to my mission without delay.

'Any sign of my nephew?' I asked.

'None,' said the sergeant.

'He has not been back?'

'He has not.'

'Very odd.'

'Very suspicious.'

An idea struck me.

'I wonder if by any chance he has gone to see his brother.'

'Has he a brother?'

'Yes. They are twins. His name is Alfred. You have probably seen him, sergeant. He is playing in the revue at the Casino. Does a conjuring act.'

'The Great Alfredo?'

'That is his stage name. You have witnessed his performance?'

'I have.'

'Amazing the resemblance between him and George. Even I can hardly tell them apart. Same face, same figure, same way of walking, same coloured hair and eyes. When you meet George, you will be astounded at the resemblance.'

'I am looking forward to meeting Mr George Mulliner.'

'Well, Alfred will probably be here this morning to have a chat with me, for he is bound to have read in the paper that I am Mr Schnellenhamer's guest. Ah, here he comes now,' I said, as George appeared on the gangway. 'Ah, Alfred.'

'Hullo, uncle.'

'So you found your way here?'

'That's right.'

'My host, Mr Schnellenhamer.'

'How do you do?'

'And Sergeant Brichoux of the Monaco police.'

'How do *you* do? Good morning, Mr Schnellenhamer, I

have been wanting very much to meet you. This is a great pleasure.'

I was proud of George. I had been expecting a show of at least some nervousness on his part, for the task he had undertaken was a stern one, but I could see no trace of it. He seemed completely at his ease, and he continued to address himself to Mr Schnellenhamer without so much as a tremor in his voice.

'I have a proposition I would like to put up to you in connection with your forthcoming Bible epic *Solomon And The Queen Of Sheba*. You have probably realized for yourself that the trouble with all these ancient history super-pictures is that they lack comedy. Colossal scenery, battle sequences of ten thousand a side, more semi-nude dancing girls than you could shake a stick at, but where are the belly laughs? Take *Cleopatra*. Was there anything funny in that? Not a thing. And what occurred to me the moment I read your advance publicity was that what *Solomon And The Queen Of Sheba* needs, if it is really to gross grosses, is a comedy conjuror, and I decided to offer my services. You can scarcely require to be told how admirably an act like mine would fit into the scheme of things. There is nothing like a conjuror to keep a monarch amused through the long winter evenings, and King Solomon is bound to have had one at his court. So what happens? The Queen of Sheba arrives. The magnificence of her surroundings stuns her. "The half was not told unto me" she says. "You like my little place?" says the King. "Well, it's a home. But wait, you ain't seen nothing yet. Send for the Great Alfredo." And on I come. "Well, folks," I say, "a funny thing happened to me on my way to the throne room," and then I tell a story and then a few gags and then I go into my routine, and I would like just to run through it now. For my first trick—'

I was aghast. Long before the half-way mark of this speech

the awful truth had flashed upon me. It was not George whom I saw before me – through a flickering mist – but Alfred, and I blamed myself bitterly for having been so mad as to mention Mr Schnellenhamer to him, for I might have known that he would be inflamed by the news that the motion picture magnate was within his reach and that here was his chance of getting signed up for a lucrative engagement. And George due to appear at any moment! No wonder that I reeled and had to support myself on what I believe is called a bollard.

'For my first trick,' said Alfred, 'I shall require a pound of butter, two bananas and a bowl of goldfish. Excuse me. Won't keep you long.'

He went below, presumably in quest of these necessaries, and as he did so George came up the gangway.

There was none of that breezy self-confidence in George which had so impressed me in Alfred. He was patently suffering from stage fright. His legs wobbled and I could see his adam's apple going up and down as if pulled by an invisible string. He looked like a nervous speaker at a public banquet who on rising to his feet to propose the toast of Our Guests realizes that he has completely forgotten the story of the two Irishmen Pat and Mike, with which he had been hoping to convulse his audience.

Nor did I blame him, for Sergeant Brichoux had taken a pair of handcuffs from his pocket and was breathing on them and polishing them on his sleeve, while Mr Schnellenhamer subjected him to the stony glare which had so often caused employees of his on the Colossal-Exquisite lot to totter off to the commissary to restore themselves with frosted malted milk shakes. There was an ominous calm in the motion picture magnate's manner such as one finds in volcanoes just before they erupt and make householders in the neighbourhood wish they had settled elsewhere. He was plainly holding himself in with a powerful effort, having decided to toy with my unhappy nephew before unmasking him. For George's opening words had been 'Good morning. I – er – that is to say – I – er – my name is Alfred Mulliner', and I could see that neither on the part of Mr Schnellenhamer or of Sergeant Brichoux was there that willing suspension of disbelief which dramatic critics are always writing about.

'Good morning,' said the former. 'Nice weather.'

'Yes, Mr Schnellenhamer.'

'Good for the crops.'

'Yes, Mr Schnellenhamer.'

'Though bad for the umbrella trade.'

'Yes, Mr Schnellenhamer.'

'Come along and join the party. Alfred Mulliner did you say the name was?'

'Yes, Mr Schnellenhamer.'

'You lie!' thundered Mr Schnellenhamer, unmasking his batteries with horrifying abruptness. 'You're no more Alfred Mulliner than I am, which isn't much. You're George Mulliner, and you're facing a murder rap or the next thing to it. Send for the police,' he said to Sergeant Brichoux.

'I *am* the police,' the sergeant reminded him, rather coldly it seemed to me.

'So you are. I was forgetting. Then arrest this man.'

'I will do so immediately.'

Sergeant Brichoux advanced on George handcuffs in hand, but before he could adjust them to his wrists an interruption occurred.

Intent though I had been on the scene taking place on the

deck of the yacht, I had been able during these exchanges to observe out of the corner of my eye that a heavily bandaged man of middle age was approaching us along the quay, and he now mounted the gangway and hailed Mr Schnellenhamer with a feeble 'Hi, Jake'.

So profuse were his bandages that one would hardly have expected his own mother to have recognized him, but Mr Schnellenhamer did.

'Sam Glutz!' he cried. 'Well, I'll be darned. I thought you were in the hospital.'

'They let me out.'

'You look like Tutunkhamen's mummy, Sam.'

'So would you if you'd been belted by a hoodlum like I was. Did you read about it in the papers?'

'Sure. You made the front page.'

'Well, that's something. But I wouldn't care to go through an experience like that again. I thought it was the end. My whole past life flashed before me.'

'You can't have liked that.'

'I didn't.'

'Well, you'll be glad to hear, Sam, that we've got the fellow who slugged you.'

'You have? Where is he?'

'Right there. Standing by the gentleman with the handcuffs.'

George's head had been bowed, but now he happened to raise it, and Mr Glutz uttered a cry.

'*You!*'

'That's him. George Mulliner. Used to work for the Colossal-Exquisite, but of course I've fired him. Take him to the cooler, sergeant.'

Every bandage on Mr Glutz's body rippled like wheat beneath

a west wind, and his next words showed that what had caused this was horror and indignation at the programme Mr Schnellenhamer had outlined.

'Over my dead body!' he cried. 'Why, that's the splendid young man who saved my life last night.'

'What!'

'Sure. The hood was beating the tar out of me when he came galloping up and knocked him for a loop, and after a terrific struggle the hood called it a day and irised out. Proud and happy to meet you, Mr Mulliner. I think I heard Jake say he'd fired you. Well, come and work for the Perfecto-Wonderful, and I shall be deeply offended if you don't skin me for a salary beyond the dreams of avarice. I'll pencil you in as vice-president with brevet rank as a cousin by marriage.'

I stepped forward. George was still incapable of speech.

'One moment, Mr Glutz,' I said.

'Who are you?'

'George's agent. And there is just one clause in the contract which strikes me as requiring revision. Reflect, Mr Glutz. Surely cousin by marriage is a poor reward for the man who saved your life?'

Mr Glutz was visibly affected. Groping among the bandages, he wiped away a tear.

'You're right,' he said. 'We'll make it brother-in-law. And now let's go and get a bite of lunch. You, too,' he said to me, and I said I would be delighted. We left the boat in single file – first Mr Glutz, then myself, then George, who was still dazed. The last thing I saw was Alfred coming on deck with his pound of butter and his two bananas. I seemed to detect on his face a slight touch of chagrin, caused no doubt by his inability to locate the bowl of goldfish so necessary to his first trick.

Our Man in America

One of the great traditions in America has always been the adding of pencilled moustaches to the faces on posters in the subway, and some superb work has been done in that line over the years. They fine you two hundred and fifty dollars if they catch you doing it, but to the artist the satisfaction of attaching a walrus moustache to the upper lip of – say – Miss Elizabeth Taylor is well worth the risk. (Moustache drawers are a proud guild and look down on the fellows who simply write 'George Loves Mabel' or 'Castro ought to have his head examined' on the walls. Hack work, they consider it.)

In an effort to keep their advertisements undecorated, the Transit Authority are now supplying at many of their stations posters measuring thirty by forty inches carrying twelve faces, together with this message to their patrons:

'Please! If you must draw moustaches, draw them on these.'

It is doubtful if the idea will catch on. A few small boys took advantage of the invitation, but the true moustache drawers shook their heads.

'One misses – how shall I put it? – one misses the *tang*,' said one of them, when interviewed. 'It's clever, but is it Art?' said another, and after having a malted milk at the refreshment counter they went off to see what could be done with the latest poster of Carol Channing in *Hello, Dolly.*

*

Let us turn for a moment to the subject of cows. You know what happens to cows in winter, they have to stick in a barn all the time with little or no cultural stimulus except what they can get from exchanging ideas with other cows, and it is very rare to find a cow with ideas to exchange. This state of things touched the tender heart of an extension service dairyman on the staff of the University of Maine, and it struck him it would ease the strain a good deal if movies were provided during the winter months. A group of farmers in North Gray, Maine, wired a barn for sound and set up a screen and the cows loved it. They mooed at the sight of fields and mooed even louder when bulls appeared on the screen. Some of the avant garde pictures fell a little flat, but the Westerns went big. The favourite star seems to be John Wayne, and the only regret these North Gray cows have is that they can't send him fan letters. Winter now passes in a flash.

*

An admirable suggestion has been made by Mr Wilfred S. Rowe, a season ticket holder on one of the local railways whose trains make a leisurely progress towards New York each day and generally fetch up there sooner or later. Mr Rowe's idea, simple as all great ideas are, is to establish a bookie at each station, prepared to accept commissions from the customers, who would queue up delightedly to wager on how late a given train would be. Heated arguments with other bettors would help pass the time, and the daily take at the betting window would soon put the road back on its financial feet. And the spectacle of a mob of eager travellers with brief cases in their hands running beside the train and shouting 'Come on, Steve' to the engine driver could not fail to strike a lively note.

*

It was some months ago that a metal fabricating firm at Long Beach, California, noticed that one of its employees, a Mr Kenneth Vosper, seemed to be putting on a bit of weight. Upon what meat does this our Vosper feed that he is grown so great, they asked one another, and when he turned the scale at nineteen stone ten, they thought it was time to take steps. 'Waddle off to some quiet rural retreat, Ken, and shed about five stone,' they said, and when he refused, they fired him.

My personal sympathies are with Mr Vosper. He feels as I do that there is far too much of this modern craze for dieting. He likes his potatoes with lots of butter on them and is partial to at least six of the more widely advertised brands of beer, and he sees no reason why a metal fabricator should be lean and slender and look as if he were about to go into a tap dance.

'Give me a bit of metal, and I'll fabricate it before you can say What ho,' he said. 'Could Fred Astaire do that?'

But no, they persisted in easing him off the pay roll, and the case is now up before the State Department of Employment.

*

Ask anyone in Memphis, Tennessee, and they will tell you that until you have spent a night at the home of Mr and Mrs Lloyd Ward of that city, you don't know what excitement is. Living dangerously is the phrase that springs to the lips when one muses on Lloyd W and helpmeet.

Take last Thursday, for instance. While watching a television show, Mr Ward fell asleep and Mrs Ward turned off the apparatus. Startled into wakefulness by the sudden silence, Mr Ward cried 'What's that?', seized a pistol, sprang to his feet, tripped over them and put three shots through a cupboard door.

Mrs Ward knew what to do, this sort of thing having presumably happened before. She grabbed the pistol and threw it away. Mr Ward went after it like a retriever and had just picked it up when he tripped over his feet again and the weapon once more exploded, this time breaking a vase containing roses and ruining a rather attractive picture of cows in a meadow, the work of Mrs Ward's mother, who went in for water colours.

Both Mr and Mrs Ward agree that it was an odd coincidence that the TV offering which started all the trouble was 'Have Gun, Will Travel', for Mr Ward unquestionably had gun and on the arrival of a sergeant and a couple of patrolmen travelled to the local police station. One is glad to report that the Judge let him off with a caution, merely telling him to keep away from firearms and to try not to fall asleep except at his regular bedtime.

When Lancelot Bingley, the rising young artist, became engaged to Gladys Wetherby, the poetess, who in addition to her skill with the pen had the face and figure of the better type of pin-up girl and eyes of about the colour of the Mediterranean on a good day, he naturally felt that this was a good thing and one that should be pushed along. The sooner the wedding took place, in his opinion, the better it would be for all concerned. He broached the subject to her as they were tucking into the *poulet rôti au cresson* one evening at the Crushed Pansy, the restaurant with a soul.

'What I would suggest,' he said, 'if you haven't anything special on next week, is that we toddle round to the registrar's and encourage him to do his stuff. They tell me these registrar fellows make a very quick job of it. The whole thing wouldn't take more than ten minutes or so, and there we would be with it off our minds, if you see what I mean.'

To his consternation, instead of clapping her hands in girlish glee and telling him that he had struck the right note there, she shook her head.

'I'm afraid it's not so simple as that.'

'What's your problem?'

'I was thinking of Uncle Francis.'

'Whose Uncle Francis?'

'My Uncle Francis.'

'I didn't know you had an Uncle Francis.'

'He was my mother's brother. Colonel Pashley-Drake. You've probably heard of him.'

'Not a word. Nobody tells me anything.'

'He used to be a famous big game hunter.'

Lancelot frowned. He was not fond of big game hunters. His own impulse, if he had met a wapiti or a gnu or whatever it might be, would have been to offer it a ham sandwich from his luncheon basket, and the idea of plugging it with a repeating rifle, as this Pashley-Drake presumably did, revolted him.

'I'm not sorry we never ran across each other, then. I wouldn't have liked him.'

'Mother did. She looked up to him very much, and when she died she left him a chunk of money which he was to hand over to me when I married.'

'Excellent.'

'Not so excellent, because I am only to get it if he approves of the man I want to marry. And he won't approve of you.'

'Why not?'

'You're an artist.'

'What's wrong with artists?'

'Uncle Francis thinks they spend all their time having orgies in studios and painting foreign princesses sitting on leopard skins in the nude.'

'Uncle Francis is a fathead.'

'Very true. But he's the one who controls the cash.'

'And you feel he won't part?'

'The betting's against it.'

'Then let's do without it. I've plenty,' said Lancelot, who was more fortunate than most artists in having a nice private income.

Gladys shook her head. It seemed to him that she was always shaking her head tonight.

'No,' she said. 'I need that money, and I won't get married without it. I'm not going to be one of those pauper wives who have to come and plead brokenly with their husbands every time they want the price of a new hat. Some of my married friends tell me it sometimes takes fully half a pint of tears before their mate can be induced to disgorge the most trifling sum. I couldn't do it. My pride forbids it.'

And though Lancelot argued eloquently with her all through the *poulet rôti au cresson* course and later during the after-dinner coffee, she was not to be moved from her decision. It was a gloomy young rising artist who saw her home and then went off and got plastered in a series of pubs. What, he was asking himself, would the harvest be and where did he go from here? He tried to tell himself that this was a mere whim on her part, but the theory brought him little consolation. He knew only too well that she had a whim of iron.

His hangover on the following day precluded for a space all thought of anything except bicarbonate of soda, but even when several beakers of the refreshing fluid had built him up physically he was no nearer to being his customary carefree self, for anguish and despair took over and he sat brooding and listless in his studio, incapable of putting brush to canvas. If a nude princess had looked in wanting her portrait painted, he would have refused the commission without hesitation, pleading in excuse that he was not in the mood. All he could do in the way of alleviating the agony that seared his soul was to play the accordion, always his solace in times of stress, and he had worked his way through *Over The Rainbow* and was preparing to tackle *Old Man River*, when the door flew open and Gladys bounded in, her manner animated and eyes shining, it seemed to him from a quick glance, like twin stars.

'Put away that stomach Steinway, my Prince Charming,' she cried, 'and listen to me, for I bring news that will make you go dancing about London like a nautch girl. Guess what arrived by the morning post. A letter from Uncle Francis.'

Lancelot was unable to see why this should be considered a cause for rejoicing.

'Oh, yes?' he said, not attempting to share her enthusiasm.

'And what do you think he was writing about? He's asked me to find him an artist to paint his portrait, to be presented to the Explorers Club. You get the job.'

Lancelot blinked, still unenthusiastic. His head had begun to pain him again, and he could imagine nothing less agreeable than painting the portrait of a big game hunter who would probably want to be portrayed with a gun in his hand and a solar topee on his head, standing with one foot on a stuffed antelope.

'Me?' he said. 'Why me?'

'Don't you see what this means? You'll be closeted with him day after day, and if you can't fascinate him under those conditions, you're not the king among men I've always thought you. By the end of a couple of weeks you'll have got him so that he can deny you nothing. You then tell him we're going to get married and he gives you his blessing and reaches for his fountain pen and cheque book. Any questions?'

Lancelot's listlessness fell from him like a garment. Even though his mind was working slowly this morning he was able to see the merits of the scheme.

'None,' he said. 'It's terrific.'

'I knew you'd think so.'

'But—'

A thought had occurred to Lancelot. As an artist he belonged to the ultra-modern school, expressing himself most readily in pictures showing a sardine tin, two empty beer bottles, a bunch of carrots and a dead cat, the whole intended to represent Paris in Springtime. He doubted his ability to work in another vein.

'Would I be any good at a portrait?'

'Good enough for a gaggle of explorers. All explorers have weak eyes through staring at the sunrise on the Lower Zambesi. They won't notice a thing.'

'Well, if you say so. Then what's the drill?'

'Uncle Francis has a house down at Bittleton in Sussex. You go there tomorrow with your paints and brushes. I'll phone him to be expecting you.'

Another thought struck Lancelot.

'I suppose I'm in for a thin time as regards meals. Don't big game hunters live on pemmican and native maize and that sort of thing?'

'Uncle Francis doesn't. He has the most sensational cook. Every dish a poem.'

'That sounds all right,' said Lancelot, brightening. Being an artist, he usually made do of an evening with the knuckle end of a ham or something out of a tin, but he was by no means incapable of appreciating good cooking and had often wished, when at the Crushed Pansy, that the *poulet rôti au cresson* had been a bit better *rôti*. 'I go tomorrow, you say?'

'Better perhaps the day after tomorrow. That'll give you time to mug up Uncle Francis's book, *My Life With Rod And Gun*, so that you can draw him out about the things he used to shoot.

He gave me a copy at Christmas, when I was expecting at least a wrist watch.'

'That's how it goes,' said Lancelot sympathetically.

'Yes, that's life,' Gladys agreed. 'And the best offer I got from the secondhand book shop was threepence, so the volume is still on my shelves. You can come and fetch it this afternoon.'

'And I leave the day after tomorrow?'

'That's right. I'll come and see you off at the station.'

As Lancelot sat in his compartment waiting for the train to start and gazing at Gladys, who was standing on the platform, he was thinking how much he loved her and what a dreadful thought it was that they were to be separated like this for who knew how long. He was to learn almost immediately that there were other dreadful thoughts going around. She now gave utterance to one of them.

'Oh, by the way, angel,' she said, 'there's one other thing. I almost forgot to tell you. Uncle Francis is rabidly opposed to smoking.'

'He is?' said Lancelot, feeling that the more he heard of this uncle of hers, the less attractive a character he appeared to be.

'So of course you'll have to knock it off for the duration.'

A strong shudder shook Lancelot. He was a heavy smoker in spite of having two aunts who belonged to the Anti-Tobacco League and kept sending him pamphlets showing how disastrous for the health the practice was. His jaw fell a couple of notches, and he stared at her incredulously.

'Knock off smoking?' he gasped, wondering if he could have heard her correctly.

'That's right.'

'For weeks and weeks? I couldn't!'

    'You couldn't, eh?'

    'No, I couldn't.'

    'Well, you'd jolly well better, or—'

    'Or what?'

    'Else,' said Gladys, and the train moved off.

It was one of those trains that have not become attuned to the modern spirit of speed and hustle, and as it sauntered through the sunlit countryside Lancelot had ample opportunity to turn over Gladys's parting words in his mind and examine them. And the more he did so, the less he liked the sound of them. Nor is this surprising. There are probably no words in the language which a lover more dislikes to hear on the lips of his loved one than those two words 'or else'. They have a sinister ring calculated to chill the hardiest.

He mused. One cannot say that he was standing at a man's crossroads, for he was sitting, but it was plain to him that he was confronted with the most serious dilemma of his lifetime. If, on the one hand, he obeyed her behest and refrained from smoking, every nerve in his body would soon be sticking out and starting to curl at the ends and the softest chirrup of the early bird attending to its worm outside his window would send him shooting up to the ceiling as if some fun-loving practical joker had exploded a bomb beneath his bed. He had once knocked off smoking for two or three days, and he knew what it was like.

If, however, on the other hand, he took a strong line and stoutly refused to keep away from the box of fifty excellent cigars which he had brought with him, what then? He knew very well what then. There would be for him no wedding bells or whatever registrars substitute for them. Gladys was as nearly as made no matter an angel in human shape, but she was inclined, like so many girls who have what it takes, to be imperious and of a trend of mind to resent hotly anything in the nature of what might be called funny business. And that she would class as funny business a deliberate flouting of her orders was sickeningly clear to him. She would return the ring, his letters and what was left of the bottle of scent he had given her on her birthday within minutes of learning of his disobedience.

There flitted into his mind an insidious line from an old poem of Rudyard Kipling's. 'A woman is only a woman,' it ran, 'but a good cigar is a smoke', and for one awful moment he found himself feeling that Mr Kipling had said a mouthful. Then he remembered Gladys's starlike eyes, her slender figure and the little freckle on the tip of her nose and was strong again. It was with the resolve that however great his sufferings he would retain her love that he alighted at Bittleton station and a short time later was meeting the man whose rugged features he was about to record on canvas.

They were features, particularly the three chins, of an undisguised opulence, and his body was in keeping with his face. Colonel Pashley-Drake was, in short, a stout man. Indeed, the thought flashed through Lancelot's mind that if he wanted to have himself painted full length, it would be necessary to send back to London for a larger canvas than any that he had brought with him. He knew from reading *My Life With Rod And Gun* that the Colonel, when hunting big game, had frequently hidden behind a tree. To conceal him in this the evening of his life only a Californian redwood would have served. And when later they sat together at the dinner table, he got an inkling as to how this obesity had come about.

The dinner was a long one and in every respect superb. It was plain to Lancelot from the first spoonful of soup that Gladys had well described his host's cook as sensational. The fish confirmed his view that she was a cook in a thousand. He mentioned this to the Colonel, and the latter, a look of holy ecstasy in his eye, agreed that Mrs Potter – for such was the gifted woman's name – was at the very head of her profession. After that he did not speak very much, being otherwise occupied.

Coffee after the meal was served in a study or library, a large room tastefully decorated with the heads of various fauna which had had the misfortune to meet the other when he was out with his gun. As they seated themselves, the Colonel wheezed apologetically.

'I am afraid I cannot offer you a cigar,' he said, and Lancelot raised a deprecating hand.

'Had you done so,' he assured him, 'I should have been obliged to decline it, with thanks of course for the kind thought. I do not smoke. Smoking,' said Lancelot, remembering a pamphlet sent to him by one of his aunts, 'causes nervous dyspepsia, sleeplessness, headache, weak eyes, asthma, bronchitis, neurasthenia, rheumatism, lumbago, sciatica, loss of memory, falling out of hair and red spots on the skin. I wouldn't smoke so much as a cigarette to please a dying grandfather. My friends often rally me on what they consider my finicky objection to having red spots on my skin, but I remain firm.'

'You are very sensible,' said Colonel Pashley-Drake with such obvious approval that Lancelot felt that the task of fascinating him would prove even easier than Gladys had predicted. He looked forward to the moment – at no distant date – when he would have the old buster rolling on the floor with paws in the air like a tickled dachshund.

* * *

The love feast became intensified as the time went on. The Colonel was plainly delighted that Lancelot had derived such pleasure from his little book and spoke fluently and well on the subject of tigers he had met and what to do when confronted with a charging rhinoceros, together with many an anecdote about the selected portions of gnus, giraffes and the like which ornamented the walls. At long last he stifled a yawn and said he thought he would be turning in, and they parted in an atmosphere of the utmost cordiality.

The dinner, as has been said, had been a long and heavy one, and it had left Lancelot with a feeling of repletion which only fresh air could relieve, and before going to bed he felt the prudent thing to do was to take a half-hour stroll in the garden. He proceeded to do so, and what with the beauty of the night and the thinking of long loving thoughts of Gladys he exceeded the estimated time by a wide margin. It was some two hours later when the advisability of going to bed presented itself, and he made his way back to the house – only to discover when he reached it that in his absence some hidden hand had locked the front door.

It was a blow which might have crushed a weaker man, but Lancelot was resourceful and the idea of trying the back door occurred to him almost immediately. He found that, too, securely fastened, and it became evident that unless he was prepared to pass the remainder of the night in the open it would be necessary to break a window. This, as noiselessly as possible, he did and climbing through found himself in what from the smell he took to be the kitchen. And he was about to grope in the darkness in the hope of finding the door, when a voice spoke, a harsh, guttural voice which jarred unpleasantly on his sensitive ear, though the most musical voice speaking at that moment would equally have given him the illusion that the top of his head had parted from its moorings. It said rather curtly:

'Who are you?'

Suavity, Lancelot felt, was what he must strive for.

'It's quite all right,' he said obsequiously. 'I was locked out.'

'Who are you?'

'My name is Lancelot Bingley. I am staying in the house. I am an artist. I am here to paint Colonel Pashley-Drake's portrait. I would not advise waking him now, but if you enquire of him in the morning, he will support my statement.'

'Who are you?'

Annoyance began to compete with Lancelot's embarrassment. If voices asked you questions, he felt, they might at least take the trouble to listen to you when you answered them. His manner took on a stiffness.

'I have already informed you in a perfectly frank manner that my name is Lancelot Bingley and that I am staying in the house in order to paint—'

'Have a nut,' said the voice, changing the subject.

Lancelot's teeth came together with a sharp click. Few things are more mortifying to a proud man than the discovery that he has been wasting his time being respectful to a parrot, and he burned with resentment and pique. Ignoring the bird's sugges-tion – in the circumstances ill-timed and lacking in taste – that he should scratch its head, he continued groping for the door and eventually found it.

After that everything was simple. Bounding silently up the stairs, he flung open the door of his room and not bothering to turn on the light flung himself on the bed. Or rather not precisely on the bed but on some squashy substance inside it which proved on investigation to be Colonel Pashley-Drake. Pardonably a little overwrought by his recent exchange of ideas with the parrot, he had mistaken the Colonel's room – first to the left along the corridor – for his own, which, he now remembered, was the second on the left along the corridor.

He lost no time in climbing off his host's stomach, on which he rightly supposed he had been nestling, but it was too late. The mischief had been done. The Colonel was plainly emotionally disturbed. He soliloquized for some moments in some native dialect which was strange to Lancelot.

'What the devil?' he enquired at length, dropping into English.

Inspiration descended on Lancelot.

'I came to ask you about the portrait. I was wondering if you wanted it full length or just head and shoulders,' he said, prudently omitting to explain why such a speculation was needed.

His room mate quivered like someone doing one of the modern dances.

'You woke me at this time of night to ask me *that*!'

'I thought it a point that should be settled.'

'No reason why you should come jumping on my stomach.'

'No, there,' Lancelot admitted, 'I perhaps went a little too far. I am sorry for that.'

'Not half as sorry as I am. I was dreaming of rogue elephants, and I thought one of them had sat down on me. Do you know what I'd have done if you had played a trick like that on me in the old days in West Africa? I'd have shot you like a dog.'

'Really?'

'I assure you. It is routine in West Africa.'

'Tell me about West Africa,' said Lancelot, hoping to mollify.

'To hell with West Africa,' said the Colonel. 'Get out of here, and consider yourself fortunate that you aren't as full of holes as a colander.'

Lancelot left the room feeling somewhat despondent. During dinner and after it he had flattered himself that he had made a good impression on his host, but something seemed to tell him that he had now lost ground.

And what, meanwhile, of Gladys Wetherby? Working on a sonnet next morning, she was conscious of a strange feeling of uneasiness and apprehension which made it hard for her to get the lines the right length. Ever since she had seen Lancelot off on the train she had been a prey to doubts and fears. She adored him with a passion which already had produced six sonnets, a ballade and about half a pound of vers libre, but all engaged girls have the poorest opinion of the intelligence of the men they are engaged to, and she had never wavered in her view that her loved one's I.Q. was about equal to that of a retarded child of seven. If there was a way of bungling everything down at Bittleton, he would, she was convinced, spring to the task, and it was only the fact that there seemed no way in which even he could bungle that had led her to entrust him with the mission which meant so much to them both. All he had to do was paint a portrait and while painting it exercise the charm she knew him to possess, and surely even Lancelot Bingley was capable of that.

Nevertheless she continued ill at ease, and it was with more anguish than surprise that she read the telegram which reached her shortly after lunch. It ran:

Drop everything and come Bittleton immediately. Disaster stares eyeball and your moral support sorely needed. Love and kisses. Lancelot.

For some moments she stood congealed, her worst fears

confirmed. Then, going to her bedroom, she packed a few necessaries in a suitcase, and hailed a taxi. Twenty minutes later she
was on the train, a ticket to Bittleton in her bag, and an hour
and forty-five minutes after that she entered her uncle's garden.
The first thing she saw there was Lancelot pacing up and down,
his manner indistinguishable from that of a cat on hot bricks.
He came tottering towards her.

'Thank heaven you're here,' he cried. 'I need your woman's
intelligence. Perhaps you can tell me what to do for the best, for
the storm clouds are lowering. I seem to remember saying in my
telegram that disaster stared me in the eyeball. That in no way
overstated it. Let me tell you what's happened.'

Gladys was staring at him dumbly. She had been expecting
the worst, and this was apparently what she was going to get.
If she had had any tan, she would have paled beneath it.

'Here, then, are the facts. I must begin by saying that last
night I jumped on your uncle's stomach.'

'Jumped on his stomach?' whispered Gladys, finding speech.

'Oh, purely inadvertently, but I could tell by his manner that
he was annoyed. It was like this,' said Lancelot, and he related
briefly the events of the previous night. 'But that wouldn't have
mattered so much,' he went on, 'if it hadn't been for what happened this morning. I had sauntered out into the garden with
my after-breakfast cigar—'

He paused. He thought he had heard a stepped-on cat utter
a piercing yowl. But it was only Gladys commenting on what he
had said. Her eyes, which under the right conditions could be
so soft and loving, were shooting flames.

'I told you you were not to smoke!'

'I know, I know, but I thought it would be all right if no one
saw me. One must have one's smoke after breakfast, or what are

breakfasts for? Well, as I was saying, I sauntered out and lit up, and I hadn't puffed more than a few puffs when I heard voices.'

'Oh, heavens!'

'That, or something like it, was what I said, and I dived into the shrubbery. The voices came nearer. Someone was approaching, or rather I should have said that two persons were approaching, for if there had been only one person approaching, he would hardly have been talking to himself. Though, of course, you do get that sort of thing in Shakespeare. Hamlet, to take but one instance, frequently soliloquized.'

'Lancelot!'

'My angel?'

'Get on with it.'

'Certainly, certainly. Where was I?'

'You were smoking your cigar, which I had expressly forbidden you to do, in the shrubbery.'

'No, there you are wrong. I was in the shrubbery, yes, but I was not smoking my cigar, and I'll tell you why. In my natural perturbation at hearing these voices and realizing that two persons were approaching I had dropped it on the lawn.'

He paused again. Once more Gladys had uttered that eldrich scream so like in its timbre to that of a domestic cat with a number eleven boot on its tail.

'Lancelot Bingley, you ought to be in a padded cell!'

'Yes, yes, but don't keep interrupting me, darling, or I shall lose the thread. Well, these two approaching persons had now drawn quite close to where I lurked behind a laurel bush, and I was enabled to hear their conversation. One of them was your uncle, the other a globular woman whom I assumed to be the Mrs Potter of whom I had heard so much, for she was sketching out the menu for tonight's dinner, which I don't mind telling you is going to be a pippin. Your uncle evidently thought so, too, for he kept saying "Excellent, excellent" and things like that, and my mouth was watering freely when all of a sudden a female shriek or cry rent the air and peeping cautiously round my laurel bush I saw that the Potter female was pointing in an aghast sort of way at something lying on the grass and, to cut a long story short, it was my cigar.'

A dull despair weighed Gladys Wetherby down.

'So they caught you?' she said tonelessly.

'No,' said Lancelot, 'I lurked unseen. And of course they didn't know it was my cigar. I gathered from their remarks that the prime suspects are the chauffeur and the gardener. It naturally didn't occur to your uncle to pin the rap on me, because after dinner last night I had convinced him that I was a total abstainer.'

Indignation brought a flush to Gladys's face. No girl likes to be dragged into the depths of the country on a hot afternoon by a telegram from her betrothed saying that disaster stares him in eyeball when apparently disaster has been doing nothing of the sort.

'Then what's all the fuss about?' she demanded. 'Why the urgent S.O.S.'s? You're in the clear.'

Lancelot corrected her gently.

'No, my loved one. In the soup, yes, but not in the clear.'

'I don't understand you.'

'You will in about two seconds flat. I am sorry to have to add that on the advice of Mrs Potter your uncle is having the cigar finger-printed.'

'What!'

'Yes. It appears that she has a brother or cousin or something at Scotland Yard, and she said that that was always the first thing they did with a piece of evidence. Taking the dabs, I believe they call it. So your uncle said he would lock it in his desk till it could be examined by the proper experts, and he picked it up carefully with his handkerchief, like they do in books. So now you see why that telegram of mine expressed itself so strongly. My fingerprints must be all over the damn thing, and it won't take those experts five minutes to lay the crime at my door.'

An expletive which she had picked up at the Poets Club in Bloomsbury burst from Gladys's lips. She clutched her brow.

'Don't talk,' she said. 'I want to think.'

She stood motionless, her brain plainly working at its maximum speed. A fly settled on her left eyebrow, but she ignored it. Lancelot watched her anxiously.

'Anything stirring?' he asked.

Gladys came out of her reverie.

'Yes,' she said, and her voice had lost its dull despondency. 'I see what to do. We must sneak down tonight when everyone's in bed and retrieve that cigar. I know where to find a duplicate key to Uncle Francis's desk. I used it a lot in my childhood when he kept chocolates there. Expect me at your bedroom door at about midnight, and we'll get cracking.'

'You think we can do it?'

'It'll be as easy as falling off a log,' said Gladys.

All artists are nervous, highly strung men, and Lancelot, as he waited for the girl he loved to come and tell him that zero hour had arrived, was not at his most debonair and carefree. The thought of the impending expedition had the worst effect on his morale. It so happened that for one reason or another he had never fallen off a log, but he assumed it to be a feat well within the scope of the least gifted, and why Gladys should think it resembled the hideous task that lay before them he could not imagine. He could tot up a dozen things that could go wrong. Suppose, to take an instance at random, the parrot overheard them and roused the house.

But when Gladys did appear, something of confidence returned to him. The mere look of her was encouraging. There is nothing that so heartens a man in a crisis as the feeling that he has a woman of strong executive qualities at his side. Macbeth, it will be remembered, had this experience.

'Sh!' said Gladys, though he had not spoken, and before they set out she had a word of advice on strategy and tactics to impart.

'Now listen, Lancelot,' she said. 'We want to conduct this operation with a minimum of sound effects. Your impulse, I know, will be to trip over your feet and fall downstairs with a noise like the delivery of a ton of coal, but resist it. Play the scene quietly. Okay? Right. Then let's go.'

Nothing marred the success of the expedition from the outset. True, Lancelot tripped over his feet as anticipated, but a quick snatch at the banisters enabled him to avoid giving the impersonation of the delivery of a ton of coals against which she had warned him. In silence they descended the stairs and stole noiselessly into the study. Gladys produced her duplicate key, and Lancelot was just saying to himself that if he were a bookie he would estimate the odds on the happy ending as at least four to one, when there occurred one of those unforeseen hitches which cannot be budgeted for. Even as Gladys, key in hand, approached the desk there came from outside the sound of stealthy footsteps, and it was only too evident that their objective was the study in which they were trapped.

It was a moment fraught with embarrassment for the young couple, but each acted with a promptitude deserving of the highest praise. By the time the door opened no evidence of their presence was discernible. Gladys was concealed behind the curtains that draped the french windows, while Lancelot, having cleared the desk with a lissom bound, was crouching behind it, doing his best not to breathe.

The first sound he heard after the opening of the door was the click of key in a lock. It was followed by the scratching of a match, and suddenly there floated to his nostrils the un-mistakable scent of cigar smoke. And even as he sought faintly for a solution of this mystery the curtains parted with a rattle and he was able to catch a glimpse of the upper portions of his betrothed. She was staring accusingly down at something beyond his range of vision, and when a sharp exclamation in Swahili broke the silence, he knew that this must be Colonel Pashley-Drake.

'So!' said Gladys.

There are not many good things one can say in answer to the word 'So!', especially if one is called upon to find one at a moment's notice, and the Colonel remained silent for a space. It was only when Gladys had repeated the word that he spoke.

'Ah, my dear,' he said, 'there you are. Sorry to have seemed a bit taciturn, but your abrupt appearance surprised me. I thought you were in bed and asleep. Well, no doubt it seems odd to you to find me here, but I can explain, and you will see how I am situated.'

'You are situated in an armchair with a whacking great cigar in your mouth, and I shall be glad to have the inside story.'

'You shall have it at once, and I think it will touch your heart. You were away from home, I believe, when Mrs Potter entered my service?'

'She had been here a year when I first saw her.'

'So I thought. She was in the employment of a friend of mine when I was introduced to her superlative cooking. When he conked out – apoplexy, poor fellow, brought on, I have always felt, by over-indulgence in her steak and kidney pies – I immediately asked her to come to me, and I was stunned when she enquired if I was a non-smoker, adding that she held smoking to be the primary cause of all human ills and would never consider serving under the banner of an employer who indulged in the revolting practice. You follow me so far?'

'I get the picture.'

'It was a tricky situation, you will admit. On the one hand, I loved cigars. On the other, I adored good food. Which to choose? The whole of that night I lay sleepless on my bed, pondering, and when morning came I knew what my decision must be. I made the great sacrifice. I told her I never smoked, and until tonight I never have. But this morning the chauffeur or somebody dropped this cigar on the lawn, and the sight of it shook me to my depths. I had not seen one for three years, and all the old craving returned. Unable to resist the urge, I crept down here and ... Well, that is the story, my dear, and I am sure you will not let this little lapse of mine come to Mrs Potter's ears. I can rely on you?'

'Of course.'

'Thank you, thank you. You have taken a great weight off my mind. Bless my soul, I haven't felt so relieved since the afternoon in West Africa when a rhinoceros, charging on me with flashing eyes, suddenly sprained an ankle and had to call the whole thing off. I shudder to think what would have happened if Mrs Potter had learned of my doings this night. She would have been off like a jack rabbit. I wouldn't have been able to see her for dust. She would have vanished like a dream at daybreak. But provided you seal your lips—'

'Oh, I'll seal them.'

'Thank you, my dear. I knew I could rely on you.'

'And you on your side will write me a cheque for that bit of cash of mine. You see, I want to get married.'

'You do? Who to?'

'You know him. Lancelot Bingley.'

A hoarse exclamation in some little known Senegambian dialect burst from the Colonel's lips.

'You mean that artist fellow?'

'That's right.'

'You're joking.'

'I am not.'

'You mean you seriously intend to marry that pop-eyed young slab of damnation?'

'He is not pop-eyed.'

'But you will concede that he is a slab of damnation?'

'I will do nothing of the sort. Lancelot is a baa-lamb.'

'A baa-lamb?'

'Yes, a baa-lamb.'

'Well, he doesn't look to me like a baa-lamb. More like something the cat brought in, and not a very fastidious cat at that.'

In his nook behind the desk Lancelot flushed hotly. For a moment he thought of rising to his feet with a curt 'I resent that remark', but prudence told him it was better not to interrupt.

'And it is not only his looks I object to,' continued the Colonel. 'I suppose he has kept it from you, but he goes about jumping on people's stomachs.'

'Yes, he mentioned that to me.'

'Well, then. You don't expect me to abet you in your crazy scheme of marrying a chap like that. I won't give you a penny.'

'Then I'll tell Mrs Potter you're a secret smoker.'

The Colonel gasped. The cigar fell from his hand. He picked it up, dusted it and returned it to his lips. His voice, when he spoke, was hoarse and trembled.

'This is blackmail!'

'With the possible exception of diamonds,' said Gladys, 'a girl's best friend.'

Silence fell. The Colonel's eyes were strained and bleak. His chins vibrated. It was plain that he was engaged in serious thought. But the clash of wills could have but one ending.

'Very well,' he said at length, 'I consent. I do it with the utmost reluctance, for the idea of you marrying that ... that ... how shall I describe him ... well, never mind, you know what I mean ... chills me to the marrow. But I have no alternative. I cannot do without Mrs Potter's cooking.'

'You shall have it.'

'And furthermore,' said Lancelot, shooting up from behind the desk and causing the Colonel to quiver like a smitten jelly, 'you shall have all the cigars you want. I have a box of fifty – or, rather, forty-nine – upstairs in my room and I give them to you freely. And after breakfast tomorrow I will show you a spot in the shrubbery where you can smoke your head off without fear of detection.'

The Colonel drew a deep breath. His eyes glowed with a strange light. His chins vibrated again, but this time with ecstasy. He said a few words in Cape Dutch, then, seeing that his companions had missed the gist, he obligingly translated.

'Gladys,' he said, 'I could wish you no better husband. He is, as you were telling me, one of the baa-lambs and in my opinion by no means the worst of them. I think you will be very happy.'

Our Man in America

It always happens. Just as one is feeling pretty good and saying to oneself that it is not a bad little world after all, along comes something to take the joy out of life. This news from Washington D.C., for instance. It seems that for many years it has been the practice of members of the United States Congress to go into the House restaurant, order a cup of coffee and reach out and grab slices of bread and butter, for which until recently there was no charge. So for the price of a cup of coffee they were able to fill themselves to the brim with nourishing food and go back to the debate with that cosy feeling of being ahead of the game.

This has now been changed. The law-giver who wants bread will have to pay for it, and it is not too much to say that consternation reigns. These starchy food aficionados get only $22,500 annually, so they have to keep a watchful eye on the budget, and if they pay out good money for a slice off the loaf it throws the whole thing out of gear. It is not unusual for visitors to Washington these days to find themselves stopped in the street by President Johnson and asked if they can spare a dime. 'My Congressmen are crying for bread,' he says.

*

It is pretty generally agreed that we are living as of even date in the times that try men's souls, and it is interesting, as one surveys the American scene, to note the steps the various states are taking to cope with them. Thus, in Grand Rapids, Michigan, the populace was conscious recently of a great wave of relief, for they knew that even if a hostile power were to start unloading unpleasant things from the skies above America, they at least would be sitting pretty. Grand Rapids has just passed a law making it illegal for any aviator to 'drop a bomb while flying over the city without leave from the city commission', and it is very improbable that such permission would be given a foreign foe.

In Wisconsin they fortify themselves somewhat differently. Reports from there reveal that last year Wisconsin – men, women and children all pulling together – drank 1,025,739,909 bottles of beer. It worked splendidly. After about the 25,739,909th bottle they simply stopped caring. 'Who's afraid of the big bad wolf?' was the slogan heard on all sides, though in one or two instances the words were so slurred as to be indistinguishable.

*

Rather sad, the way America's most cherished customs and traditions are dying out nowadays. The latest to become one with Nineveh and Tyre is the annual woolly bear hunt on Bear Mountain. Each Autumn for nearly a decade it has been the practice of Dr C. H. Curran, curator of insects and spiders at the Museum of Natural History, to take a paper bag and set forth, accompanied by Mrs Curran and a bevy of friends and well-wishers, to collect specimens of the caterpillar of that name and inspect them with a view to seeing what sort of Winter we were going to have.

The idea has always been that if in the Autumn the brown bands on the woolly bear were wide, conditions from December to March would be clement, while if they were narrow the populace was in for ice and snow and all the trimmings. And now Dr Curran has rocked the country with a bombshell.

'This,' he said, as the hunters returned to the hunting lodge and were gloating over the bulging paper bag, 'is the last woolly bear hunt we will conduct. Statistics over the last nine years show that the width of the little chiseller's brown bands can tell us nothing whatsoever about the weather. The woolly bear stands stripped of its mask at the bar of world opinion.'

Well, naturally, everyone was pretty appalled. Mrs Curran fought to keep back the tears and many of those present paled visibly. A reporter from the *New York Herald-Tribune*, who had come along because there was a free lunch, was heard to cry 'Oh, Doctor Curran, say it ain't so!', but the doc was adamant. He had had it.

'Look what happened last year,' he said.

One knows what was in his mind. Last October every woolly bear you met was sporting the widest possible bands, and the Winter should have been Springlike. But was it? Not by a jugful. It was a stinker. No wonder Dr Curran had felt compelled to take this strong line. As he rather aptly puts it, you can fool all the people some of the time, you can even fool some of the people all the time, but you can't fool all the people all the time. From now on the woolly bear means nothing in his life. He will take the high road and it the low road, and if they happen to meet he will merely nod coldly, if that.

*

It is unlikely, perhaps, that Mr Ernest Crowley of Watkins Glen, N.Y., will ever invite me to spend a long week-end at his home, but if he does I shall certainly tell him I can't possibly fit it in, for, according to an interview he has given to the press, he has a singing dog on the premises. According to him the animal has a repertory ranging from 'My Wild Irish Rose' to 'Happy Birthday'.

Buster, for such is his name, presumably confines himself to rendering the music of these items, omitting the words like a citizen joining in 'The Star-Spangled Banner' and possibly sings only in his bath, but even so the whole thing strikes me as fairly sinister.

In his interview Mr Crowley says he is in the habit of taking Buster to hospitals 'to entertain the aged and mentally ill', and no one more surprised than he, one imagines, when the performance scares the pants off them. I am aged myself – eighty-five next birthday – and mentally not very bright, and I know that if I were lying in bed and a dog came in and suddenly started singing the 'Jewel Song' from *Faust*, I would shoot straight up to and through the ceiling, sustaining bruises and contusions.

Mr Bunting, of the legal firm of Bunting and Satterthwaite, looked at his watch and saw with satisfaction that it was getting on for lunch time. His digestion being none too good, he seldom took more for his mid-day meal than a glass of hot water, but he enjoyed the agreeable break it made in the morning's routine. He also welcomed the prospect of being able to stop trying to explain the law of Great Britain to his visitor Freddie Threepwood.

'Well, as you will have gathered,' he said, 'it's all pretty compli-cated and one never knows how these cases are going to go with a jury, so I think the best thing is to try for a settlement out of court. You agree, Satterthwaite?'

Mr Satterthwaite said he did.

'And you, Freddie?'

'Not for me to say, is it? Up to old Donaldson, surely?'

'Quite right. It's for him to decide. I'll get him on the trans-atlantic phone and ask him how he feels about it.'

'Good idea,' said Freddie, relieved, for the discussion had begun to make his head ache. Sent over to England from Long Island City by his employer Mr Donaldson of Donaldson's Dog Joy, his task a roving commission to ginger up the English end of the business, he had looked in on Bunting and Satterthwaite to learn how that law suit of Mr Donaldson's was coming along and had been unable to make much of what Mr Bunting had told him. Legal minutiae were not in his line. His genius lay in selling dog biscuits.

'You must enjoy these visits of yours to the old homeland, Freddie,' said Mr Bunting, becoming chatty now that the conference was concluded. 'How did you leave Donaldson, by the way? Fit, I hope?'

'Oh, very. Still inclined to bark at one a bit.'

'I remember that trait of his. Like a seal surprised while bathing. When do you go back?'

'In about three weeks.'

'I suppose you have been hobnobbing with all the friends of your youth?'

'Well, actually, no. I've been too busy. I ran into Joe Cardinal yesterday. He tells me he's given up his painting and is working in a bank. You know Joe, don't you?'

'Very well indeed.'

'Then perhaps you can give me his address? I forgot to ask him.'

'I'll write it down,' said Mr Bunting, and as he spoke the inter-com sounded.

'There's a girl out there wants to see you, Bunting,' said Mr Satterthwaite, having answered it. 'Some name like Riddell.'

'It must be young Dinah Biddle. Haven't you ever met her?'

'Not to my recollection. Who is she?'

'Arnold Pinkney's secretary.'

At the mention of that name a close observer might have seen Freddie wince as if troubled by an old wound. It was a name more or less graven on his heart. In his whirlwind tour of the British Isles as ambassador for Donaldson's Dog Joy he had achieved many notable triumphs: he had secured gratifying orders from – to cite but a few – McPhail and McPherson of Edinburgh, Wilks Brothers of Manchester and Beatle Beatle and Beatle of Liverpool, but Arnold Pinkney of Pinkney's Stores had been one of his failures. He had not been able even to obtain an interview with him, and this rankled.

'Tell her to come in,' said Mr Bunting, and a few moments later Miss Biddle appeared, preceded by an animated dachshund on a leash.

Those who like girls to be tall and statuesque would not have been greatly impressed by Dinah Biddle, for she was on the small side. What there was of her, however, was excellent. Freddie, whose standards in feminine comeliness were high, would not perhaps have gone so far as to place her among the absolute stupefiers, but he would readily have conceded that she pleased the eye, while the Joe Cardinal of whom he had been speaking had fallen in love with her after a single meeting – one at which only twenty-two words had been exchanged, she contributing eighteen, he four.

Mr Bunting greeted her warmly. They were old friends.

'Come in, young Dinah. Nice to have you with us. We need more of your sort to brighten up this dingy office. My dingy partner, Mr Satterthwaite. And – an added attraction – Mr Threepwood, the Anglo-American tycoon.'

'How do you do? I just came to give you this letter from Mr Pinkney. He wanted it delivered by hand. I hope you don't mind me bringing the dog.'

'Not at all. Any friend of yours. A recent purchase?'

'I've just bought him for Mr Pinkney. It's a present for his fiancée.'

It takes a good deal to make an old established solicitor betray emotion, but at these words Mr Bunting started visibly. Arnold

Pinkney was a client of his, but not a crony. He was a pompous man who took life heavily, and Mr Bunting, who though well stricken in years had never quite shaken off the frivolity of youth, found association with him damping to the spirit.

'His fiancée?' he cried incredulously. 'You mean to tell me that superfatted poop is engaged to be married?'

'Ought I to listen to you calling my employer a superfatted poop?'

'Well, that's what he is. Ask anyone. Who is the purblind female he's marrying?'

'A Mrs Cheever. She's Judson Phipps's sister.'

A sharp gasp escaped Freddie. During the recent exchanges he had been giving only a minimum of his attention to what was being said, for he was thinking of dog biscuits, but at this piece of information he became suddenly electrified, like a war horse hearing the sound of a bugle.

'Judson Phipps!'

'A young American plutocrat whose erratic affairs we handle.'

'Oh, I know Juddy. Known him for years. Is Pinkney really marrying his sister?'

'Unless Dinah here is pulling our legs.'

'I wouldn't lay so much as a finger on your legs. It's official.'

'Well, well,' said Freddie.

He was profoundly moved. So consistent had been Mr Pinkney's elusiveness that though not easy to discourage he had about written him off as a prospect. But if he was going to marry Juddy's sister, hope dawned again. Obviously this sister must have a pull with the man and Juddy presumably a pull with his sister. A word with Juddy, and the thing would be in the bag.

'Think I'll be getting along,' he said, for he wanted to be alone to brood over this new development.

'If you feel you must,' said Mr Bunting. 'Here's Joe Cardinal's address.'

'Oh, thanks.'

The short pause that always follows the departure of one of a group was broken by Mr Bunting.

'So that sister of Phipps's is in circulation again. Husband dead?'

'She divorced him, I think.'

'What a woman! We used to act for her at one time. You remember her, Satterthwaite?'

'I do indeed.'

'She's even crazier than Judson, wouldn't you say?'

'A close thing, of course, but perhaps you're right.'

'Do you remember when she smuggled her pearls through the New York Customs?'

'Inside a Mickey Mouse which she bought at the ship's shop. When she told us what she was planning to do, we tried to dissuade her, but she carried on regardless.'

'It's always surprised me that she has never acquired a long prison sentence. For years she's been asking for it.'

'Pleading for it. Do you remember that other time when she—'

'Listen,' said Dinah. 'I suppose you two old gossips are going to sit here for the rest of the afternoon swopping reminiscences, but I can't stop to hear them. Goodbye.'

'Come, come,' said Mr Bunting, 'you can't leave us as abruptly as that. Let me at least see you out. What's your hurry?' he asked, as they passed into the corridor.

'We're in a great rush these days. Mr Pinkney is sailing for New York on Thursday.'

'Running him out of the country, are they?'

'He has a merger cooking with some New York store.'

'Is he taking you with him?'

'Of course. I'm indispensable.'

'What boat?'

'The *Atlantic*.'

'I'll send you some flowers. Well, it's been nice seeing you even for such a brief time. I always relish these visits of yours. It's like an April breeze blowing into the office.'

'And interrupting you in the middle of a conference.'

'We had finished.'

'I'm glad of that. Who was the man who said he knew Judson Phipps?'

'That was Freddie Threepwood, Lord Emsworth's younger son. He emigrated to America some years ago, joined the staff of Donaldson's Dog Joy, married the boss's daughter, and is now, I understand, a force to be reckoned with in the dog biscuit industry. You probably noticed that he gave your hound a sharp look, seeing in him no doubt a potential customer. It's curious about Freddie. When I first knew him, he was just a young fellow about town, a sort of Judson Phipps, incapable, one would have said, of anything in the nature of coherent thought, but America has turned him into as high-powered a salesman as ever breathed the rarefied air of Madison Avenue. Quite a startling metamorphosis.'

'What was that name you mentioned to him? Cardinal, was it? I wonder if it's the same Mr Cardinal I met the other day.'

'Did you meet a Mr Cardinal?'

'Yes, he came wanting to see Mr Pinkney.'

'Then that was Joe. Pinkney's his uncle.'

'What does he do?'

'He works in a bank.'

'He's very shy, isn't he?'

'What gave you that impression?'

'It was just that he hardly said a word. He simply stood and looked at me and made funny noises.'

'Obviously he must have fallen in love with you at first sight. Like Romeo. If I were forty years younger,' said Mr Bunting, 'I'd make funny noises at you myself. Well, Dinah, I wish I could ask you to lunch, but, as you know, I confine myself to a glass of hot water and the spectacle would depress you.'

'And I couldn't have come, anyway. I'm lunching with Judson Phipps.'

A frown appeared on Mr Bunting's face. Normally it resembled that of an amiable vulture. He now looked like a vulture dissatisfied with its breakfast corpse. He had a paternal fondness for this girl and did not like to see her getting into dubious company. Judson Phipps in his opinion was lacking in character and serious purpose and he disapproved of him.

And yet Judson was a young man who, starting from nothing, had made good in a big way. He was the son of the late Mortimer Phipps, the Suspender King, who sold so many suspenders in America and braces in Great Britain that for years and years the money had simply poured in. On his decease his fortune had been divided equally between Judson and Judson's sister Julia, so that now several safe deposit boxes bulged with Judson's millions and he could write a cheque for almost anything he pleased. It was a real success story, the sort of thing Horatio Alger used to write about, and one might have expected Mr Bunting to admire rather than shake his head in disapproval.

Nevertheless, he did so shake his head.

'I didn't know you knew Phipps. Where did you meet him?'

'At a party somewhere.'

'Do you see much of him?'

'Quite a good deal.'

'Tut, tut.'

'Why the double tut? What's wrong with Judson?'

'He's an irresponsible playboy.'

'Don't you like irresponsible playboys?'

'No, though the business they bring in is a great help towards paying office expenses. Judson Phipps keeps us working day and night. Already we have had to see him through two breach of promise cases. I've just written him a very severe letter on the subject.'

'Has he anyone in mind at the moment?'

'The last time I saw him he was raving about your Mr Pinkney's daughter Arlene, but the fervour may have spent itself since then. Has he ever proposed to you?'

'Oh no. We're what they call just good friends.'

'Strange!'

'I think he likes them taller than I am.'

'All the same, I'd avoid him, if I were you.'

'It won't be easy. He's sailing on Thursday, too.'

'On your boat?'

'Yes. There's some sort of boxing championship fight at Madison Square Garden two weeks from now and he doesn't want to miss it.'

'Well, see as little of him as possible. Don't stroll with him on the boat deck in the moonlight. Be careful how you partner him at shuffleboard. In short, shun him.'

'I certainly shan't shun him till I've had this lunch. I'm a hungry working girl and I want that caviare or possibly that smoked salmon...'

'Don't mention such things in my presence,' said Mr Bunting with a shudder. 'I don't like to think of them.'

* * *

The lunch at Barribault's famous hotel had fulfilled Dinah's most glowing expectations. Judson Phipps might have his defects – Mr Bunting could have mentioned a dozen – but he was a princely host. No nervous watching of the prices in the right-hand column for him. He did his guests well. When they had finished being entertained by him, they knew they had been at a luncheon.

The meal had reached the coffee stage, and Judson produced an ornate cigarette case.

'Turkish this side, Virginian that,' he said, offering it. 'Who are you grinning at?'

'Actually I was smiling respectfully. At my boss, Mr Pinkney. He's at a table near the door.'

'I don't see him.'

'You wouldn't. He's right behind you. Did you know he was a superfatted poop?'

'Who says so?'

'Mr Bunting. I saw him this morning.'

'Oh, did you?' said Judson, speaking without enthusiasm. To others Mr Bunting might be a kindly friend, but to him he had always been a source of fear and discomfort, like something out of a horror film.

If it had not been for the padding which a prudent tailor had inserted in the shoulders of his coat, Judson Phipps would have provided a striking illustration of what Euclid had meant when he spoke of a thing having length without breadth. As a boy he had gone through the process of what is known as completely outgrowing his strength, and now in his riper years there was much too much of him from south to north and not nearly enough from east to west. Though never stinting himself in the matter of calories, he presented the appearance of one to whom square meals were unknown. He had a pleasant, vacant face, mostly nose and horn-rimmed spectacles, and his disposition was unvaryingly amiable.

'He doesn't approve of you. He's just written you a very severe letter, he tells me.'

'He's always writing me very severe letters. Well, I won't get this one. I'm off to Paris tomorrow morning.'

'To Paris? I thought you were sailing with us.'

'I am. I'm getting on at Cherbourg.'

'What are you going to Paris for?'

'My sister's there, and I've had a letter from her asking me to come. There's something she wants me to do for her.'

What she had heard of Judson's sister in Mr Bunting's office had been enough to whet Dinah's interest in her. She had sounded an intriguing personality.

'Tell me about your sister, Judson.'

'What about her?'

'What's she like?'

'To look at, do you mean? Sort of blonde and fluffy.'

'I was thinking more of character and disposition and all that. Mr Bunting says she's crazier than you are. Surely he was exaggerating? I wouldn't have thought anyone could be.'

Judson reflected.

'Yes, I'd say he was about right. I'm not in Julie's class. She's the hell-raising type, always apt to be starting something. Take this letter she's written me. I won't tell you what it is she wants me to do for her, but it's something that'll rock civilization.'

'She sounds what you might call a live wire.'

'She is.'

'Then I wonder what she saw in my esteemed employer. He's not exactly rollicking.'

'She'll jazz him up.'

'Poor Mr Pinkney. I ought to warn him of what he's letting himself in for. Or would you rather do it?'

'Me?'

'I thought you might like the chance of talking to his daughter Arlene. She has just joined him.'

Judson started violently.

'Has she seen us?'

'No, she's facing the other way.'

'Thank heaven for that.'

Dinah found herself unable to follow his train of thought.

'But I was given to understand that you were madly in love with her.'

'Who told you that?'

'Mr Bunting. He said you raved about her.'

'Old Bunting talks too much. Maybe I did rave about her, but it wasn't long before I thought it over and could see she wasn't my type at all. You know her and you know what she's like.'

'Strenuous? Athletic?'

'Exactly. If we were married, she'd have me up before breakfast for eighteen holes of golf.'

'She's wonderful at golf. She only just missed going to America with the Curtis Cup team.'

'And on top of that she's bossy. I didn't spot it at first, but I soon got on to it. She wouldn't let me call my soul my own. It's lucky I'm leaving. No telling what might have happened if I'd kept on seeing her.'

Once more Dinah was conscious of not being equal to the intellectual pressure of the conversation.

'I don't get it,' she said. 'You apparently don't even like her, and you're talking as if you'd only have to be with her for five minutes and you'd be asking her to marry you.'

Judson hunted for a phrase.

'Fatal fascination,' he said, having found it. 'When I'm with her, I feel a powerful impulse to ask her to be mine, and I don't *want* her to be mine, dammit.'

'Oh, I see. She casts a spell on you, and you wish she wouldn't.'

'That's right.'

'Has it ever occurred to you that she might refuse you?'

This surprised Judson. The idea that any girl in these enlightened days was capable of refusing someone as rich as he was had never struck him.

'It's possible, of course, but I can't take a chance. The thing to do is to get out while the going's good. What are they doing now? They haven't seen us? Not coming in our direction?'

'No, Mr Pinkney is drinking coffee, and Arlene is touching up the face that fascinates you so much. Why, do you want to sneak out?'

'You don't mind?'

'Of course not. I was hoping for some more coffee, but your safety is paramount. I'll fetch the dog from the cloakroom and meet you outside.'

'Do just that,' said Judson. 'Waiter, l'addishiong.'

At his table near the door Mr Pinkney had reached that comfortable state of repletion which Barribault's Hotel is always anxious to encourage in its clientele. He was a man of what is sometimes called full habit, not yet perhaps quite the superfatted poop of Mr Bunting's description but certainly one who would have to be watching his weight before long. It would not, indeed, have been a bad thing if he had started doing so already.

He had had a most enjoyable lunch, and he did not disguise it from himself that one of the things that had made it so agreeable was that his daughter Arlene had not been there to share it. Too often a meal taken in her society resolved itself into a battle of wills, he ordering rich foods, she telling him he ought not to, because one should eat lightly and so keep oneself fit. It was pleasant to think that she would not be sailing with him on the *Atlantic*, for her criticisms following the nightly dinner at the Captain's table would have been hard to bear. She had a depressing way of saying 'Father, *really!*' whenever he was trying to enjoy one of those simple forms of nourishment which a man needs if he is to keep body and soul together.

The waiter was bringing him his coffee now and with it the tray of petits fours to which he had been looking forward. And he was concentrating his powerful mind on the problem of which to select, when a voice spoke behind him.

'Father, *really!*' it said, and having jumped in his seat like a rising trout he turned belligerently.

'Oh, it's you?' he said. 'What do you mean, "Father, *really*"?'

'You know what pastry does to your tummy.'

'Never mind about my tummy.'

'You ought to avoid everything like sugar, custards, cakes, pies, rich gravies, fat meats, nuts, cream, fried foods and creamed soups, and particularly those petits fours things.'

It is frequently assumed that stout men are easy-going and quiet. Mr Pinkney exploded this theory. No slender man could have exceeded the irascibility with which he addressed the attendant waiter.

'Gimme that one with the chocolate on it and that one there,' he said in a voice that rang out like the Last Trump. 'What,' he asked, now addressing his child, 'was that you said?'

'The observation I made was, "Oh, well, if you don't *mind* looking like Nero Wolfe".'

'It was, was it?'

'It was.'

Mr Pinkney champed sullenly at that one with the chocolate on it, and there was silence for a space.

'You mustn't eat too much on the boat,' said Arlene, seeming to have been following a train of thought, and Mr Pinkney, who had now consumed not only the one with chocolate on it but also that one there and was feeling in consequence that he had won a moral victory, decided to be amiable. He considered the remark offensive and he detected in her manner the bossiness of which Judson Phipps had complained, but he told himself that women say these things. His late wife had said them frequently, and Arlene took after her.

'It's a pity,' he said with something approaching – if not very closely – geniality, 'that you won't be there to watch over me.'

'Oh, but I shall,' said Arlene. 'That's what I came to tell you. I've got to sail right away. The Curtis Cup people want me.'

'The what people?'

'Haven't you ever heard of the Curtis Cup? Golf. British females versus American females. I had expected to be picked by the selectors, but they passed me over, the fatheads. And now one of the team has broken a leg and they've cabled me to hurry across and fill in.'

Mr Pinkney stared at her dumbly. Not even Judson Phipps's jaw could have fallen more limply at this news than did his.

* * *

It was at about the moment when Mr Pinkney was receiving the bad news that Joe Cardinal entered the lobby of Barribault's Hotel and made his way to the desk. Barribault's, that Mecca of the rich, was not a customary haunt of his, but he had come to leave a note for Freddie Threepwood, who had made the place his headquarters while in London, giving him his address. He delivered the note and having done so returned as quickly as possible to the street outside, for the lobby was full of Texas millionaires and Duchesses with miniature poodles, and their presence seemed to mock his honest poverty. They gave him the feeling that he was wearing trousers that bagged at the knees and shoes that had been polished, if they ever had been polished, somewhere in the distant past.

Out in the street, he lit a cigarette and stood thinking, as he did almost incessantly these days, of Dinah Biddle.

With regard to their one and only meeting he had total recall. Every detail of it was imprinted on his memory in letters of fire. He had called at Mr Pinkney's office, gone in, seen what looked like an angel of the better sort sitting behind a typewriter, and instantly there had permeated his system a peculiar tingling sensation accompanied by the ringing of cow bells in his ears. It was the suddenness and unexpectedness of the vision that had unmanned him. The last time he had visited his uncle, some months previously, he had been received by the other's elderly secretary, a Miss Prebble, and nobody had told him that she had recently retired to Bournemouth on a pension and that her place had been taken by a girl who, he saw at a glance, was the girl he had been looking for all his life. He stood staring at her, entranced. It was improbable, he knew, that an unseen hand had struck him behind the ear with a stuffed eelskin, but the illusion that it had done so was perfect.

The following dialogue had then taken place:

HE: Er.

SHE: Good morning. Do you want to see Mr Pinkney? He's out, I'm afraid. What name shall I say?

HE: Eh? Oh, Cardinal.

He had then withdrawn.

It is a very unintelligent young man who after an interview like that does not have the feeling that he has failed to show himself at his best, and Joe required no one to point out to him how widely in these conversational exchanges he had differed from the debonair Joe he would have liked to present to this girl's attention. She had probably told her friends that evening that she had met the weirdest man that morning. A Trappist monk I think he must have been, she had probably said, he just stood there not uttering. No doubt a mental case, the friends would have suggested, and she would have agreed that there might be a good deal in the theory.

He yearned for an opportunity of showing her his better and more attractive side and was wondering wistfully if he would ever see her again, when he did. She came through the swing door, leading a dachshund on a leash.

In addition to the dachshund she was accompanied by a rich-looking young man with a large nose and horn-rimmed spectacles, at the sight of whom a shudder of disgust ran through him. The thought that she had any male acquaintances but himself revolted him, and the last male acquaintances he would have wished to see in her company were rich-looking young men, whether spectacled or not spectacled.

Addressing this obvious multimillionaire, she said:

'Thanks for that wonderful lunch, Judson. Where are you headed for now?'

'I thought I'd look in at the steamship office and see if they can't give me a better stateroom.'

'What's wrong with the one you've got? No swimming pool?'

'Ha ha,' said the plutocrat and passed on his way, and the girl, turning, saw Joe and a look of pleased surprise came into her face.

'Oh, hullo,' she said.

In describing Joe to Mr Bunting as shy Dinah had erred. Normally he was quite the reverse, and his taciturnity at their previous meeting had been merely a passing weakness. Any man is entitled to have trouble with his vocal cords when the girl he has been looking for all his life suddenly pops up out of a trap at him without a word of warning. He was now himself again, and that self was an exuberant one. To say that he beamed would be understating it. His smile of gratification nearly split his face in half. A miniature poodle which was passing sneered at him, but he did not even notice it.

The dachshund, however, did and took instant offence at the sneer – directed, he mistakenly supposed, at himself. A rasping sound like that of someone gargling mouth wash burst from his lips, and the next moment battle had been joined.

Most people, seeing Joe Cardinal, would have put him down as an ordinary young man, and he was an ordinary young man, but it so happened that in the matter of stopping dog fights he was rather exceptional. He owned an animal of mixed ancestry whose touchy disposition led it to become embroiled with others of its kind at the drop of a bone. A good deal of his leisure had been spent in detaching it from the throats of a variety of antagonists. So now, where many a man would have hesitated, he acted. There was a rending sound, and the two belligerents came apart in his hands.

Dinah for the next few moments was busy apologizing to the poodle's Duchess owner, but when the latter had gone off in her limousine, she turned to Joe with shining eyes. She did not actually say 'My hero!' but her manner implied it.

'That was very adroit,' she said. 'You must have had a lot of practice.'

'A good deal, yes – but these brawls never amount to much. Fighting to a dog is just the normal way of passing the time of day. It's his way of saying "Hello, there".'

'You seem to understand dogs.'

'They have few secrets from me.'

'You must be fond of them.'

'I am. Are you fond of dogs?'

'Yes, very.'

'So am I. There's something about dogs.'

'Yes.'

'Of course, there's something about cats, too.'

'Yes.'

'But, still, cats aren't dogs.'

'No.'

Dinah was feeling a little bewildered. The discovery that Joe, who at their first meeting had seemed to be giving an impersonation of Lot's wife when turned into a pillar of salt, was in reality a brilliant conversationalist, gave her the sensation of being in the presence of a changeling. It was as if a statue had suddenly become loquacious. Her surprise was increased when his next remark was an invitation to her to lunch with him.

'But I've just had lunch.'

Joe winced. He was only too well aware of this, and a spasm of jealousy shook him as he thought who her host had been.

'Well, some other day?'

'I'd love to.'

'Tomorrow?'

'All right. Where?'

'Here,' said Joe. 'I'll book a table.'

His guardian angel whispered to him that he was being rash, for pay day was not for another two weeks and it would mean digging deeply into his little savings, but he had his answer to that. No lesser place than Barribault's was worthy of a girl like this, he told his guardian angel, and his guardian angel agreed that he had a point there.

The directors of Barribault's Hotel, knowing how fastidious are the Duchesses, the Maharajahs and the Texas oil millionaires on whom they rely for patronage, had spared no expense on its lobby. The result had been something that would have satisfied Kubla Khan when passing the specifications for the stately pleasure dome which he had decreed in Xanadu, and on his previous visit Joe, as we have seen, had found its magnificence oppressive. It amazed him as he sat waiting there on the following afternoon that he could ever have disliked it. In excellent taste he considered its decorations. He liked the faces of his fellow lunchers, too. Duchesses passed, and he thought what nice Duchesses they were. Texas millionaires came by, and he hoped their latest gushers were working out satisfactorily. He had an indulgent eye for the Maharajahs and the miniature poodles. He was in a mood of overflowing benevolence towards all created things.

He had been sitting there for perhaps ten minutes when a burst of sunshine filled the lobby, harpsichords and sackbuts began to play soft music, and he saw Dinah coming through the swing door.

'Am I late?' she said.

'Not a bit,' said Joe. 'Beautiful day.'

'Except for the rain.'

'Is it raining?'

'Rather hard.'

'Probably all for the best. I hear the farmers need it.'

'Are you fond of farmers?'

'I love them.'

They went into the grill-room, and a waiter took their order.

'Nice-looking fellow,' said Joe, following him with an appreciative eye. 'I like the way he walks.'

'You seem to be liking everything this morning.'

'I am.'

Dinah's conscience was troubling her.

'You know,' she said, 'this is all wrong.'

'All *wrong*?' said Joe. 'I don't see how it could be righter.'

'I mean you ought not to be taking me to lunch at a place like this.'

'Why not?'

'Too expensive. You can't afford it.'

'Who told you that?'

'Mr Bunting.'

A wave of emotion at the thought that she had felt enough interest in him to make her discuss him with Mr Bunting swept Joe.

'What did he tell you?'

'That you were in a bank. Do you like it?'

'Not much. Do you like being a secretary?'

'Yes, though I wish the job carried a bit more money. I love money as much as you love dogs and farmers. Not that I've ever had any.'

'Tell me about yourself.'

'There's nothing much to tell.'

'Well, we might start with your name.'

'Biddle,' said Dinah, and Joe thought he had never heard anything so musical. 'Dinah Biddle. Though it ought to be Dinah Micawber.' She gave a little laugh. 'My father was just like Mr Micawber. I suppose he was about the most impractical man who ever lived. When he died, I was brought up by an aunt and learned shorthand and typing, and here I am. Now tell me the story of *your* life.'

'It's rather dull.'

'I won't be bored.'

'Well, like you, I was brought up by an aunt.'

'Were you fond of her?'

'Very.'

'I was of mine.'

'Nobody could have done more for me than she did. She paid all my expenses at school, Cambridge, art school in Paris.'

'Oh, were you an artist?'

'I started out as one, but I didn't make much of a go of it. I thought I would do better in time, but I couldn't get my uncle to see eye to eye with me.'

'Mr Pinkney?'

'Yes. And he insisted on my going into a bank.'

'But what had he to do with it?'

'Unfortunately, when my aunt made her will, leaving all she had to me, he persuaded her to leave it in trust, making him my trustee. So he was in a position to dictate. He said I was wasting my time painting pictures which nobody would buy and ought to be embarking on a business career like every other young man. So he put me in the New Asiatic Bank, of which he is a director. I could see his point of view. I'm not saying I liked it, but I could see it.'

'But don't you ever get your money?'

'Not for another three years, unless he cares to give it to me. It can be released at the discretion of the trustee, but so far he's shown no signs of having reached years of discretion.'

Dinah felt her heart warming to him. He had spoken cheerfully and with no trace of self-pity, a weakness for which she had little tolerance. During the worst of the crises which her Micawber-like father had brought on the home in the old days she had never felt sorry for herself.

'What will you do when you get it? Go back to painting?'

'You bet.'

'Well, three years isn't so long to wait.'

It was, Joe felt, if you wanted to get married in the next week or so, but this was not the moment to mention it.

'Well, that's the life story you asked for. I hope it didn't bore you.'

'I told you I wouldn't be bored. Oh, heavens!' said Dinah, looking at her watch.

'What's the matter?'

'I'd no idea it was so late.'

She reached for her bag, and rose. Joe uttered a cry of protest.

'You aren't going?'

'I must, I'm afraid. We're in a terrible rush now that we're sailing.'

'Sailing?'

'Mr Pinkney is leaving for New York on Thursday.'

A horrible thought chilled Joe to the marrow.

'You're not going, too?'

'Yes.'

Joe had often heard the expression 'Everything went black', and now he knew what it meant.

'How long will you be in New York?'

'I don't know. A long time, I expect.'

'What boat are you sailing on?'

'The *Atlantic*. So I have to get back to Mr Pinkney to see if he wants me for anything.'

They were in the lobby now. She held out her hand.

'Goodbye.'

She was gone, and Joe roused himself from the coma which had gripped him and started to walk to Chelsea. It was a long walk, but in his present state of mental turmoil he needed it.

Arriving at the studio which was still his home, he was further depressed, when he entered it, to find Freddie Threepwood there. He was fond of Freddie, but a man who has been told by the girl he loves that she is sailing for New York on Thursday for an indefinite visit wants solitude.

'I've been looking at your pictures, Joe,' said Freddie.

'Oh?' said Joe.

'I like that one where the girl's lying on a mossy bank and the fellow's bending over to kiss her.'

Joe regarded it with an eye that could not have been less enthusiastic if he had been an art critic.

'That's a rotten thing I did years ago. I thought I had burned it. It wouldn't be a bad idea to burn the whole damn lot of them,' he said, and so charged with gloom was his voice that Freddie looked at him, concerned.

'What's wrong, Joe?'

'Nothing.'

'Don't try to fool me. At Donaldson's Dog Joy we are trained to observe. What's the matter?'

Except in the older type of musical comedy a man in love seldom pours out his heart in confidences to a friend or chorus of friends, but Joe's morale at the moment was extremely low and the urge to cry on someone's shoulder imperative. There was, moreover, something in Freddie's personality, the quality of persuasiveness which had enabled him to sell dog biscuits to Wilks Brothers of Manchester and Beatle Beatle and Beatle of Liverpool, that made him hard to resist. With some surprise Joe found himself telling all, and Freddie scratched his chin thoughtfully with the handle of his umbrella.

'You love this girl?'

'Yes.'

'And she spurns your suit?'

'There hasn't been any suit.'

'Then there had better begin to be, or you won't get anywhere. You can't just stand there. Now in the matter of pressing one's suit,' said Freddie, 'there are various schools of thought. Aggie and I,' he said, alluding to the daughter of Mr Donaldson of Donaldson's Dog Joy, to whom he had been happily married for some years, 'clicked with such rapidity that there wasn't any need for finesse and science, but in most cases, I imagine, something in the nature of a systematic approach would be required. One of my colleagues at Dog Joy, who was recently distributing cigars to celebrate the coming on the scene of his bouncing first-born, told me that he had ensnared the little woman by means of what he called the Rockmeteller Method. His name is Bream Rockmeteller. His plan was to go at it gradually. Having located the prospect, he started by looking at her.'

'Looking at her?'

'Yearningly. Wherever she went, there would be Bream Rockmeteller getting the daily eyeful, and of course it wasn't long before she was saying to herself "What's all this in aid of?". Her initial supposition that her slip must be showing soon passed and the conviction began to steal over her that this nonstop goggling meant something. Then he began to send her flowers, books of poetry and what not, and when she was thoroughly softened up, he proposed. The whole operation took about six weeks. Why do you laugh?'

It was intelligent of Freddie to have diagnosed the sound which had proceeded from Joe as a laugh. By a less acute ear it might have been mistaken for the groan of a fiend in torment.

'I was amused by your suggesting a system that takes six weeks. I told you she was sailing for New York on Thursday.'

'But of course you're sailing too?'

'How can I? I haven't got the money for the fare.'

Freddie was astounded.

'But I always thought you had a wad of money. Didn't an aunt of yours leave you a packet?'

'Yes, in trust. Pinkney's my trustee. I don't get it till I'm thirty.'

'And you can't touch him for a bit in advance?'

'No.'

'H'm. This complicates things. Can't you sell one of your pictures?'

'No.'

'I could.'

'Then you must be a marvel as a salesman.'

'So the boys at Dog Joy often tell me. Yes, I think I know the very man on whom to unload that girl-on-mossy-bank one. If I now, I shall probably catch him at the Drones. Shall I take the picture along with me and give him the hard sell?'

'If you like,' said Joe.

Anything that removed Freddie from his presence suited him. He wanted to be alone with his sombre thoughts.

Half an hour or so after Freddie had departed on his mission Judson Phipps came into the Drones Club to have a look at the smoking-room tape. He wanted to see what had won the fifth race at Hurst Park that afternoon.

As he was passing through the bar, the man behind it addressed him.

'Mr Threepwood was looking for you, Mr Phipps.'

'Freddie Threepwood? But he's in America.'

'He wasn't ten minutes ago.'

Though Mr Bunting would have denied it hotly, Judson Phipps was capable at times of ratiocination. He showed this now.

'He must be over in England.'

'That's what I thought.'

'Is he in the smoking-room?'

'He was headed that way.'

'I'll go and say Hello. Old Freddie with us again! Fancy that. What won the fifth at Hurst Park?'

'Aspidistra.'

'Hell,' said Judson, who had wagered on the speed and endurance of a horse named Lemon Drop.

'Hi, Freddie,' he was saying a few moments later, and Freddie came out of a waking dream about dog biscuits.

'Oh, there you are, Juddy. I was looking for you.'

'So McGarry told me. You're back in London, are you?'

'In person.'

In the short space of time it had taken him to move from bar to smoking-room the obvious explanation of his friend's presence in England's metropolis had come to Judson.

'So they've fired you?' he said.

'Eh?'

'Those dog biscuit guys of yours. I thought it was only a question of time.'

It was with considerable dignity that Freddie corrected this mistaken view.

'What do you mean, fired me? Of course they haven't fired me. I was sent over by the big chief to buck up the English end of the business, and I don't mind telling you I've booked some orders which'll make him do the dance of the seven veils all over Long Island City. The only blot on my escutcheon is that I haven't been able to contact Pinkney of Pinkney's Stores, and that brings me to what I want to talk to you about.'

'What's that thing you've got there on the floor?'

'A picture. Never mind that for the moment. We'll be touching on it later. The item at the top of the agenda paper is Pinkney. Is it true what I hear about him being going to marry your sister?'

'Sure.'

'So I take it that you stand fairly high in his estimation? The brother of the woman he loves.'

'Well, I wouldn't say we were bosom buddies, but we get along all right.'

'Then you can do me a signal service by introducing me to him so that I can bend him to my will in the matter of stocking up Dog Joy in his emporium. I only need ten minutes of his undivided time to make him see the light. You'll do this for me, Juddy?'

'But I'm leaving for Paris tomorrow morning.'

'Then when you get back?'

'I won't be back. I'm sailing for New York on Thursday. I get aboard at Cherbourg.'

'Can't you go by a later boat?'

'Impossible. That fight.'

'What fight?'

'There's the light-heavyweight fight at Madison Square Garden a day or two after I land. If I went by a later boat, I'd miss it, and I've been looking forward to it for months.'

'You could fly.'

'Me? I wouldn't go up in one of those things if you paid me.'

'Not to help a pal?'

'Not to help a hundred and forty-seven pals. My sister Julie's flying over the week after next, but you don't catch me doing it. And anyway it wouldn't do you any good me cancelling my passage, because Pinkney's sailing, too.'

All the go-getter in Freddie sprang to life. He could not be said to have been thinking on his feet as recommended by the memoranda which hung on the wall of every office at Donaldson's Dog Joy, for he was seated, but it was plain that a thought had come like a full-blown rose, flushing his brow.

'He'll be on your boat?'

'Yes.'

'Then so will I. I wasn't meaning to leave for another three weeks, but this is an opportunity that may not occur again. You're sailing on the what?'

'The *Atlantic.*'

'I'll book a passage tomorrow. This'll bring the roses to Aggie's cheeks. She wasn't expecting me till the middle of next month. She'll go singing in the streets. How long does it take the *Atlantic* to get across?'

'About five days.'

'Five days during which I shall be constantly at Pinkney's side guiding his thoughts in the right direction. If by the time we land I haven't got him signing on the dotted line, I'm not the man I think I am.'

'Well, I wish you luck.'

'Thanks.'

'You'll need it.'

It was apparent that something was amusing Judson. A sound like water going down the waste pipe of a bath showed that he was chuckling.

'And I'll tell you why,' he said. 'Because once the voyage has started I doubt if Pinkney will be in the mood to give his mind to dog biscuits. Want to hear something funny, Freddie? I told you my sister was flying to New York in a week or so. Well, by way of filling in the time before she leaves she has been buying out most of the Paris stores, concentrating particularly on the jewellers. One of the things she's bought, she tells me, is a diamond necklace costing about thirty thousand dollars. Well, you know what that means when you get to the other end.'

'Lot of duty to pay.'

'Yes. And she doesn't approve of paying duty.'

'Many people don't.'

'So she's giving me the thing to give to Pinkney to smuggle through. I can just see his face when I slip it to him,' said Judson, once more chuckling.

Freddie was staring, aghast. His friend had described this

appalling piece of news as 'something funny', but its humour eluded him. Only too clearly could he see that, as Judson had said, his prospect would not be in the mood to concentrate his mind on dog biscuits.

'When are you planning to give him the thing?'

'As soon as I get on board.'

'No! Do me a favour, Juddy.'

'Such as?'

'Wait till the last day of the voyage. That'll give me time to make my sales talk.'

'Yes, I could do that.'

'Apart from anything else, it would be the humane course to pursue. You don't want to spoil the poor blighter's trip, do you?'

'I see what you mean.'

'So you'll do it? Last day of voyage?'

'Sure.'

'That's a promise?'

'Sure.'

Freddie drew a relieved breath.

'Thanks, Juddy. I knew you wouldn't let me down. And now a very important point. Has Pinkney any hobbies?'

'Hobbies?'

'In working on a prospect my first move is always to find out what he's interested in, so that I can endear myself to him by bringing the subject up. P. P. Wilks of Wilks Brothers Manchester, for instance, from whom I obtained a substantial order, is a staunch supporter of the Manchester United football team. My spies informed me of this and I attribute my success entirely to my shrewdness in asking around till I had all the facts relevant to the United's recent performance at my fingertips and was able to discuss them intelligently. By the time we parted we were like ham and eggs. He patted me on the back and showered cigars on me.'

'Pinkney won't do that.'

'Not pat?'

'Not shower. He's a big wheel in the Anti-Tobacco League.'

'How fortunate you told me this. I might have approached him blowing smoke rings. Well, many thanks for your invaluable co-operation, Juddy. You have clarified the whole picture. And talking of pictures,' said Freddie, remembering his mission. 'You were asking just now about this one. Take a glance at it.'

In the matter of pictures, Judson, if questioned, would have said that he did not know much about them, but he knew what he liked, and it was plain from his expression that this one of Joe's did not fall into that category.

'It doesn't look much.'

Freddie had foreseen some such reaction.

'At first sight, no,' he agreed. 'A doll asleep on a mossy bank and a guy bending over her to kiss her. Corny, you say to yourself, the kind of thing that went out in the Victorian age. But think again. The guy is wearing a sort of bath robe, right?'

'Right.'

'But if he was wearing pants, what then? How about his braces?'

'You mean suspenders?'

'All right, suspenders if you like. If he was wearing suspenders and stooped like that, he'd bust them, wouldn't he? No, sir, he would not bust them, not if they were Phipps's, because Phipps's will stand the strongest strain. See what I'm driving at, Juddy? Buy that picture, get a staff artist to put the guy in pants and a polo shirt, fix him up with a pair of Phipps's Tried and Proven, and you've got a full colour page in all the magazines which'll send your sales soaring into the empyrean. I know you don't take an active part in the business, but it won't do you any harm to get known in the firm as an ideas man. The rank and file work with more enthusiasm if they feel that the fellow up top isn't just sitting on his fanny clipping coupons, but is right on the job and setting company policy. So how about it?'

Considering that the Wilks Brothers of Manchester and Beatle Beatle and Beatle of Liverpool had been wax in Freddie's hands, it would have been remarkable if Judson Phipps had been able to resist him. He made no attempt to do so.

'How much would the fellow want? What's his name, by the way?'

'Cardinal. Joe Cardinal. I think two hundred pounds would be about the right price.'

'Two hundred pounds!'

'A mere nothing to you.'

'I dare say. But two hundred pounds!'

Freddie saw that the crux of the negotiation had been reached and that the time had come to step up the pressure.

'Listen, Juddy, I'll tell you the whole story, and I'm sure it will overcome any objection you may have to parting, because you're a man of sentiment. You must be, to have had two breach of promise cases. Joe Cardinal has fallen in love with a girl and before he'd had time to start pressing his suit he finds she's sailing on the *Atlantic* on Thursday. A nice bit of news for him to get out of a blue sky, you'll admit.'

Judson conceded that the discovery could not have been pleasant.

'So naturally he wants to drop everything and go with her.'

'In the hope of bringing home the bacon?'

'Exactly. You're very quick, Juddy.'

'I always have been.'

'So I've heard. Well, the snag is he's not got the money to pay for his passage. He works in some minor capacity in a bank. So his whole future happiness depends on you. Come on, Juddy, be a sport and strew a little happiness as you go by. You probably have your chequebook on you. Out with it, and start writing. You'll never regret it.'

With the unfailing accuracy of the trained dog biscuit sales-man Freddie had struck the right note. It would be difficult to say whether Judson's eyes filled with tears, for they were always a little watery, but the dullest observer could see that he was melted.

'You'd better make the cheque out to me,' said Freddie. 'I am empowered to act as Joe's agent. If you'll excuse me, I'll go and phone him the good news, and I have no doubt he will strew roses from his hat and call down blessings on the head of his benefactor.'

The S.S. *Atlantic* was under way, moving in a slow and thought-ful manner down the Solent. Friends and relatives had gone ashore, baskets of fruit had been deposited in staterooms, yacht-ing caps donned by those who liked yachting caps. The Captain was on the bridge, pretty sure that he knew the way to New York but, just to be on the safe side, murmuring to himself 'Turn right at Cherbourg and then straight on'. The ship's doctor was already playing shuffleboard with the more comely of the female passengers. Mr Pinkney was getting up an appetite for the eleven o'clock soup. His daughter Arlene was keeping fit by walking round and round the promenade deck. And on the boat deck Freddie Threepwood was standing talking to his friend Joe Cardinal.

The start of the voyage found Freddie in the best of spirits, as voyages always did when the liner's nose was pointed westward. These periodical visits of his to the land of his birth were all very well, and he enjoyed them, but his heart was in his home at Great Neck with Aggie popping the toast out of the toaster and the 8.15 train waiting to take him to Long Island City. Spreading the light in England had its attractions, but he always longed to be back in the pulsating centre of the dog biscuit world, standing shoulder to shoulder with Bream Rockmeteller and the rest of them like the boys of the Old Brigade.

His thoughts for the moment, however, were not on Dog Joy.

'Tell me of this girl of yours, Joe,' he was saying. 'Would I know her? What's her name?'

'Dinah Biddle. She's my uncle's secretary.'

'Then I do know her. At least, we've met. She came to Bunting's office when I was there. I liked her looks.'

'Me, too.'

'Nice girl. I'm not surprised you're dashing after her like this. Good luck to you, say I, though I doubt if Pinkney will take the same kindly view. If I remember rightly, you told me it was he who put you in your bank job?'

'Yes, curse him.'

'And he doesn't know you're playing hooky?'

'No.'

'It will dawn on him when he sees you pacing the deck.'

'Yes, I thought of that.'

'And bim will go any chance you may have had of inducing him to scatter purses of gold. H'm,' said Freddie. 'You had better leave this to me, Joe. It calls for constructive thinking. Go and lie low in your stateroom till I've had time to formulate a policy.'

'I don't see what policy you can formulate.'

'Nor as of even date do I.'

But it is rarely that an executive of Donaldson's Dog Joy is baffled for long. It was only a minute or two before Freddie saw the way – which, as it turned out, was a good thing, for it was only a minute or three before a voice spoke and he found that he had been joined by a stout man – one of the stoutest, indeed, whom he had ever encountered.

'Pardon me,' said this obese character.

Mr Pinkney, as has been said, was looking forward to his eleven o'clock soup and thoughts of it had been occupying his mind to the exclusion of all else. But when he had suddenly seen his nephew Joseph where no nephew Joseph should have been, soup was temporarily forgotten. A man of his build could never move from spot to spot at any high rate of speed, but he had made for Freddie at as high a rate of speed as was possible.

'Pardon me,' he said. 'Would you mind telling me who that young man was that you were talking to.'

'His name's Cardinal. Joe Cardinal.'

'I thought as much!'

'You know him?'

'I'm his uncle, and perhaps you can tell me—'

'You're not Mr Pinkney?'

'I am.'

'Of Pinkney's Stores?'

'I am. And perhaps you can tell me—'

It has already been hinted that Arnold Pinkney was not a feast for the eye and would have had to taper off quite a good deal before entering for a beauty contest with any confidence of success. Nevertheless, Freddie was gazing on him as he might have gazed on some noble work of Nature like the Grand Canyon of Arizona.

'This is a great pleasure, Mr Pinkney. I heard you were on board and was hoping that we should meet.'

'Thank you. But perhaps you can tell me what in the world my nephew is doing on this boat.'

'I thought you might be surprised to find him here. The explanation is very simple. The men up top at the bank think so highly of his abilities that they are transferring him to the main office in New York.'

To say that Mr Pinkney was surprised would not be to over-state it, for he found it difficult to understand how anyone could think highly of the abilities of his nephew Joseph, but he accepted this curious state of things without disbelief.

'Oh?' he said. 'I see. I was wondering. Thank you, Mr—'

'Threepwood. Of Dog Joy.'

'Of what?'

'Donaldson's Dog Joy.'

'What is Donaldson's Dog Joy?'

Freddie was only too happy to inform him, though amazed that he needed to be informed.

'Donaldson's Dog Joy,' he said, a hand stealing to his hat as if he were about to bare his head, 'is God's gift to the kennel, whether it be in the gilded palace of the rich or the humble hovel of the poor. Dogs raised on Donaldson's Dog Joy become fine, strong, upstanding dogs who look the world in the eye with their chins up and both feet on the ground. Get your dog thinking the Donaldson way! Let Donaldson make your spaniel a super-spaniel. Place your wirehaired terrier's paws on the broad Donaldson highway and watch him scamper away to health, happiness, the clear eye, the cold nose and the ever-wagging tail. Donaldson's Dog Joy—'

'It's a sort of dog biscuit,' said Mr Pinkney, groping.

'*Sort* of dog biscuit?' said Freddie, wounded to the quick. 'It's the dog biscuit supreme.'

'The only dog biscuit we carry at my Stores is Peterson's Pup Food. Good morning, Mr Threepwood,' said Mr Pinkney, and he removed himself abruptly, for some sixth sense had told him that the eleven o'clock soup was now being served.

Freddie stared after him, aghast. He felt like a clergyman who has found schism in his flock. It was an axiom at Donaldson's Dog Joy that its leading rival Peterson's Pup Food was a product lacking in many of the essential vitamins and that dogs who indulged in it were heading straight for rheumatism, sciatica, anaemia and stomach trouble. He began to see that his task of leading Arnold Pinkney into the true faith was going to be more difficult than he had supposed.

But though a Dog Joy executive may be down, he is never out, and by the time the tender at Cherbourg had deposited its cargo of passengers on board the *Atlantic* Freddie had found the solution of the problem of how to cope with Mr Pinkney's sales resistance.

Your prudent go-getter always likes, on the principle of trying it on the dog, to get an outside opinion from some independent source, and seeing Judson Phipps hastening towards him Freddie decided that here was the captive audience he required. As he put it to himself, he would run up the flag and see if Judson saluted.

'Ah, Juddy,' he said. 'Welcome aboard. You'll be interested to hear that I've met Pinkney and stunned, no doubt, to learn that he had never heard of Donaldson's Dog Joy and carries only Peterson's Pup Food in his store. But I have the matter well in hand. I propose to give him Treatment A.'

'Listen,' said Judson, and a less self-centred man than Freddie would have noticed that his manner was agitated and the eyes behind his horn-rimmed spectacles bulging. His air was that of one who has had disconcerting news.

'Treatment A involves ocular demonstration. Our demonstrator stands out in plain view of the consumer public and when the audience is of sufficient size takes a Donaldson's biscuit and chews it. And not only does he chew it, he enjoys it. He rolls it round his tongue and mixes it with his saliva, thus showing that Donaldson's Dog Joy is so superbly wholesome as actually to be fit for human consumption. I have a sample biscuit in my stateroom. I shall draw Pinkney aside and eat it before his eyes, and I shall be greatly surprised if he doesn't immediately—'

'Listen,' said Judson. 'Freddie, I'm in a spot.'

It irked Freddie to have to stop talking about Dog Joy while so much of his music was still within him, but he was essentially kindly and always at the service of a friend in distress.

'What's your problem?' he asked.

Now that he had succeeded in obtaining Freddie's attention, Judson became a little calmer, though still presenting the appearance of a man who has rashly looked for a leak in a gas pipe with a lighted candle.

'Well, I must begin by telling you that Pinkney has a daughter.'

'Proceed.'

'I saw a good deal of her in London.'

'And?'

'I've just found out she's on board. It knocked me sideways. I'm trembling like a—'

'Leaf?'

'Aspen. I'm all of a twitter.'

Donaldson's Dog Joy has very few employees on its pay roll who are not as quick as lightning.

'Say no more,' said Freddie. 'I grasp the situation. You love this girl and you want me to take her aside and give you a build-up – tell her what a splendid fellow you are and so forth, so that when you come to do your stuff you will find her all eagerness to co-operate. That's the idea, isn't it?'

'No, it isn't. I particularly want to avoid her.'

'I didn't know you ever avoided girls. Don't you like her?'

'She fascinates me.'

'Then why do you want to avoid her?'

'Because if I go on seeing her, especially aboard an ocean liner, I know I shall ask her to marry me. I don't want to, but I won't be able to help myself. It's like a bird and a snake. Have you ever seen a snake hypnotizing a bird? The bird would prefer to let the whole thing drop, but the snake exercises a spell on it and it has to carry on against its better judgment. It's like that with me. The last thing I want to do is ask Arlene Pinkney to marry me, but I know I shall do it if we're going to be together for five days on an ocean liner. I should explain that she looks like something out of a beauty chorus.'

'Ah!' said Freddie, enlightened. 'Yes, I follow you now. You mean that in spite of the fact that she gives you a pain in the gizzard you can't help being intrigued by her outer crust.'

'Exactly. I realize perfectly well that I'd be crazy to propose to her, but when I see that profile of hers I feel the only thing worth doing in this world is to grab her and start shouting for clergymen and bridesmaids to come running.'

'Have you tried not looking at her sideways?'

'It wouldn't do any good. The effect full face is just the same.'

Freddie pondered.

'It's a tricky situation,' he agreed. 'Oddly enough, I had a similar experience myself once, before I met Aggie. There was a girl who attracted me like billy-o and at the same time repelled me like a ton of bricks. If it hadn't been for Pongo Twistleton, goodness knows what might have happened. By the greatest good luck he, too, had fallen under her spell, and he clustered round her to such an extent that there was no getting her alone. It was the most impressive case of adhesiveness since Mary had a little lamb.'

Into Judson's haggard face there had come the light that shows that hope has dawned.

'Then that's exactly what you must do, Freddie. You must be constantly at Arlene Pinkney's side. Never leave her for an instant. Begin where Mary's lamb left off.'

'But you say she's more or less the Sheik's Dream of Paradise.'

'I'd certainly put her in the Top Ten.'

'Then I'm sorry. It can't be done. If Aggie learned that I had been Mary's-lambing with a girl of that description, I'd never hear the end of it. Aggie's the sweetest thing on earth, but her views on how a husband should behave when her eye is not on him are rigid. However, an idea presents itself. Why don't you get someone to cluster round *you*? What you want is a bodyguard, the sort of thing Prime Ministers have. If there's always someone with you when you meet this Pinkney, you can't do anything rash. Your lips will be sealed.'

Judson's spectacles leaped from his nose, so great was his enthusiasm.

'Freddie, you've hit it! You shall be my bodyguard.'

'I certainly shan't. I need every moment of my time for casting a spell on Pinkney.'

'Then who can I get?'

'Oh, anybody, anybody,' said Freddie absently. His thoughts were once more on Treatment A.

And it was at this moment that Judson saw Dinah Biddle approaching.

As a general rule Judson was a slow thinker. He would not have lasted a week at Donaldson's Dog Joy. But peril sharpens the intellect, and the idea of casting Dinah for the vacant role came to him in a flash. She was accompanied by the dachshund and at any other time its presence would have given him pause, for he was always a little nervous in the society of strange dogs, but there was too much at stake now to permit of any worrying about dachshunds. A moment later he was at her side, placing the facts before her.

'You see what I mean?' he said, having done so, and Dinah assured him that she had not missed the gist. In the intervals of thinking about Joe Cardinal she had been giving not a little thought to what Judson's reactions would be when he found Arlene Pinkney on board.

'I think it's a wonderful idea,' she said.

'You'll do it?'

'Of course. The first thing to do is to get two deck chairs side by side.'

'And never move from them.'

'Not an inch. And in the evening we'd better dance together a good deal. The dance hour is the dangerous one.'

Judson drew a deep breath. He removed his spectacles and polished them with something of a flourish. It would be exaggerating to say that even now his soul was altogether at peace, but the illusion that it was being churned up by an egg whisk had unquestionably diminished in intensity.

* * *

At about the time when Judson and Dinah were settling them-selves in their deck chairs Joe Cardinal came out of the state-room in which he had been lurking. Freddie having reported that owing to his, Freddie's, quick thinking no awkward ques-tions would be asked when he met Mr Pinkney, he was in buoy-ant mood. No doubt immunity from the latter's wrath would be merely temporary and a painful scene with him some time in the future inevitable, but this was a trifle he could not bother about now. His step, as he ranged the boat in quest of Dinah Biddle, was light and his spirits effervescent.

These conditions prevailed till he came on to the promenade deck where the deck chairs were, when his view that everything was for the best in this best of all possible worlds underwent an abrupt revision. For there, side by side and obviously on the most intimate terms, were the girl he was seeking and the man who had been with her at Barribault's Hotel and had looked so rich. He was looking even richer now, for he was wearing a yachting cap.

Not much ensued in the way of dialogue. Sparkling give-and-take is scarcely to be expected when two members of a group of three are feeling breathless and the third is a man never much given to small talk. Dinah said, 'Mr Cardinal! I didn't know you were on board,' and Joe said Yes, he was on board. Dinah said 'Do you know Mr Phipps?' and Joe nodded jerkily in Judson's direction, and then there was a pause of some duration, at the end of which Judson said the weather seemed to be keeping up, and Joe said Yes and withdrew, tripping slightly over his feet. Not, as has been said, very brilliant stuff and scarcely, one feels, worth recording.

Judson looked after Joe's receding form with an interest that had not been provoked by the brightness of his conversation.

'Cardinal did you say that guy's name was?'

Dinah's faculties were still a good deal disordered, but she was able to reply in the affirmative.

'I'll tell you something about him. Do you know why he's on this boat?'

'I suppose he's going to America.'

'Very probably, but do you know why he's going to America? It's a most romantic story. I had the facts in the case from Freddie Threepwood. He's sailing because he wants to press his suit with some girl who's on board.'

'What!'

'That's right. It appears that he fell in love with this girl at first sight, found she was sailing and packed a toothbrush and came along too, so as to press his suit. What are you looking so starry-eyed about?'

'Am I looking starry-eyed? Just because I'm feeling happy, I suppose.'

'Why are you feeling happy?'

'Who wouldn't, being with you?'

'Something in that,' said Judson.

Leaving the promenade deck and making for the bar, for he felt greatly in need of its services, Joe encountered Freddie, who had been down to his stateroom for his sample dog biscuit.

'Hullo, Joe,' said Freddie. 'Have you seen Pinkney anywhere?'

'Freddie,' said Joe simultaneously. 'Do you know a man called Phipps?'

'I want to demonstrate to him how superlatively wholesome ... Phipps, did you say? Juddy Phipps? Known him for years. He's on board.'

'I've just met him. Who is he?'

'Suspenders.'

'What about them?'

'That's who he is. Phipps Tried and Proven Suspenders, though I shall never waver in my view that they ought to be spoken of as braces. Excluding those who wear belts, practically the whole of America's male population use Phipps's suspenders. Otherwise their pants would fall down.'

Joe's worst suspicions were confirmed.

'Then he's rich?'

'*Rich*? Add the adjective "stinking". He and his sister inherited the late Phipps Senior's pile, which years of selling suspenders had rendered stupendous. Why do you ask?'

'Oh, I just wondered. I'm going to have a drink. You coming?'

'Sorry, no. I have to give Pinkney Treatment A.'

As Joe went on his way, his heart was heavy, for he was brooding on Dinah Biddle. Remembering as he did every word she had said in their brief acquaintanceship, he recalled that observation of hers at the luncheon table. At the time it had not seemed to him significant, but now it came back to him fraught with sinister meaning. 'I love money as much as you love dogs and farmers,' she had said, and he realized now that it had been no idle pleasantry, but a cold statement of fact. She stood revealed as calculating and mercenary, the sort of girl who makes a bee line for the nearest millionaire and snuggles up beside him in a deck chair, however limited – apart from the ability to write cheques – his attractions. Most of Judson Phipps had been concealed by a steamer rug, but enough of him had protruded to make it manifest to Joe that he was totally lacking in any kind of charm, and he tottered blindly towards the bar like a camel making for an oasis after a hard day at the office.

But he was not destined yet to reach journey's end, for while he was still distant from his objective a voice hailed him. It was that of his cousin Arlene, a loud, authoritative voice that always reminded him of the sergeant who had come to teach drill at his preparatory school. She was staring at him in the manner usually described as agog.

'Joe! What in the world are you doing here?'

Joe's state of mind was still chaotic, but thanks to Freddie's quick intelligence he was able to answer that.

'I didn't know you were sailing,' he said, having done so.

'They want me on the Curtis Cup team.'

'That's good.'

'Yes. But if I'd had an ounce of sense, I'd have flown.'

'Don't you like ocean travel?'

'As a rule I do, but this time it's different.'

'What's wrong with this time?'

'I'll tell you what's wrong. I was watching the crowd coming off the tender, and you could have knocked me down with a number seven iron. One of the first to step aboard was a frightful man called Phipps.'

'Phipps!'

'You know him?'

'I've met him.'

'So have I,' said Arlene with a bitter laugh. 'He's been in my hair for weeks. He'll be in it again the moment he sees me, and the fear that haunts me is that he'll ask me to marry him and I shall accept him in a weak moment because of his money. But now you're here, Joe, I breathe again.'

'Why's that?'

'Because you must be always at my side, never leaving me for an instant. He can't possibly propose with you sitting in the front row all the time. I shall be all right after we've landed, because

I go straight on to Chicago or somewhere, but the thought of five days on a boat with Judson Phipps haunting me like a family spectre gives me gooseflesh.'

Joe, with a sombre note in his voice, informed her that in his opinion these precautions were unnecessary, Judson having other commitments, but she was not to be convinced. Not even his story of the contiguous deck chairs impressed her. Judson, she said, might be festooned in girls at the moment, but he was not yet aware of her presence on board. When he did become aware, she predicted, he would forsake all others and resume his place in her hair. Joe, she said, must not fail her.

'Oh, all right,' said Joe.

It was not how he had originally planned to pass his time during the voyage, but nothing mattered now.

In the printed brochures put out by transatlantic steamship companies the discerning reader always seems to detect a note of uneasiness. The writers are trying not to be pessimistic, but they are plainly prepared for the worst and keeping their fingers crossed. They hint nervously at the possibility of typhoons and waterspouts and there is always, they feel, the chance of mutiny on the high seas and piracy. It is pleasant, therefore, to be able to report that the S.S. *Atlantic* won through to the final day of the voyage without disaster. No water had spouted, no typhoon had blown, no pirates had put in an appearance, and so far from being mutinous the crew had been amiability itself. If the vessel's luck held for a few more hours, she would be safe.

The last day of an ocean voyage is usually an occasion for universal rejoicing. The Captain is happy because he is sure now that he has not taken the wrong turning and is going to fetch up in Africa. The doctor is congratulating himself on having come through one more orgy of deck tennis and shuffleboard without committing himself to anything definite. The stewards are totting up prospective tips, always an invigorating task, while those of their number who are bigamists have long since got over the pang of parting from their wives and children in Southampton and are looking forward with bright anticipation to meeting once more their wives and children in New York.

Nevertheless, not all the lips on board the *Atlantic* were wreathed in smiles. Joe Cardinal's were not. Nor were Dinah Biddle's. And least of all were those of Freddie Threepwood as he stood watching the after-dinner dancing in the lounge.

Much had occurred to prevent Freddie being at his blithest. For one thing, Mr Pinkney had saddened him by failing to respond to Treatment A. He had eyed Freddie stolidly as he consumed his sample biscuit, but had shown no signs of having got the message. He had looked throughout like the fat proprietor of a department store watching a rather tedious parlour trick, and Freddie's thoughts had strayed nostalgically back to the Wilks Brothers of Manchester, both of whom had been electrified by the demonstration.

For another thing, his wife Aggie had informed him by wireless that he would not find her at their Great Neck home on his arrival, for she was spending a few weeks with her father at Westhampton Beach. She had expressed herself delighted at his early return, but regretted that she could not disappoint Daddy, a feat which Freddie could have performed without a qualm, indeed, for Mr Donaldson was a little difficult at times, with a good deal of pleasure.

And finally, like Dinah Biddle, he had been mystified and exasperated by the peculiar behaviour of Joe Cardinal. For four days Joe, who should have been inseparable from Dinah, had been inseparable from Arlene Pinkney. He was dancing with her now, and the spectacle affected Freddie with an indignation similar to that which he felt when somebody praised Peterson's Pup Food in his presence. As the music stopped and Arlene, detaching herself, went off, no doubt to her stateroom to do some packing, he swooped down on Joe like a hawk that intends to demand a full explanation.

He did not beat about the bush. With no preamble he asked Joe what was the idea, and when Joe said 'Idea of what?' he replied that Joe knew what the idea of what was all right. He found himself unable, he said, to fathom Joe's mental processes. Here, he said, was a man who had thrown up his job, thereby ruining any chance he had ever had of inducing old Pinkney to kick in, simply in order to be on the same ocean liner as the girl he loved – call her Girl A – and all he had done since the start of the voyage was stick like Scotch tape to another girl – call her Girl B. Why? Freddie asked. Was this, he demanded, a system?

Joe's reply was prompt and more than merely tinged with bitterness. What, he asked, was the point of trying to get so much as a word with what Freddie called Girl A when she so obviously preferred the society of Judson Phipps? So when his cousin Arlene had begged him to take on the role of chaperone in order to ensure that she was never left alone with this Phipps, he had seen no reason not to oblige her.

Now that he lived in America Freddie no longer wore the monocle which had been a feature of his London years. His father-in-law had happened to ask him one day would he please remove that damned window pane from his eye because it made him look like something out of a musical comedy chorus, and he always respected his father-in-law's wishes. But had it been functioning at this moment, it would undoubtedly have parted from its moorings, for at this statement of Joe's his eyebrows rose sharply.

'This Pinkney beazel asked you to be her bodyguard?'

'That's what it amounted to.'

'Well, fry me for an oyster! This opens up a new line of thought. Wait here,' said Freddie. 'I'll be back in a minute. I just want to have a word with Juddy.'

His search for Judson ended in the bar, which curiously enough was the first place he tried. Declining the other's invitation to join him in one for the tonsils, he came without delay to the *res*.

'Juddy,' he said, 'I want you to throw your mind back for a moment. You remember what we were talking about the day you came on board, about enlisting the services of a bodyguard?'

Judson said he had not forgotten.

'You went ahead with the scheme?'

'Sure. After you let me down I got Dinah Biddle to take on the assignment.'

'And that was the only reason you've been closeted with her throughout?'

'That's right.'

'No question of the sex motif? No idea in your mind of starring her in your next breach of promise case?'

'Certainly not. I explained the whole situation to her at the outset, and she thoroughly understood my motives. I owe that girl more than I can say, Freddie, and I'd like to give her some little present as a reward for her services. But what little present? She's not the sort of girl who would accept anything that cost a lot. Do you think I could get something at the ship's shop?'

'You mean chocolates?'

'I was thinking more of those weird animal things they sell

there – toy dogs and cats and Mickey Mice and so on. Girls like those. My second breach of promise case had a whole collection, and when I told her everything was off and there would be no centre aisleing she threw them at me one by one. Would that be all right for Dinah, do you think?'

'Make her day, I should imagine. Have you any idea where I can find her?'

'She's on the boat deck. What do you want her for?'

'I am hoping to adjust a rather tricky tangled hearts sequence.'

'I don't follow you.'

'You don't have to. So long, Juddy.'

'So long. Oh, by the way, about that necklace of Julie's. I shall have to give it to Pinkney tonight. I hope it doesn't upset your plans.'

'Don't worry about that,' said Freddie bitterly. 'I've no further interest in Pinkney. I've written him off as a prospect. If a man can't listen to reason, there's no sense in bothering about him. One crosses him off the list.'

Joe, sitting in the lounge after Freddie had left him, woke a few moments later from a dark reverie to find his cousin Arlene at his side. Her presence surprised him, for he had supposed that she had retired for the night.

It had always puzzled him a little that in all the years he had known her he had never fallen in love with this cousin of his, for he could see that it was the logical thing for any young man to do. But there had always existed between them a pleasant camaraderie, and while he would have preferred to be alone he was not displeased to see her.

'I thought you had gone to bed,' he said.

'No, I went to see Father.'

She settled herself on the settee beside him and plunged into the subject she had come to discuss with a directness which would have won the approval of Mr Donaldson of Donaldson's Dog Joy.

'That money of yours he's holding. You've had several tries at getting it out of him, haven't you?'

'One or two.'

'But no luck?'

'None.'

'Do you know why?'

The answer to that was simple – viz. that Mr Pinkney was a pig-headed old bohunkus to whose finer feelings it was futile to appeal, because he had not got any, but he forbore to explain this lest he wound a possibly loving daughter. He said No, he did not know why.

'I'll tell you. Because you probably saw him during office hours. That was your strategic error. What you didn't realize was that Father during office hours and Father after a good dinner are two substantially different personalities. I don't approve of his dining habits and if I've told him so once I've told him a hundred times, but there's no getting away from it that six courses including caviare have a remarkable effect on him. After such a meal, accompanied by champagne and topped off with old brandy, he becomes so mellowed that a child could play with him. Whereas if the child was ass enough to try to touch him for a trifle before the dinner bell rang, he would probably bite a piece out of its leg. I imagine you have grasped where all this is heading. Condensing it from a drive to a short putt, I went to him just now and told him that if you were starting out in a strange country and in a city like New York where everything is twice as expensive as in London, you would need some extra cash, and he said he would give you that money that's coming to you. I don't say he said it immediately. I had to reason with him. But I was so grateful to you for keeping Judson Phipps out of my hair these last days that I didn't spare myself in the way of eloquence. So that's the final score. He's parting.'

For a long moment Joe sat speechless. He was thinking, as the late Thomas Hardy used to do, how ironical life was. Life's little ironies always exasperated Thomas Hardy, and they exasperated Joe. For years he had been looking forward to the day when he would get that money, and now that he had got it, what was the use of it? Girls like Dinah Biddle, when they have Phipps Suspender millions in view, do not turn from them to men who have inherited comparatively small legacies from their aunts; they do the sensible, practical thing and stick to the source of those millions like, to borrow Freddie's powerful image, Scotch tape.

But though what Arlene had been instrumental in securing for him was nothing but Dead Sea fruit, it was only polite to thank her, and he did so.

'Just the Pinkney service. Do you want to tread the measure again?'

'I don't think so.'

'Then I'll be getting along,' said Arlene. 'I always like to do some practice putting into a tooth glass before turning in.'

She had scarcely departed with this praiseworthy end in view, when Freddie appeared.

Freddie's hair was a little disordered by the breeze on the boat deck, and on his face was the self-satisfied look which go-getters wear when they have go-got.

'Well, Joe,' he said, coming to the point with a promptness equal to Arlene's, 'you'll be glad to hear that I have made your path straight. You have the green light. Carry on and fear nothing.'

Joe found him obscure. He expressed a wish to know what he was talking about.

'I'll tell you what I'm talking about. You and young Dinah Biddle. I've just been revealing to her your motives in attaching yourself to Arlene Pinkney. I have also seen Juddy, and I have cleared up that angle. She was merely bodyguarding him as you were bodyguarding Arlene P. One of those laughable misunderstandings.'

'What!'

'You may well say "What!"'

'Do you mean—?'

'I don't see how I can put it plainer. You will find La Biddle on the boat deck, and I rather gathered from the way she looked and the emotional nature of her breathing that she will be in co-operative mood. But before you go there are one or two things we ought to thresh out in debate. First, we must ask ourselves if you are really doing the square thing in asking her to marry you. Do you mind me being frank?'

'What are you going to be frank about?'

'Your financial position.'

'Oh, that?'

'Yes, that. Let's face it. You've no job and no money, and you won't have any money for another three years. Is it fair to ask her to wait all that time? Why do you smile?'

'I wasn't smiling, I was beaming. Stirring things have been happening since you left me, Freddie. Condensing it from a drive to a short putt, Arlene has persuaded Pinkney to release my money. I shan't be rich, but I shall be able to afford matrimony on a modest scale.'

Freddie gaped.

'Is this official?'

'Arlene said it was. And now, if you will excuse me—'

'But wait. There's another thing we ought to give a thought to – your method of wooing. Don't forget that you will have to cram into a few short hours the suit-pressing which should have been stretched over five days. You'll have to work quick, and this being so I strongly recommend the Ickenham System.'

'The what?'

'As outlined by old Ickenham, Pongo Twistleton's Uncle Fred. Pongo explained it to me once, and I think I can quote the old buster's words verbatim. Stride up to the subject, Ickenham said, and grab her by the wrist. Then, ignoring her struggles, if any, clasp her to your bosom and shower kisses on her upturned face. You needn't say much – just "My mate" or something of that sort. And in grabbing her by the wrist don't behave as if you were handling a delicate piece of china. Grip firmly and waggle her about a bit.'

Joe had never had the pleasure of meeting the fifth Earl of Ickenham, Pongo Twistleton's redoubtable Uncle Fred, and he was sorry not to have done so, for it was plain to him that they were kindred souls who thought along the same lines. Grabbing Dinah Biddle and waggling her about a bit was the very mode of approach he had had in mind. With no further words he hurried away, and when we say hurried, we mean precisely that. Freddie, watching him disappear, was reminded of a jack rabbit he had once encountered while selling dog biscuits out Nebraska way, and as he adjusted himself comfortably to the cushions of the settee he was conscious of feeling all in a glow. There is nothing that so induces this sensation as the knowledge that one has done one's day's good deed. Boy Scouts, habituated to performing acts of kindness, probably in time grow blasé and lose that first electric thrill, but to the novice it is as if a soothing mustard plaster had been applied to his soul.

He was still glowing when a 'Say, Freddie' at his elbow jerked him out of his pleasant thoughts, and he saw that he had Judson Phipps with him.

Judson was carrying, tucked under his arm, a furry object which was probably its creator's idea of a cinnamon bear, and on his face in addition to his horn-rimmed spectacles there was a look that suggested that something had occurred to perplex him.

'Got a moment, Freddie?' he said, and Freddie replied that he had no immediate calls on his time and would be happy to give Judson audience.

'What's on your mind, Juddy?'

'It's this fellow Cardinal.'

'What about him?'

'He's been acting very strangely. I went up to the boat deck to give this bear or whatever it is to Dinah Biddle and there he was, kissing her.'

'I see nothing unbalanced in that.'

'I do. It struck me as odd. Considering that he came on this boat simply in order to press his suit with Arlene Pinkney.'

'What gave you that idea?'

'You said so yourself.'

'I didn't say anything of the sort. His objective from the kick-off was the Biddle.'

'But he's been with Arlene ever since we left Cherbourg.'

'Oh, I can explain that. There's a man on board whom she wanted to keep away from her and she drafted Joe to act as interference. Same idea as you had when you engaged Dinah Biddle's services.'

Judson was astounded. His spectacles trembled on their base.

'You're kidding!'

'No. Joe told me.'

'Well, I'll be darned. Who was the man?'

'Ah, that we shall probably never know.'

'Must be a repulsive sort of specimen.'

'So one would suppose.'

Judson lit a relieved cigarette.

'You've taken a weight off my mind. I'm very fond of Dinah, and I wouldn't like to think she had fallen under the spell of a smooth operator who would play her up and break her heart. But Cardinal's okay, isn't he? He'll—'

'Do right by our Nell? Yes, nothing to worry about in that respect.'

Judson was looking grave. A thought had struck him.

'What about the money end of it? When you were selling me that picture of his, you told me he hadn't a nickel.'

'He hadn't then. He's getting some from Pinkney.'

'Pinkney?' Judson could make nothing of this. 'Are you sure you haven't got the name wrong? Pinkney's one-way pockets are a byword in the circles in which he moves. I can't see him handing out money.'

'It's Joe's money. Pinkney's his trustee.'

'Oh, I see.'

'For years he's refused to let Joe have the stuff, but tonight he agreed to come across.'

'You don't say!'

'So I learn from a source close to him.'

'Very remarkable.'

'Very.'

'But does him credit.'

'Yes. And now, Juddy, I must ask you to leave me. You're interrupting my glowing.'

'Your what?'

'When you came up, I was glowing.'

'What about?'

'Oh, nothing special,' said Freddie. 'Just glowing.'

Judson, as he removed himself, was also feeling quite a glow. It was caused by the discovery that his future brother-in-law Arnold Pinkney, whom he had always supposed to be totally lacking in the milk of human kindness, was in reality well stocked up with it. He had told Freddie that he and Mr Pinkney 'got on all right', but this was merely because he kept out of the latter's way as much as he could. Privately he considered Mr Pinkney a dangerous specimen and had never suspected him of having a softer side. As Freddie had said, he was a sentimentalist, and what a motion picture magnate would have called The Cardinal Story had touched him. This evidence that it had also touched Mr Pinkney warmed his heart and it seemed to him that it would be a graceful act to seek him out and tell him how greatly his magnanimity was appreciated.

He found him in his stateroom reading a balance sheet.

'Oh, it's you,' said Mr Pinkney, plainly resentful at being interrupted in this congenial task and by Judson of all people.

In becoming betrothed to Judson's sister, Mr Pinkney had realized that he must accept Judson as part of the package deal, but that did not mean that he had to give him an effusive welcome when he came uninvited to his stateroom.

'What's that damned thing?' he asked, eyeing the cinnamon bear with obvious dislike.

'Just a small tribute of my esteem for Dinah Biddle,' Judson explained. 'I think she'll like it, don't you? Its head screws off and you put candy inside and pass it around at parties, causing great fun and laughter.'

'Well, don't point it at me.'

'I'll put it down on this chair here while we talk.'

The last three words struck Mr Pinkney as sinister.

'Are you intending to make a long stay?'

'No, no, I shan't keep you a minute. I just came to give you something Julie asked me to slip to you. But first I would like to tell you that in my opinion you're doing the big, generous thing in giving Cardinal that money. I had the story from Freddie Threepwood and was greatly impressed. Many men in your position would have been sore at him for throwing up his job at the bank and dashing off after a girl just because he couldn't bear being parted from her. But you took the romantic view. Love's love, you said to yourself, and in my opinion it was the right spirit.'

Judson paused. He was interested to see that the recipient of these stately compliments was turning purple. Not so purple as he was going to turn later when the subject of the necklace was broached, but purple enough to cause concern.

'Do you mean—' said Mr Pinkney, and he too paused. 'Do you mean to tell me—' He paused again. 'Do you mean to tell me,' he demanded, at last becoming coherent, 'that my nephew Joseph has given up the post I got for him at the New Asiatic Bank and has come on this ship because he is infatuated with some girl?'

'That's it. I thought you knew.'

'Guk!' said Mr Pinkney, or something that sounded like 'Guk!' and made for the door. 'I am going to find that young idiot and tell him what I think of him,' said Mr Pinkney, and was gone with an agility remarkable in so stout a man.

Left alone, Judson removed his spectacles and polished them with a thoughtful handkerchief, his habit when life was not running smoothly. He found the sudden purpling of Mr Pinkney's face and the abruptness of his departure disturbing, and the conviction had begun to steal over him that he had said the wrong thing. Even to him, though he was not a quick thinker, it had become plain that in supposing that Mr Pinkney had been touched by Joe Cardinal's romantic story he had erred. So far from touching him, it seemed to have aroused his worst passions and there could be little doubt that if and when he found Joe Cardinal, their encounter would for the latter not be an agreeable one.

Heavy breathing sounded outside the open door, and Mr Pinkney reappeared. Judson regarded him anxiously.

'Did you find him?'

'I did, and I told him that if he thinks he is going to get any money from me, he is very much mistaken.'

'You aren't going to give him his money?'

'I am not.'

'Then,' said Judson severely, 'you ought to be ashamed of yourself, and I hope those Customs guys catch you with your pants down and you get sent up the river for ten years.'

'What are you talking about?'

'This.'

'What's that?'

'A necklace Julie bought in Paris. She gave it to me to give to you to smuggle through the Customs.'

'What!'

'And here's a letter she wrote that goes with it.'

If Judson had been offering him a cobra di capello, or some other poisonous serpent, Mr Pinkney might have looked more perturbed, but not much. In predicting that his face would take on an even deeper tinge of mauve than it had worn as he listened to the Cardinal Story, Judson had made no miscalculation.

'She disapproves of paying duty,' he explained, 'and I don't have to tell you what the duty on a chunk of ice like this would tot up to. As I see it,' said Judson, feeling that Mr Pinkney would like to know where he stood, 'three courses are open to you. You can disregard Julie's wishes, which I wouldn't advise because you know what Julie's like when her wishes are disregarded, or you can have a shot at smuggling the thing in, which, as I say, will probably lead to your being jugged for several years, or you can pick up the tab yourself, paying the duty out of your own—'

'Get out!' said Mr Pinkney, and Judson did so. He had plenty more to say, but this did not seem to him the moment.

It was probably the relief of being freed from his future brother-in-law's company that after a short while enabled Mr Pinkney to start thinking with a certain measure of coherence. Judson, goggling at him through his spectacles like some rare fish in an aquarium, had precluded thought. He was able now to examine the problem confronting him with something of the efficiency which he brought to those which were always cropping up during business hours.

It was, he could not but see, a problem that called for the exercise of his fullest powers. His opinion of Judson's intelligence was low, but he was unable to deny that in his parting speech that not very gifted young man had spoken sound sense, outlining the position of affairs with a lucidity which would have done credit to someone with a far higher I.Q.

There were, he had said, three courses which he, Pinkney, could pursue, and he, Pinkney, found it difficult to decide which of them he liked least. At the thought of what his betrothed would have to say if he refused to carry out her instructions his flesh crept; but so it did at the thought of being arrested for smuggling. And as for paying the duty out of his own pocket, it became positively agile at the prospect. He had always been a careful man with his money.

What he wanted was a fourth alternative, and there did not appear to be one.

It was as he reached this depressing conclusion that his eye was caught by the letter from his betrothed which Judson had laid on the bed table, and he picked it up and opened it. He was not expecting to derive any solace from it, but reading it was something to do.

It was a short letter, written by a practical woman who believed in keeping to the point. Smuggling, she said, was pie. All he had to do was go to the ship's shop and buy a Mickey Mouse – or, if he preferred it, a Felix the Cat – and go ashore with the necklace in its interior. She could testify to the efficiency of this routine, for she had tried it with gratifying success. The only reason she was not handling the thing herself, she explained, was that her purchases in Paris would have made her a marked woman, for these darned shops always notified the Customs people who had bought what, and they went through your belongings with a fine tooth comb. He, of course, would have none of this inconvenience. She concluded with a cheery 'Best of luck' and said that she was looking forward to seeing him again.

'Guk!' said Mr Pinkney, and flung himself into a chair. And as he did so he became conscious of an odd feeling that he was not alone. He seemed to sense an unseen presence. It was as if he were being watched by ghostly eyes, which was curious when you came to think of it because it was unlikely that a stateroom on the C deck of a reputable ocean liner would be haunted.

Then, scanning his surroundings more closely, he saw that his room mate was not a spectre but the woolly cinnamon bear which Judson, when getting out as requested, had omitted to take with him.

Most of Mr Pinkney's business successes had been the outcome of flashes of inspiration, and it was a flash of inspiration that lightened his darkness now, though he would have been the first to admit that he owed much to his Julia and her letter. He had remembered something Judson had said on entering the stateroom.

It was not often that Judson's remarks lingered in people's minds, but his words on this occasion came back to Mr Pinkney as if played on a record. Its head screws off and you put candy inside, he had said, speaking of this cinnamon bear, and he had mentioned that he was giving it to Mr Pinkney's secretary Dinah Biddle as a token of his esteem.

What Customs official, Mr Pinkney reasoned, was going to enquire too closely into the cinnamon bear of a charming young girl whose honest face and modest secretarial position obviously placed her above suspicion. The fellow would probably not even know that the heads of ship's shop cinnamon bears do screw off. Mr Pinkney was a man of wide experience and knowledge of the world, and this was the first time he had learned of it.

To remove the creature's head, insert the necklace and screw the head on again was with him the work of an instant – which was fortunate, for he had scarcely completed the operation when there was a knock on the door and Judson entered.

'I forgot my bear,' said Judson, speaking haughtily, for they had parted on bad terms.

He was surprised to find Mr Pinkney quite genial.

'Ah, yes, there it is. You are giving it to Miss Biddle?'

'That's right.'

'I am sure she will be pleased.'

'She ought to be. Have you decided what to do about Julie's necklace?'

'I'm thinking it over,' said Mr Pinkney.

'He told me he was thinking it over,' said Judson.

'Well, he seems to have thought to some purpose,' said Freddie. 'He's as calm as a halibut on ice.'

The S.S. *Atlantic* had come to journey's end, and they were standing in the P–T section of the New York Customs sheds, watching Mr Pinkney as a stern-faced man in uniform examined his baggage. And, indeed, there was nothing in Mr Pinkney's aspect to suggest that that baggage harboured a guilty secret which might at any moment be exposed to the pitiless light of day by a flick of the inspector's fingers. Despite the fact that the latter, as deficient in simple faith as he was in Norman blood, was being very thorough in his researches, his face was untroubled and his whole demeanour, as Freddie had said, as nonchalant as that of a fish on a fishmonger's slab.

His placidity smote Freddie like a blow.

'There's no justice in the world,' he complained. 'There stands a man who thinks Peterson's Pup Food superior to Donaldson's Dog Joy and on top of that refuses to give Joe Cardinal the money he is morally entitled to, and does the wrath of heaven strike him? Not by a jugful. With a light laugh he flouts the most sacred laws of the United States of America and gets away with it. See! The bloodhound has let him through. We know that necklace must be concealed somewhere in his effects, but he's managed to tuck it away so shrewdly that even an experienced Customs inspector failed to find it. It's uncanny. Well, I'm getting out of this,' said Freddie, surveying his surroundings with an unappreciative eye. 'I always say these Customs sheds are all right for a visit, but I wouldn't live here if you gave me the place. I'm going to take a taxi to Great Neck and drop my lighter things and get my car and drive back and have lunch at the Plaza. Perhaps you will join me?'

Judson was obliged to refuse the invitation. He had, he said, a date.

'But you only landed about twenty minutes ago.'

'I fixed it up just now on the phone.'

'A girl?'

'Yes.'

'Well, God bless you. Then I'll be pushing along. Hullo,' said Freddie, his attention drawn for the first time to a cinnamon bear of repellent aspect which sat on the top of Judson's steamer trunk. 'I thought you were giving that thing to Dinah Biddle.'

'She didn't want it.'

'I'm not surprised. Ashamed to be seen in public with it, eh? What are your plans for its future?'

'I was thinking of dropping it in a litter basket.'

'You can do better than that. Give it to me.'

'You don't mean you want the beastly thing?'

'Not for myself,' Freddie hastened to assure him. 'But I've a friend named Bream Rockmeteller who recently added a Junior to the strength ... well, of course, actually Mrs Bream did most of the heavy work, but Bream gets his name on the bills ... and an object like that will be just the infant's cup of tea. I don't know if you've noticed it, but all babies are practically dotty. Where you and I shrink from this cinnamon bear, the young Rockmeteller will be all over it. No accounting for tastes. Right, then, let me have it.'

* * *

Freddie's bijou residence in Great Neck was near what had been the Soundview golf course till the developers took it over, and a swift taxi brought him there in a short space of time. His return to the metropolis was delayed for some twenty minutes by Lana Tuttle, the cook whom Mrs Freddie had left in charge. Lana was an immigrant from the Bottleton East section of London and was anxious for information as to how the old town had been getting on since she left it. She also had interesting local news to impart – items of public interest such as that there had been a burglary at the Witherspoons down the road and others of a more private nature such as that she was going to wash her hair that afternoon. It was a little past one o'clock when Freddie entered the Plaza's dining-room and began his lunch. And he had just finished it when, like Mr Pinkney in his state-room, he became aware of a presence. Looking up, he saw that he had been joined by Judson Phipps. He greeted him cordially.

'Welcome to the Empire City, Juddy. Have you been lunching here? I didn't see you.'

'We were over in a corner.'

'Where's the girl?'

'She left. She had to go to a rehearsal,' said Judson. He took a chair. His manner was grave. 'Do you know what?'

'What?'

'We're engaged.'

'You are? When did this happen?'

'Over the coffee.'

'You work quick, don't you? Well, heartiest congratulations and all that.'

'Thanks. But I'm beginning to wonder if I've done the smart thing.'

'Already?'

'It came over me as I was putting her in her taxi. I'm not sure she's my type.'

'Still, she isn't Arlene Pinkney.'

'No, there's that,' said Judson, cheering up a little. 'But I think I could use a drink. One for you as well?'

'No, thanks. I've got to phone Aggie. I tried to get her before lunch, but she was out.'

Freddie's route to the telephone booths lay through the lobby, and as he approached the newsstand his eye fell on a man buying a paper there, and he was struck by his extraordinary likeness to Mr Bunting of the legal firm of Bunting and Satterthwaite. Looking more closely, he saw that the resemblance was due to the fact that the other *was* Mr Bunting, the last person he would have expected to see in mid-town Manhattan.

'You?' he said, astounded.

'Ah, Freddie. I thought we might run into one another before long.'

'But what are you doing over here?'

Mr Bunting had a ready explanation.

'If you remember, when we parted I was about to get your father-in-law on the transatlantic telephone to discuss with him the idea of settling that law suit of his. Being a man whose slogan is "Do it now", he asked me to fly over and confer with him, which I was very happy to do. They tell me at the office that he's out of town.'

'He's down at Westhampton Beach. I was planning to go there this afternoon. Give you a lift, if you like.'

'That would be capital.'

'We might start as soon as I've phoned Aggie. How long will it take you to pack?'

'Not long.'

'Then I'll meet you in the lobby. We'll stop off for a moment at my place in Great Neck and pick up my things and on the way I'll tell you something about Arnold Pinkney that will make you sit up a bit. Oh yes, and also the latest about Judson Phipps. How about lunch? Have you had yours?'

'Just my usual glass of hot water,' said Mr Bunting. 'They serve an excellent hot water here.'

Judson had had his drink and was taking a slightly more cheerful view of his matrimonial future. He was still not quite sure that he had done the right thing in becoming betrothed to Miss Elaine Jepp of the personnel of the ensemble at the Alvin Theatre, but, as Freddie had said, she was not Arlene Pinkney, and it was in quite a tranquil frame of mind that he paid the waiter, asked him which of the two contestants for the forthcoming light-heavyweight contest he fancied, and sauntered out into the lobby. He had scarcely reached it when the door of one of the elevators opened and Mr Pinkney shot out – a purple and agitated Mr Pinkney who attached himself to his coat sleeve with a feverish grasp and asked him where that Thing was.

'Thing?' said Judson, not unnaturally at something of a loss, and Mr Pinkney explained that he was alluding to the bear or whatever it was that he had brought into his stateroom on the previous night. He understood, he said, from Miss Biddle that she had given it back to him.

'Oh, that?' said Judson. 'Yes, she didn't seem to want it.'

'Well, I want it. Where is it?'

'I gave it to Freddie Threepwood.'

'What!'

'He was going to hand it on to the infant son of some buddy of his.'

It was impossible for Mr Pinkney actually to turn pale, but his face became noticeably less mauve.

'You must get it back from him.'

'Why?'

'Never mind why. I have urgent need of it.'

'I think he took it to his house at Great Neck.'

'Where is Great Neck?'

'Just outside New York.'

'Do you know where Threepwood lives?'

'Oh, sure. I've been there lots of times.'

'Then go now. Hire a car and drive there immediately. I can't go myself. I have an important conference in my suite here this afternoon.'

As Judson steered his hired car through the traffic in the direction of Great Neck, he found himself wondering, not for the first time, what was the peculiar quality in Arnold Pinkney that made it impossible for a fellow to meet his most unreasonable demands with a curt 'Go fry an egg'. He was still wondering as he turned off the main road and drew up outside the Threepwood home.

It also perplexed him that Mr Pinkney should be entertaining this positive yearning for the society of a synthetic cinnamon bear for which at their first meeting he had shown such distaste. If ever the stout proprietor of a department store had given the impression of not being fond of cinnamon bears, this stout proprietor was that stout proprietor.

These were deep waters, and Judson soon gave up the attempt to plumb them, for sustained thinking always made his head ache. Alighting from the car, he rang the front door bell. Nothing happened. He rang again, and once more nothing happened. The house appeared to be uninhabited, and there presented itself the problem of what to do next.

There were windows on each side of the front door, and peering through them he saw suitcases. And on top of one of the suitcases was the cinnamon bear, its customary silly smile on its face, and it suddenly occurred to Judson that in the middle of the day like this the front door would probably not be locked. He tested it, and found that his supposition had been correct.

He did not hesitate. If this had been some stranger's house, it would have been different, but a lifelong friend like Freddie would naturally have no objection to him treating the place as his own. 'Go to it,' Freddie would have said, and he went to it. And he had just picked up the cinnamon bear and was about to return with it to his car, when a voice behind him, speaking with a startling abruptness, said 'Hands up!', and turning he perceived a young woman in a pink dressing gown and slippers. Her mouth was set in a determined line, and her tow-coloured hair was adorned with gleaming curling pins. In her right hand, pointed at his head, she held a revolver.

The burglary at the Witherspoons down the road had made a deep impression on Lana Tuttle, causing her to purchase from her own private funds the firearm without which in her opinion no American home was complete. Only this morning she had offered to give the mail man attractive odds that marauders would be around at Chez Threepwood before either of them was much older, and here, just as she had predicted, was one of them, a nasty, furtive, spectacled miscreant probably well known to the police, who are notorious for their fondness for low company.

It is not given to every girl who makes prophecies to find those prophecies fulfilled within a few short hours of their utterance, and the emotions of Lana Tuttle were akin to those of one who sees the long shot romp in ahead of the field or who unexpectedly solves the crossword puzzle. Mixed, therefore, with her disapproval of Judson was a feeling almost of gratitude to him for being there. Of fear she felt no trace. She presented the pistol with a firm hand.

One calls it a pistol for the sake of technical accuracy. To Judson's startled senses it appeared like a bazooka, and so deeply did he feel regarding it that he made it the subject of his opening remark – which, by all the laws of etiquette, should have been a graceful apology for and explanation of his intrusion.

'You shouldn't point guns at people,' he urged.

'Well, you shouldn't come breaking into people's houses,' said Lana, and Judson felt a good deal reassured by the level firmness of her tone. This was plainly not one of those neurotic, fluttering females whose index finger cannot safely be permitted within a foot of a pistol trigger.

'I only came to get something.'

'I'll bet you did.'

'This bear. Freddie wants it, Mrs Threepwood.'

'Who are you calling Mrs Threepwood?'

'Aren't you Mrs Threepwood?'

'No.'

'You aren't married to Mr Threepwood?'

'No, I'm not.'

Judson was a broadminded young man.

'Ah, well, in the sight of God, no doubt.'

'I'm the cook.'

'Oh, that explains it.'

'Explains what?'

'It seemed a trifle odd for a moment that you should be popping around here with your hair in curlers and your little white ankles peeping out from under a dressing gown.'

'Coo!' said Lana in a modest flutter. She performed a swift adjustment of the garment's folds. 'Keep your hands up.'

'But I'm getting cramp.'

'Serves you right.'

'But listen, my dear little girl—'

'Less of it!' said Lana austerely. 'It's a bit thick if a girl can't catch a burglar without having him start to flirt with her. I'm going to call the cops.'

'And have them see you in curling pins?'

'What's wrong with my curling pins?'

'Nothing, nothing,' said Judson hastily. 'I admire them.'

'And they won't see me in curling pins, because I shan't call them till I've dressed. I'm going to put you in the cellar and lock you in till they come. Skip lively.'

Judson did as directed.

When coping with the New York traffic, Freddie was always a driver of silent habit. It was not till the Triborough Bridge was passed and the road had become somewhat clearer that he embarked on the narrative which he had predicted would make Mr Bunting sit up a bit, starting Chapter One with the tale of Arnold Pinkney's smuggling activities.

'I wouldn't have thought it could be done,' he concluded. 'There was Pinkney, his baggage literally bursting with diamond necklaces, and there was this Customs bloke, all eagerness to catch him bending, and not a thing happened. The trunks were opened, the bloke went through them like a dose of salts, and what ensued? Not a trace of any diamond necklace. Where, one asks oneself, could he have concealed the ruddy thing? It's inexplicable. Old Pinkney isn't a man I'm fond of . . . he's utterly unsound on dog biscuits, and he refuses to loosen up for poor old Joe . . . but I don't mind telling you all this has given me a grudging respect for him. You have to take your hat off to a man who can do down the New York Customs.'

Mr Bunting agreed that it was a feat to be proud of, and expressed surprise that Mr Pinkney should have been capable of it. It just showed, he said, that there is unsuspected good in all of us.

'Well, you promised to make me sit up, my dear Freddie,' he said. 'And I am sitting up. Have you similarly sensational news to tell me of Judson Phipps? You hinted, if you remember, that you could a tale unfold about him whose lightest word would harrow up my soul, freeze my young – or, rather, elderly – blood and make my two eyes, like stars, start from their spheres. What is the latest concerning Judson?'

'Oh, Juddy? Yes, I was coming to that. You know he's a two-time loser?'

'I beg your pardon?'

'I mean he's had two breach of promise cases already. Well, he's engaged again.'

'You don't say!'

'I don't know who she is, but he took her to lunch today and proposed over the coffee.'

Mr Bunting blessed his soul.

'Amazing! The effect of the sea air, no doubt. I have often speculated,' said Mr Bunting, 'as to why our Judson does these things. Is it because he is unusually susceptible or does he ask them to marry him just because he can't think of anything to say and feels he must keep the conversation going somehow? Well, more work for Bunting and Satterthwaite.'

'You think there's another breach of promise case in the offing?'

'Inevitable, I should say.'

'He may not want to get out of this one.'

'I doubt it. Did you ever see Gilbert and Sullivan's *Trial by Jury*? I played the Usher in *Trial by Jury* once in my younger days. At a village in Hampshire in aid of the church organ fund.'

'I wish I'd been there.'

'Yes, you missed an unforgettable experience. But what I was going to say was that Judson Phipps always reminds me of the Defendant in that operetta. To refresh your memory, he was constantly getting engaged and then changing his mind and sneaking out of it. Judson does the same, and it always ends in him having to come to Bunting and Satterthwaite to arrange a settlement.'

Mr Bunting fell into a reverie, no doubt on the subject of prospective fees, and did not speak again till the car arrived at its destination, when he said that Freddie had a nice place here, to which Freddie responded that it was a home and he liked it.

They entered the living-room, conversing amiably, and up in her bedroom Lana Tuttle, removing the last of the hair curlers, heard their voices and burned with justifiable indignation. That a solitary burglar should have invaded her privacy was more or less what a girl had to expect if she left Bottleton East and came to America, but a group or flock of marauders, chatting with one another as if the place belonged to them, was too much. Seizing her revolver, she descended the stairs three at a time and burst into the living-room.

'Hands up!' she cried. 'Oh, it's you, Mr T. Sorry, ducks, I thought you were a burglar.'

'At this time in the afternoon?'

'They keep all hours. I've got one in the cellar now. I'll bring him up, shall I, so you can have a look at him.'

'Tell me, Freddie,' said Mr Bunting, 'is this sort of thing the normal run of life in America? It is my first visit to that great country, and I should like to know the ropes. Sugar daddies, I learn from the Press, are frequently surprised in love nests, but does the domestic help go about with guns as a general rule and deposit burglars in cellars?'

'If you ask me, I think the girl has flipped her cork.'

'The expression is new to me, but I gather that you feel that she is mentally unbalanced. Do you?'

'Looks like it. What on earth would a burglar be doing ... Good Lord! Juddy!'

Judson had entered, slightly soiled from his sojourn among the coal, and he was closely followed by Lana Tuttle, who seemed to be prodding him in the small of the back with her weapon. At the sight of Freddie his sombre face lightened, excluding the portions of it which were covered with coal dust.

'Freddie! Thank God!'

'What on earth is all this about, Juddy?'

'It's a long story. Would you mind telling this girl to take her damned pistol out of my ribs.'

'It's all right, Lana. This is a friend of mine.'

'Well, why didn't he say so? I caught him getting away with your plaything.'

'My what?'

'That bear,' said Lana Tuttle. 'If it is a bear.'

'I can explain everything, Freddie. Just get rid of this female.

That's all I ask. Oh, hullo, Mr Bunting,' said Judson, seeing him for the first time. 'What are you doing in America?'

'A business trip. But I'm not too engrossed in my business to listen to what should be an interesting story.'

'Nor me,' said Freddie. 'You can leave us, Lana.'

'Pop off?'

'That's right.'

'Well, if you think it's safe, love,' said Lana Tuttle.

When Judson told a story, as he sometimes did when flushed with wine, it was not often that he riveted the attention of his hearers, they being inclined to interrupt at an early point in the proceedings and start to tell what they considered better ones, but on this occasion it would not be too much to say that he held his audience spellbound.

All Freddie could find to say, when he had concluded his narrative, was that the evidence seemed to point to Arnold Pinkney having, as he had unjustly suspected Lana Tuttle of doing, flipped his cork, but Mr Bunting with his special knowledge saw deeper into the matter.

'Tell me, Judson,' he said, 'have you looked inside that object?'

'No. Why?'

'Has Arnold Pinkney ever had access to it?'

'Of course not. Yes, he has, though. I left it in his stateroom last night.'

'And are you aware that some years back your sister smuggled in her pearls in the interior of a Felix the Cat which she had purchased at the ship's shop?'

Freddie was staring at Mr Bunting as if the latter had been a beautiful picture, which was far from being the case.

'You aren't suggesting—?'

'It is more a matter of stating than suggesting. I have had the pleasure of a long acquaintance with your sister, Judson, and I know how considerate she is. She would never have asked her loved one to smuggle her necklace through the Customs without giving him kindly advice on how to do it. I think if you were to open the animal, Freddie ... Ah, you have done so, and, as I foresaw ...'

Freddie was staring at what he held in his hand. So was Judson.

'Do you mean,' said the latter, appalled, 'that that old crook let me go through those Customs sheds with *that*? Why, I might have got jugged for life!'

'He would naturally prefer that you and not he did the stretch you allude to. You spoke, Freddie?'

'If you can call saying "Ha!" speaking.'

'Did you say "Ha!"?'

'Yes, I did, and I'll tell you why. I am now in a position to go to Pinkney and dictate terms.'

'Could you sketch them out for us?'

'In a few simple words. I'm going to give Pinkney a buzz at the Plaza ... What's the number?'

'I can tell you that. Plaza 3-3000.'

'And inform him that I am holding this necklace in ... what's the word?'

'Escrow?'

'That's right. I'm holding it in escrow till he comes through with a substantial order for Donaldson's Dog Joy and gives Joe Cardinal his money and ... Have you anything to suggest?'

'You might make it a condition that he goes on a diet.'

'I will.'

Most people, meeting Freddie Threepwood, were struck by his remarkable resemblance to a sheep, but if they could have seen him now as he strode to the telephone and dialled, they would have realized that this was no ordinary run-of-the-mill sheep they were looking at, but a keen, brisk, alert sheep, the sort of sheep that knows all about drive and push and has been trained to develop its initiative.

'Plaza Hotel?' he said curtly. 'Put me through to Mr Arnold Pinkney's suite.'

'He'll have a fit of apoplexy,' said Judson, awed.

'He couldn't do better,' said Freddie. 'Ah, Pinkney, is that you? This is Threepwood speaking. Listen, Pinkney . . .'

Time Like an Ever-rolling Stream

I must confess that often I'm
   A prey to melancholy
Because I do not work on *Time*.
   Golly, it must be jolly.
No other bliss, I hold, but pales
   Beside the feeling that you're
One of nine hundred – is it? – males
   And females of such stature.

   How very much I would enjoy,
   To call Roy Alexander 'Roy'
   And hear him say 'Hullo, dear boy!'

     Not to mention mixing on easy
       terms with
       Louis Banks
       Richard Oulahan Jr
       Edward O. Cerf
       Estelle Dembeck
       Cecilia I. Dempster
       Ed. Ogle
       Robert Ajemian

> *Honor Balfour*
> *Dorothy Slavin Haystead*
> *Mark Vishniak*
>   *Old Uncle Fuerbringer and all.*

The boys who run the (plural) *Times*
    Are carefully selected;
Chaps who makes puns or Cockney rhymes
    Are instantly rejected.
Each day some literary gem
    By these fine lads is written,
And everyone considers them
    A credit to Great Britain.

    But dash it all – let's face it, what? –
    Though locally esteemed as hot
    For all their merits they are not,

        Well, to take an instance at random,

> *Robert W. Boyd Jr*
> *Lester Bernstein*
> *Gilbert Cant*
> *Edwin Copps*
> *Henry Bradford Darrach Jr*
> *William Forbis*
> *Barker T. Hartshorn*
> *Roger S. Hewlett*
> *Carl Solberg*
> *Jonathan Norton Leonard*
>   *Old Uncle Fuerbringer and all.*

Alas, I never learned the knack
   (And on *Times'* staff you need it)
Of writing English front to back
   Till swims the mind to read it.
Tried often I've my darnedest, knows
   Goodness, but with a shock I'd
Discover that once more my prose
   Had failed to go all cockeyed.

So, though I wield a gifted pen,
There'll never be a moment when
I join that happy breed of men.

   I allude to (among others)

> *Douglas Auchincloss*
> *Louis Kronenberger*
> *Champ Clark*
> *Alton J. Klingen*
> *Michael Demarest*
> *Bernard Frizell*
> *Theodore E. Kalem*
> *Carter Harman*
> *Robert Shnayerson*
> *Harriet Bachman*
> *Margaret Quimby*
> *Elsie Ann Brown*
> *Shirley Estabrook*
> *Marion Hollander Sanders*
> *Danuta Reszke-Birk*
> *Deirdre Mead Ryan*

F. Sydnor Trapnell
Yi Ying Sung
Content Peckham
Quinera Santa King
   Old Uncle Fuerbringer and all,
   Old Uncle Fuerbringer and all.

Printer's Error

As o'er my latest book I pored,
   Enjoying it immensely
I suddenly exclaimed 'Good Lord!'
   And gripped the volume tensely.
'Golly!' I cried. I writhed in pain.
'They've done it on me once again!'
   And furrows creased my brow.
I'd written (which I thought quite good)
'Ruth, ripening into womanhood,
Was now a girl who knocked men flat
And frequently got whistled at,'
And some vile, careless, casual gook
Had spoiled the best thing in the book
   By printing 'not'
   (Yes, 'not', great Scott!)
     When I had written 'now'.

On murder in the first degree
   The Law, I knew, is rigid:
Its attitude, if A kills B,
   To A is always frigid.
It counts it not a trivial slip

If on behalf of authorship
You liquidate compositors.
This kind of conduct it abhors
    And seldom will allow.
Nevertheless, I deemed it best
And in the public interest
To buy a gun, to oil it well,
Inserting what is called a shell,
    And go and pot
    With sudden shot
        This printer who had printed 'not'
            When I had written 'now'.
I tracked the bounder to his den
    Through private information:
I said 'Good afternoon' and then
    Explained the situation:
'I'm not a fussy man,' I said.
'I smile when you put "rid" for "red"
And "bad" for "bed" and "hoad" for "head"
    And "bolge" instead of "bough".
When "wone" appears in lieu of "wine"
Or if you alter "Cohn" to "Schine",
    I never make a row.
I know how easy errors are.
But this time you have gone too far
By printing "not" when you knew what
    I really wrote was "now".
Prepare,' I said, 'to meet your God
Or, as you'd say, your Goo or Bod
    Or possibly your Gow.'

A few weeks later into court
   I came to stand my trial.
The Judge was quite a decent sort,
   He said 'Well, cocky, I'll
Be passing sentence in a jiff,
And so, my poor unhappy stiff,
If you have anything to say,
Now is the moment. Fire away.
   You have?'
      I said 'And how!
Me lud, the facts I don't dispute.
I did, I own it freely, shoot
This printer through the collar stud.
What else could I have done, me lud?
   He's printed "not" . . .'
    The Judge said '*What!*
     When you had written "now"?
God bless my soul! Gadzooks!' said he.
'The blighters did that once to me.
   A dirty trick, I trow.
I hereby quash and override
The jury's verdict. Gosh!' he cried.
'Give me your hand. Yes, I insist,
You splendid fellow! Case dismissed.'
   (Cheers, and a Voice 'Wow-wow!')

A statue stands against the sky,
   Lifelike and rather pretty.
'Twas recently erected by
   The P.E.N. committee.

And many a passer-by is stirred,
For on the plinth, if that's the word,
In golden letters you may read
'This is the man who did the deed.

His hand set to the plough,
He did not sheathe the sword, but got
A gun at great expense and shot
The human blot who'd printed "not"

When he had written "now".
He acted with no thought of self,
Not for advancement, not for pelf,
But just because it made him hot
To think the man had printed "not"

When he had written "now".'

A Note on Humour

It will not have escaped the notice of the discerning reader that the foregoing stories and in-between bits were intended to be humorous, and this would seem as good a time as any for me to undertake the What-is-Humour essay which every author is compelled by the rules of his Guild to write sooner or later.

In the sixteenth century they called humour 'a disorder of the blood', and though they were probably just trying to be nasty, it is not a bad description. It is, anyway, a disorder of something. To be a humourist you must see the world out of focus. You must, in other words, be slightly cock-eyed. This leads you to ridicule established institutions, and as most people want to keep their faith in established institutions intact, the next thing that happens is that you get looked askance at. Statistics show that 87.03 of today's askance looks are directed at humourists, for the solid citizenry suspect them and are wondering uneasily all the time what they are going to be up to next, like baby-sitters with charges who are studying to be juvenile delinquents. There is an atmosphere of strain such as must have prevailed long ago when the king or prince or baron had one of those Shakespearian Fools around the castle, capering about and shaking a stick with a bladder and little bells attached to it. Tradition compelled him to employ the fellow, but nothing was going to make him like it.

'Never can understand a word that character says,' he would

mutter peevishly to his wife as the Fool went bounding about the throne-room jingling his bells. 'Why on earth do you encourage him? It was you who started him off this morning. All that nonsense about crows!'

'I only asked him how many crows can nest in a grocer's jerkin. Just making conversation.'

'And what was his reply? Tinkling like a xylophone, he gave that awful cackling laugh of his and said "A full dozen at cock-crow, and something less under the dog star, by reason of the dew, which lies heavy on men taken with the scurvy." Was that sense?'

'It was humour.'

'Who says so?'

'Shakespeare says so.'

'Who's Shakespeare?'

'All right, George.'

'I never heard of any Shakespeare.'

'I said all right, George. Skip it.'

'Well, anyway, you can tell him from now on to keep his humour to himself, and if he hits me on the head just once more with that bladder of his, he does it at his own risk. Every time he gets within arm's reach of me – socko! And for that I pay him a penny a week, not deductible.'

Humourists are often rather gloomy men, and what makes them so is the sense they have of being apart from the herd, of being, as one might say, the eczema on the body politic. They are looked down on by the intelligentsia, patronized by the critics and generally regarded as outside the pale of literature. People are very serious today, and the writer who does not take them seriously is viewed with concern and suspicion.

'Fiddle while Rome burns, would you?' they say to him, and treat him as an outcast.

I think we should all be sorry for humourists and try to be very kind to them, for they are so vulnerable. You can blot the sunshine from their lives in an instant by telling them you don't see what's so funny in *that*, and if there is something funny in it, you can take all the heart out of them by calling them facetious or describing them as 'mere humourists'. A humourist who has been called mere not only winces. He frets. He refuses to eat his cereal. He goes about with his hands in his pockets and his lower lip jutting out, kicking stones and telling himself that the lot of a humourist is something that ought not to happen to a dog, and probably winds up by going in for 'sick' humour like Lenny Bruce, and the trouble about being like Lenny Bruce is that the cops are always arresting you, which must cut into your time rather annoyingly.

This is no doubt the reason why in these grey modern days you are hardly ever able to find a funny story in print, and in the theatre it is even worse. Playwrights nowadays are writing nothing but that grim stark stuff, and as about ten out of every twelve plays produced perish in awful agonies, I don't think they have the right idea. If only the boys would stop being so frightfully powerful and significant and give us a little comedy occasionally, everything would get much brighter. I am all for incest and tortured souls in moderation, but a good laugh from time to time never hurt anybody.

And nobody has laughed in a theatre for years. All you hear is the soft, sibilant sound of creeping flesh, punctuated now and then by a sharp intake of breath as somebody behind the footlights utters one of those four-letter words hitherto confined to the cosy surroundings of the lower type of bar-room. (Odd to reflect, by the way, that when the word 'damn' was first spoken on the New York stage – in one of Clyde Fitch's plays, if I remember rightly – there was practically a riot. Police raided the joint, and I am not sure the military were not called out.)

The process of getting back to comedy would, of course, be very gradual. At first a laugh during the progress of a play would have a very eerie effect. People would wonder where the noise was coming from and would speculate as to whether somebody was having some sort of fit. 'Is there a doctor in the house?' would be the cry. But they would get into the way of it after a while, and it would not be so very long before it would be quite customary to see audiences looking and behaving not like bereaved relatives at a funeral but as if they were enjoying themselves.

The most melancholy humour today is, I suppose, the Russian, and one can readily understand why. If you live in a country where, when winter sets in, your nose turns blue and has to be rubbed with snow, it is difficult to be rollicking even when primed with two or three stiff vodkas.

Khrushchev in the days when he was out and about was probably considered Russia's top funny man – at least if you were domiciled in Moscow and didn't think so, you would have done well to keep it to yourself – and he never got beyond the Eisenhower golf joke and the Russian proverb, and if there is anything less hilarious than a Russian proverb, we have yet to hear of it. The only way to laugh at one was to watch Khrushchev and see when he did it.

'In Russia,' he used to say, making his important speech to the Presidium, 'we have a proverb – A chicken that crosses the road does so to get to the other side, but wise men dread a bandit,' and then his face would sort of split in the middle and his eyes would disappear into his cheeks like oysters going down for the third time in an oyster stew, and the comrades would realize that this was the big boffola and that if they were a second late with the appreciative laughter, their next job would be running a filling station down Siberia way. There may come a time when Russia will rise to He-and-She jokes and stories about two Irishmen who were walking along Broadway, but I doubt it. I cannot see much future for Russian humourists. They have a long way to go before they can play the Palladium.

I see, looking back on what I have written, that I have carelessly omitted to say what Humour is. (People are always writing articles and delivering lectures telling us, generally starting off with the words 'Why do we laugh?' One of these days someone is going to say 'Why shouldn't we?' and they won't know which way to look.) I think I cannot do better than quote what Dr Edmund Bergler says in his book on *The Sense of Humour*.

Here it comes:

> 'Laughter is a defence against a defence. Both manoeuvres are instituted by the subconscious ego. The cruelty of the super-ego is counteracted by changing punishment into inner plea-sure. The superego reproaches the ego for the inner pleasure, and the ego then institutes two new defences, the triad of the mechanism of orality and laughter.'

What do you mean, you don't know what he means? Clear as crystal. Attaboy, Edmund. Good luck to you, and don't laugh at any wooden nickels.